Under Carico's Moons
Book 1

Distant Trails

by

Nan C Ballard

Published in the United States by
Not a Pipe Publishing
www.NotAPipePublishing.com

Paperback Edition

ISBN-13: 978-1-956892-10-9

Cover art by Don Aguillo
Photo of Nan C Ballard by Jonathan Billing,
PNWPortraitEFX.com

For Joyce,
in memory of all the imaginary adventures
we shared as kids.
I hope I've brought some fragments of them to life.

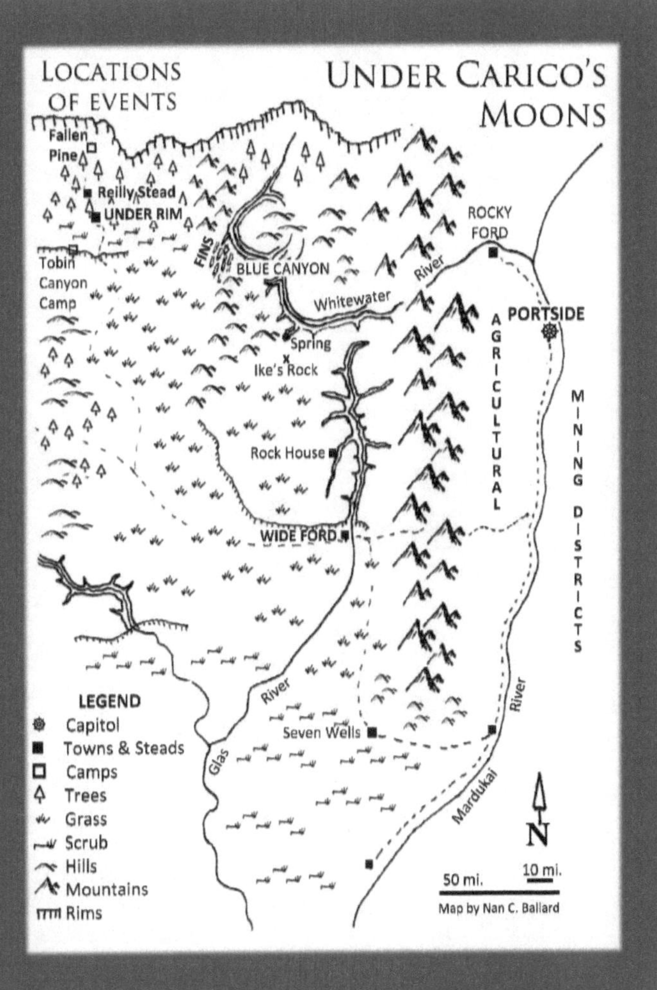

LOCATIONS OF EVENTS
UNDER CARICO'S MOONS
Fallen Pine
Reilly Stead
UNDER RIM
Tobin Canyon Camp
FINS
BLUE CANYON
ROCKY FORD
Whitewater
River
PORTSIDE
Spring
Ike's Rock
AGRICULTURAL
MINING DISTRICTS
Rock House
WIDE FORD
River
LEGEND
Capitol
Towns & Steads
Camps
Trees
Grass
Scrub
Hills
Mountains
Rims
Glas
Seven Wells
Mardukai
River
N
50 mi.
10 mi.
Map by Nan C. Ballard

Chapter 1

Seth

Seth Reilly danced, his boots scuffling in amber-green sand, leading the young horse through the steps as it learned to focus and to follow, to read the language of Seth's body, to partner with the man. The horse's attention slid away, locking on someone standing outside the gate. Seth caught the colt's eye, drew it back, a step this way, a step that, until the animal followed him, nose by his hip, in a winding curve across the pen. Seth stopped, stepped back, and turned away, disengaging.

"You about done for the day?" Kieron Dougherty asked. Crinkles from a ready smile and Carico's sun etched the man's mahogany skin.

Seth glanced at Carico's two moons, Lander and Damele, beginning their own dance in the eastern sky, pale in the light of the setting sun. It was almost dinnertime. "Finally getting somewhere with this one."

"How'd it go earlier?"

"Fine, boss. Got 'em all assigned." Across the Seven Wells barnyard, a crew jostled and joked their way to the cookhouse. Seth shook his head. "Sometimes I hate turning the young horses over. Half those riders are sure they are great horse trainers, and I'll have to correct their messes in a few months."

"Job security." Dougherty pulled a slip of paper out of his shirt pocket. "You've got a blip from your sister. I figured it must be important since it's not a holiday or your birthday."

"From Gwyn?"

Dougherty passed him the paper.

Seth read the message quickly, then reread it thoughtfully.

"Trouble?" his boss asked.

Seth shook his head. "No, but it sounds like they need me home to ride for the spring Migration this year." He tried to make it sound routine.

"You haven't been back in a while."

"Five years," he admitted. He folded the paper.

Dougherty frowned. "Will you go?"

Seth studied the piece of paper and slowly nodded. "Truth is I've been thinking it was time for a visit." He shrugged. "Might as well be now. I'll leave in a couple of days."

"That's all right with me."

"Then I'll have a job when I get back?"

"Anytime. Why don't you leave your horses here and have someone come pick you up?"

"Thanks, boss, but I'd rather ride. I was seventeen when I left. Three weeks on the trail to Under Rim ought to be about enough to settle into the idea of going back."

Dougherty chuckled. "Better go get your dinner before that crew cleans the pot."

"Yes, sir," Seth replied, then added, "Could you do me a favor?"

"What would that be?"

"Could I take a horse for part of my pay?"

The older man thought for a moment. "One of the two-year-olds?"

"Yes, the blaze-faced sorrel filly."

"I expect we can work something out. Why the sorrel?"

"She's my sister's kind of horse. Besides, she'll be the only sorrel on the place." He grinned at that thought.

"Okay, she's yours. I'll put it on the books."

"Thank you." Seth settled his hat on honey-colored hair and walked across the wide yard between the various buildings and the corrals. One of the other riders sat on the steps of the bunkhouse, leaning back on her elbows. Her brush of dark red hair stood up, damp with sweat.

"Bad news?" she asked. Kiri Devlin was ten years or so his senior and tended to treat him like a baby brother, but they had become good friends in the two years he had ridden for Seven Wells.

"Want to hear it?" he asked. Without waiting, he went ahead and read the note out loud. "It says—

Twin, it's your turn. I've taken care of things at home for five years while you've had your fun. Now I've got a chance to do something I want. Don't blow it for me. I'm going to Portside in a month. Be here by then."

"Your sister," Kiri determined. "Any idea what it's about?"

"None, but whatever it is, maybe it's time I go back."

"You have been thinking about it."

"Yup. You want to come along?"

She shook her head. "I don't think so. You don't need some stray tagging along when you go home."

"Migration time — plenty of work," he offered.

"Need someone to hold your hand?" she teased.

"That must be it, Babysitter. I just couldn't make such a long ride by myself."

"Sorry, but you are on your own this time." She ran her hand over her hair one more time and stood up. "Let's get cleaned up."

"Don't say anything to the crew. I'll tell them tomorrow."

"When are you going?"

"In a couple of days. I need to bring in my personal horses and get supplies together."

"We'll miss you, Seth."

"No, you'll just miss my horse training."

Chapter 2

Anni

"Under Rim? What would a Central like you be wanting in a far-out village like that?"

Anni Dulci pulled herself up to her full five feet two inches. "May I ride with you to Under Rim or not?" She knew her inner-world attire and carefully cultivated posture of inexperience didn't fit the frontier village where she was headed.

"No offense meant." The man shrugged. "Hop aboard. They'll be done loading any minute. Where're your bags?"

"Just these." She handed him her carry bag, keeping her tote in hand. He shook his head and climbed into the driver's seat of the well-used cargo jumper.

"Get comfortable. We'll be together for a while. Under Rim is my last stop on today's run. You can call me Al." He went through his final checks while the crew finished loading the crates of supplies for the far-flung communities lying west of Portside. In a few minutes, they lifted smoothly from the pad on the edge of the port and sailed away from the rising sun.

Her pilot-guide proved talkative, apparently pleased to have company. "Nice world, Carico. Sixty years we've been here, and we've kept the footprint pretty small. See this river valley, these grasslands. There's our wealth — plants for all sorts of medicines, and food, of course."

"I thought Carico produced copper."

"That's out east of Portside. You want technology, go out to the mines. But they couldn't survive without the botanicals.

"Under Rim's not along the river, is it?"

"Not by a long shot. We'll swing south over the desert, around the mountains to the west, and then back north under the Rim where you're headed."

"I've heard most of the communities are pretty rustic."

"You won't find a lot of fancy techno gadgets away from the mines, just what we need to get by, but we like it that way."

"What do you mean?" she encouraged him to elaborate.

"Jumpers and skimmers for transport, micro power generation, the credit net — we use those, but mostly we do things ourselves and don't get in a hurry about it. Satellite real-time is limited and costs. We mostly use compressed blips that can be delivered when there's bandwidth free."

"You must have communications and navigation satellites."

"Comm sat covers Portside and the mines. We're ground-based over here. No point buying up a lot of pricey gadgets from out there somewhere that we can't rebuild or repair ourselves.

Anni tried to hide her dismay at such a lack of basic services. "How big is Under Rim?"

"Not more than a hundred people live in the village with another two or three hundred or so in the district. They're stock raisers up there so the homesteads — they call them steads — they're pretty spread out. They have a local market with an order store, a small education center and library, and the usual public safety support."

"Any place a girl might get a job?"

"Could be. The café has live waiters, and there are two or three steads with broad enough interests to keep offices. Then there's Central Services of course, but you need some skills with them. Once in a while the Steaders' Co-op hires someone. About the only regular openings are for riders to work livestock." She recognized his unspoken skepticism about her qualifications for that work.

He spoke truly about it being a long day. They stopped at a dozen different villages and steads, leaving behind various goods at each. One stead called Seven

Wells was almost like a town in itself with its cluster of cabins, its own store, and other buildings. From there they followed an arc of hills west and north, crossed a large river, stopping at a community on its banks, then hopped from one small stead to another. She heard about the histories, the major products, how many settlers had survived the pandemic forty years earlier.

"It was worst in the outlying districts where medical care was scarce in those days," he explained. "Some places lost nearly every adult between thirty and fifty. You'll not find many elders in Under Rim."

Late in the afternoon, Al swung around a green spot in the sparse scrub of the desert hills. "See those. Those are tarbh, the local livestock." Anni looked down at the animals scattered across the little meadow around the spring. They had chunky, very wide, horse-size bodies and broad heads with horns lying flat on the skull like a helmet then curling down and forward. Four dark eyes, two forward and two to the sides, lay under the edge of the horns. Their hides were mottled greenish-brown and gray with short, wide, feather-like scales.

"They look like they're wearing shawls," she said with surprise. Something lay over the top of the necks, extending back onto their shoulders.

"Just wait until you see one with that frill standing straight up, flushed bright blue. Quite a sight! It's not all display though. They use it to control body temperature. On a hot day, they'll all be hiding under waving blue fans."

The scrub got thicker and turned to mixed trees and shrubs. Then grassy understory and meadows appeared. Her guide pointed out the great fault scarp that cut east to west across the region. "That's the Rim," he said. "It runs a couple hundred miles. Marks the north edge of the settled country."

"No one lives above there?"

"Not yet," he replied. "Haven't needed the territory. Let us get recovered from the pandemic, and someone will start pushing that way. Good country I hear but cold in the winter."

They finally circled Under Rim. Broad, paved walkways led out from each point of the triangular central plaza. Buildings lined the walkways with vehicle parking in back. The pavement turned to dirt trails at the edge of town. Al set down behind the store.

"Get pretty much anything you want here," he told her. "'Course, you have to order anything not produced locally. That's what keeps me in business." He shut down the jumper. "I like you, Anni. I'm going to give you some advice. Be best if you got a new haircut and hung those glow-clothes in the closet. Blend in a little; help you get by out here. Now come along and meet the storekeeper. She manages the apartments; probably has an opening this time of year. Unless you have family meeting you?"

"No."

"Didn't think so. Family coming in I usually hear about. Now, you take care, and if you need help with anything, see the Marshal. He's a good man."

"Thank you." She gave him a grateful smile.

Another hour found her settled into a tiny, one-room apartment in a long, low building across the plaza from the store. She was without a haircut or new wardrobe. Her dozen articles of clothing filled two needs, maximum mix-and-match and minimum packing space. All fit the description of "glow-clothes" with bright colors and fringe or ruffles that caught the light. She had let the storekeeper talk her into a long overcoat they called a duster to help her survive the late winter weather, something she had failed to consider when leaving Portside. Any other shopping would have to wait for a job. The rent left her barely enough to eat for the next few days.

She stared at the blank walls. What had she gotten herself into? The town was hardly larger than some of the steads they had stopped at and, while it had the essential medical, safety, and education services, seemed devoid of simple conveniences like public transportation and real-time communication beyond its boundaries. She had thought she was prepared for this, but now she wondered. She had never been so alone in her life.

Chapter 3

Seth

Twenty days of cold spring weather and some four hundred miles from Seven Wells, Seth stopped his horse at the edge of the village of Under Rim. "Well, old boy, we made it," he said, rubbing the dusty bay neck. He urged his weary gelding forward and tugged gently on the lead rope to encourage his pack horse and the two-year-old filly to come along. He rode up the broad promenade between the education and medical centers on the left and communications and public safety on the right. The blocky buildings lay quiet in the early spring twilight.

The promenade, restricted to non-motorized traffic, opened into a central plaza. The Gathering Hall, where the community came together for celebrations or district meetings, lay dark and empty to the left. Nothing had changed. He turned right, past the Marshal's Office, to the livery stable where he dismounted. The old wrangler that he expected didn't come out to greet him. With a shrug, he stepped up to the kiosk and laid his thumb on the pad by the door to activate the registration system. He keyed in for a corral and storage for his packs and saddles and led his animals into the wide aisle of the barn. Cabinets lined both sides for several feet with an open area in between for loading and unloading. Further back were box stalls. The far end opened outside into an alleyway between long lines of corrals. As Seth entered, the lights came up and the slot on his assigned locker blinked at him.

With sure hands, he pulled his packs off the horse and stowed them in the locker. Next, he unsaddled the two geldings and brushed them off. He took a minute to run the brush over the filly too before leading all three out through the far end of the barn and turning them into an empty corral. He carried hay out to them and checked the water to be sure it was fresh. Satisfied, he closed up the locker and left the barn.

He strolled across the plaza in no great hurry. Rajir's Café sat on the right at the beginning of the western walkway, just beyond the tall hedge hiding the parking that lined the third side of the plaza triangle. Dim light spilled from the café windows, the one place in the village showing signs of life. Food and warmth drew him, but he paused on the threshold, thinking about who he might run into. He shook the dust from his wide-brimmed hat and settled it low over his face. Opening the door, he stepped inside.

Light pooled around the tables, overlapping to wash the room in a golden glow. He rapidly ran his eyes over the occupants, finding several familiar faces in a group at the long wooden table off to the right. Three men and four women, pillars of the community, relaxed over after-dinner drinks, a clutter of napkins and dessert dishes still scattered before them. Silently, Seth found a seat left of the door where he could watch the big man at the head of the long table without attracting attention.

The table had no self-serve console, just a printed menu. A pretty girl about his own age came over to take his order. Her dark hair drooped along one side of her face, half hiding it when she lowered her head. The other side was cut short in an odd fashion for Under Rim. She had eloquent brown-gold eyes and a shy smile.

When she left with his order, he hooked the wide hat on the rack above the table and looked out of the window. Things hadn't changed much in the five years he'd been gone. Across the promenade, the office fronts stood dark. The store next to them had closed for the day. The village was a supply hub for the surrounding district more than an actual town. Except for the café and the inn and tavern next door, nothing much stayed open after sundown on a weeknight.

The girl brought his food promptly, getting his thumbprint on her tablet. He smiled, and she hurried away. He dug into his meal, savoring the rich, spicy aroma as much as the taste. He knew he wouldn't have long to enjoy it. Across the room, the members of the group, quietly jovial in their own company, were getting ready to leave.

Beyond them, the girl cleared dishes for a man alone at a table. He reached out and took her hand possessively. She deftly slid it away. The big man Seth was watching rose from the group and stepped in between the two. In low tones with unmistakable dislike, he said, "Leave the help alone, Jerdix. You've finished your meal ..."

The other man stood with a smirk. "Sure, Marshal, I'll just be about my business. Perhaps you have a personal interest in the sweets?"

The Marshal, ignoring the insinuation, stepped aside. The two were of a height, both in their mid to late fifties, but the Marshal was broad in the shoulder, fit and solid, while the other was less physical but no less imposing. Not the first encounter they had had, Seth judged from their attitudes.

Jerdix nodded to the girl. "Good evening, Anni." He stopped as he passed the Marshal's group and said good night to them. He noticed Seth and stared hard for a second before going out the door.

The waitress spoke quietly once the man had gone. "I could have handled that myself, Marshal."

"You shouldn't have to."

"Thanks, I guess." The girl brushed past him to the kitchen. A moment later she came out to work through the few customers on Seth's side of the room. When she asked if she could get him anything else, he shook his head, still watching the gathering across the room. She followed his gaze to the man who had intervened for her and quickly looked back to him with a little gasp. He knew the resemblance was unmistakable. He had his father's honey-brown hair, dark eyes, and expressive mouth. Joe Reilly could speak volumes with a quirk of that mouth when he chose to.

You're Seth!" she whispered.

He nodded and winked. "Don't give me away."

"No, no, I won't. He'll be so …" Her eyes sparkled with excitement.

He laid a finger to his lips. She grinned conspiratorially and took his dishes away.

The group began to trail out. Seth lifted his hat from the rack and stepped into his father's path.

The Marshal stopped, looking him over for a moment, expressionless. "Back, are you?" he asked flatly.

"Yes, sir, for a while." The two eyed each other before the older man grinned widely.

"Good to see you, boy." Seth found himself in a bear hug, being thumped soundly on the back. "It is good to see you."

Seth extricated himself gently. "Glad you feel that way."

"And why wouldn't I, you young rascal? You're back."

Seth withstood the scrutiny, aware of the trail dust and sweat he carried with him. "For a while," he repeated.

"We can talk about that later. Let's go home."

The girl hovered, watching the reunion. Seth was startled to see his father hook an arm casually around her shoulders and draw her close. "Anni, this is my son, Seth, come home to see the old man. Seth, this is Anni Dulci."

She smiled shyly. "Hi," she said.

When she tried to slip out of the encircling arm, the Marshal held her a moment longer. "You come out to the house for dinner tomorrow and join the celebration. Gwyn can give you a ride."

"You know how she feels about me. I'd rather walk," the girl said, dropping her eyes.

"That's a long walk. Don't let her get to you. Just be there."

She nodded. "I'll come."

He lifted his big arm and let her go back to work, then led Seth out the door. The promenade and plaza were empty. Laughter came from the parking area, but they were alone on the porch.

His father faced Seth and asked bluntly, "Okay, why?"

Seth returned the bluntness. "I guess Gwyn didn't tell you she ordered me home."

The older man shook his head. "Ordered? No. She's been acting edgy the last few days, but she didn't tell me you were coming."

Seth laughed. "She sent for me. I didn't let her know I was on the way."

"Did she say why?"

"She'll have to tell us both when we get to the house."

"Let's go then. Where's your gear?"

"The livery." As they turned toward the plaza, Seth saw a light come on across the way in one of the offices, outlining the man his father had confronted in the café. "Who is that?" he asked.

"C.T. Jerdix," his father said with an edge to his voice. "He's playing the big man around here these days. He's out to cause trouble for me, but I can fill you in later. Come on. Let's see what your twin has to say for herself. They were riding today. Probably be in late."

"She and Nick?" Seth pictured the dark, wiry young man who had shared uncounted childhood adventures with the Reilly twins.

"Nick's still waiting on her to know her mind. Your sister can be a fool sometimes." The older man shook his head. "He'll be looking twice at someone like Anni if she isn't careful."

"Seemed like you were looking twice there yourself," Seth said with a grin.

His father laughed. "Once maybe. It would be an insult to the kid not to look. Besides, she reminds me of someone. Now, let's get home. You can come back for your horses tomorrow. Gwyn'll be heading to town midday."

They went by the barn to get his packs. Seth grinned at the possessive look his father got when he saw the sorrel filly.

"Bribing your way back into the family?" Joe asked.

"Into Gwyn's good graces."

"Gwyn, huh. So you think that filly will smooth some things over with her, do you?" His father chuckled.

"Can't hurt! She was pretty upset with me when I left."

"Wasn't she though. You were two sides of a coin growing up. Then you up and took off on your own."

"It was time." He didn't try to explain.

"I know. Don't think I blame you, Seth, but we've missed you." He picked up one of Seth's packs and headed out of the barn.

Seth grabbed the other and followed. "I'm not promising to stay, you know."

"So you've said. It's been what, five years now? You haven't settled anywhere yet?"

Seth shrugged in the dark. "I've been at Seven Wells for a couple of years now, starting colts and working tarbh."

"Kieron Dougherty still around the Wells?"

"Running it."

"He's a good man. I knew him years back."

"He says my job's waiting for me."

"Sounds like him."

They hauled Seth's gear next door and loaded it into his father's patrol vehicle where it was parked behind the Marshal's Office. As Seth climbed into the vehicle, he remembered very well that his father rarely considered himself off-duty. The two-seat skimmer hummed smoothly as it glided just above tree height, heading north. After months on horseback, the rise and speed felt strange to Seth although he appreciated the warmth of the enclosed vehicle.

They rode on in surprisingly easy silence, given his long absence, but he had usually been comfortable with his father. That had not been the problem. The fact was that Joe Reilly cast a big shadow, and Seth had tired of always being seen as his father's son.

Seth stared into the darkness. They followed a line of narrow meadows winding between patches of tall, winter-bare brush and the rounded silhouettes of taller trees. What appeared to be a huge basin when seen from a distance was actually a jumble of ridges, draws, and pocket valleys. Against the far skyline loomed the black bulk of the thousand-foot-high rim at the northern edge of the settled country. He'd missed that towering barrier. It had defined his world most of his life until, at seventeen, he had ridden away.

A few minutes later, the skimmer swung around the edge of the meadows and dropped down near a log house. Built in a tradition centuries old, it had weathered into its surroundings. He'd loved this place but, at some point, it had ceased to feel like home to him. He had taken to the trail and not looked back. He felt an unexpected rush of nostalgia.

"The place doesn't feel much different." Seth climbed out of the skimmer and took in the damp earth smell, the light wind in the trees, the touch of the cool air. Spring wavered in and out, there one day and gone the next. Winter hadn't quite given up its grip yet. He shivered. The time on the trail had helped him adjust, but he'd spent the winter down on the desert, a long way from the cold.

They leaned his packs against the wall on the wide, open porch running across the east face of the house. He was surprised to find the door locked. He couldn't remember that ever happening. His father released the door and programmed the system to accept Seth's thumbprint.

"Locks now?" Seth asked.

The Marshal shrugged. "Times have changed. Get what you need from your packs. I'll take them down to the barn while you get cleaned up."

Seth carried his saddlebags inside. He vividly remembered the big room paneled in light-colored wood where the log walls didn't show. The kitchen with its well-worn plank table lay to his right. To the left a comfortable and much-abused leather couch faced two equally used armchairs in front of the stone fireplace, just as they'd been all through his childhood. On each side of the fireplace, arches opened into the sunroom beyond it. Directly ahead of him, a hallway led to a small office and a generous bath with a luxurious whirltub that his father swore was a necessity, given all the bumps and sprains suffered over the years.

Seth climbed the half-log steps to the second floor and found that his old room had become a storeroom. Amid miscellaneous clutter, treasures of his childhood still hung on the walls and sat on the shelves — pictures of him and Gwyn and Nick; the first bridle he had made with crooked beginner's tooling cut into the leather; a collection of stones and bones. Slowly, he rearranged the various boxes and bags to clear the bed so he could sit down.

He had not expected to come back to this house, this room, not yet. He had been content with his footloose life since he had left. And it wasn't like he hadn't stayed in touch with his family. They exchanged blips a few times a year, but their messages ran to the doing-fine-how-are-you variety rather than lengthy updates. Yet he was here as suddenly as if pulled by an elastic band. He tried to convince himself he had been planning to come for a visit anyway but, in his heart, he knew he would always come to help out his twin if she needed him.

Seth pulled his least worn change of clothes from his saddlebags and headed for the downstairs bath with the deep whirltub. He'd been riding the last four days without a break, camping where night found him. He felt the grit of dust on his skin, deep in every crease. Better clean up before his sister got home. With a twisted smile, he wondered what she would be like by now.

She'd been a tall, slender girl when he had left, with a line of riders hoping she would look at someone other than Nick. He pictured her clearly, headstrong, loving, willful and passionate. She'd envisioned the two of them, together with Nick, taking over the stead and being their father's strength and help in his old age. He chuckled. No wonder pretty little Anni said that Gwyn didn't like her. He couldn't picture two more different girls.

He dozed in the luxury of hot water until a sharp rap on the door woke him. A familiar voice called out, "Hey, Dad? What's up? Whose packs are out front?"

He took a breath and pulled a condescending big brother tone from his memory. "Just mine, kid. Don't bug me. I'm soaking." Trust his father to disappear and leave him to face Gwyn alone.

"Seth? No! Is that you? Seth, get out here right now."

"Yes, it's me. Now give me a few minutes."

"But Seth!"

"All right." He got out of the tub and wrapped a towel around his narrow hips. Bracing for the storm, he opened the door.

By the Four Elements, could that really be his twin? In the brief moment before she threw her arms around him, he took in the face of a grown woman, eyes dark with tears. Surprised, he held her close and let her hide her face against his bare shoulder until she got control of herself.

"I am so furious with you." She shrugged off the tears. "How dare you show up without a word! I was sure you weren't coming."

"What, no faith in me?" he questioned.

"Not a bit, Twin. Not now."

"Well, I'm here. You look great, Sis."

"Well, you don't. Hmmm, new scar. That hurt." She ran a finger along the jagged mark left where a panicky colt had run him into a tree and tore his shoulder open to the bone. "You could use a few good meals. Can't take care of yourself?"

"Three weeks on the trail getting here, at your request." He grinned. "Is Nick here?"

"No, he went straight home."

"Oh." Seth was disappointed.

"Hurry up. You can help with dinner."

"We ate in town."

"Well, I'm starved." She started for the door, then turned back to give him a hug. "Thanks for coming." She left with a bounce in her step.

As he dried off, he realized how drained he was. Warm, fed, and clean, he wanted to collapse into bed and sleep about half a day. He'd pushed himself and his horses. He hoped he could stay awake long enough to find out why.

Gwyn perched on a stool at the kitchen peninsula with a fat sandwich and a salad. Seth sat down opposite her and plucked a tart orange globeberry off her plate. "So why am I here, Twin? What's going on?"

She put down the sandwich. "I haven't said anything to Pa yet."

"I guessed that when I ran into him in town."

"He's home?" She stood up abruptly.

"Somewhere."

She slowly settled back on her seat. "I'm going to school," she said quietly. "I got a slot for full communications specialist qualification. I've been going crazy trying to figure out how to manage things since you didn't answer my blip."

"Comm Spec?" He popped another globe into his mouth to hide his surprise.

"I'm going. If you hadn't come, Nick was going to stay and try to handle everything himself."

"Why not tell Pa?" Seth remembered nothing but encouragement from their father.

She stood up again and paced restlessly. "You don't know how he's been recently. He is totally wrapped up in work, almost never here. Nick and I have been running the stead for the last year. He doesn't seem to be interested anymore." She started at the sound of footsteps on the porch and sat back down, picking at meat hanging out of her sandwich.

Their father came in, pulling off his boots and adding them to the row by the door. "Now that is a picture I have missed — both my kids home. Who wants to tell me what's up?"

Seth looked at Gwyn. She looked away nervously. He leaned back against the counter. "Gwyn sent me a blip, asking me to come home and help out for a while."

"Five years and you come home because your sister asks?" The older man walked over, helping himself to the last globeberry from the salad, and leaned his elbows on the counter. "Gwyn, your turn — why?"

"I ..." She straightened. "I'm going Portside next week to finish up my specialist qualification."

"You got a slot? Why didn't you say something?" He came around the counter and hugged her right off her feet. "I am so proud of you."

She buried her face against his shoulder and took a deep breath before stepping back. "I wasn't sure how you'd feel, I mean about me leaving with Migration coming. But Nick will take care of things, and now Seth's home to help, and you won't have to worry about anything around here."

"Whoa, slow down. You might have saved yourself a lot of worry by telling me. We would have figured something out."

"You've been so busy ..." she began.

"We'll not talk about that right now. Gwyn, I know how hard those slots are to get. How did you manage without me hearing anything about it?"

"I had Lije give me a recommendation and Doc Legat and a couple of the steaders. I told them I wanted to surprise you."

"Well, you did that, daughter, and you got this rambler back here. I am a happy man."

Gwyn mouthed "Thank you" to Seth who found himself drawn in, warmed by his sister's gladness and his father's enthusiasm, but something overshadowed his pleasure. Somewhere in the back of his mind he heard the sound of a trap gate latching firmly behind him.

Chapter 4

Seth

Breakfast was strangely like stepping back into the past, like he was seventeen again and none of the time between had happened. The three of them sat at the table talking about the day's work with Gwyn assuming he would pick up his old chores like he had never left. Then his father mentioned the afternoon's celebration and the guest he had invited.

Gwyn went silent and glared. Their father glared back. Seth could see how his sister might feel Anni was intruding on a family gathering. Gwyn never had been one to hide it when she didn't like someone. The tension between father and daughter thickened until Seth found an excuse and left the room.

Once he and Gwyn were on their way to town in the same battered Steadhand Model T-1 skimmer they'd had when he left home, Gwyn relaxed a little and chattered about the local gossip, but mostly she told him about going to work at the tech center, first doing clerical tasks, then providing extra hands to the technicians until she learned enough to start doing some of the work herself.

Seth stared at her. "You, messing with antennas and frequencies? Hard to picture."

"I love it — the challenge, the rush when I solve a tough problem." She laughed. "Tarbh are dull and predictable. You can have them."

"What does Nick think of all of this?" he asked.

She went silent for a moment. "He won't say, just tells me to do what I need to do. He is really glad you're here though. He didn't want to take on Migration by himself."

"What's the deal? He's done it for years."

"Did I forget to tell you that we're in charge at Tobin Canyon Camp?" She slowed the skimmer and swung around the east side of the village.

"In charge? You did leave that out." His mind began to run uneasily through what that meant — feeding, housing and bossing a crew, care and maintenance of equipment and horses, not to mention the underlying purpose of accounting for, vaccinating, and implanting chips in a few hundred uncooperative tarbh. "No wonder Nick's been too worried to get upset about his girl leaving him."

She set the skimmer on the ground behind the Tech Center, shut it down, and said, "I am not leaving him. I asked him to come with me, but you know how he hates town."

"Sure, Twin." He climbed out. "Don't forget to pick up Pa's guest."

That earned him a glare. "Right now, you come with me," she said. "I need to check you in at the Co-op, transfer the responsibility to you, and cut Nick and me loose. You are going to be very busy for the next few days."

While they went across the plaza and put the metaphorical lock on his trap gate, Seth's mind wandered to the dark-haired girl his father had invited to the party. He couldn't figure that out.

"Seth ... Seth!" Gwyn nudged him out the Co-op door. "What are you thinking about?"

"Sorry. What's next, now that we've set you on your road out of town?"

"I go to work making communications happen, and you head for home. Think you can find the trail?"

"I haven't been gone that long. Don't be late for the party." He headed for the livery.

As he settled his saddle on the back of his bay gelding, the horse's ears locked on the doorway. Seth turned to see Anni silhouetted there. "How's your day?" he greeted.

"Fine. I thought maybe I could ride out with you instead of waiting for your sister," she said.

He looked her over with a hint of skepticism. Under a stiff new duster, she wore a brightly colored tunic of some soft, ruffled fabric over patterned leggings. Her boots had probably never been near a horse, looking more fitted for city walkways on some world a long ways from Carico. "Get your horse, then," he agreed.

"Well, I hoped maybe you had an extra. Didn't you take your things home last night?" She tucked her hair behind an ear to have it promptly escape. "Besides, then I won't have to worry about getting a horse back here tonight. The Marshal is unlikely to let me ride back alone in the dark. He thinks I need protecting."

"Going out with Gwyn would be a lot faster."

"She just reminds me so much of someone I went to school with. So competitive." She looked up at him appealingly with just the slightest hint of charm. "Besides, I would rather ride with you."

"Do you have a saddle?"

"Well, no."

He considered for a moment. "Here, you get Buster brushed off." He directed her to the sturdy old brown gelding he used as a packhorse most of the time. "One of us is going to have to ride the pack saddle."

"I suppose that I should do that," she conceded with a frown.

"If you really want to come along." He had a twinge of conscience, knowing how uncomfortable she would be, but decided it was her choice. He placed the pack saddle on Buster's back.

Anni stepped in and fumbled with the cinch and breast collar. He let her figure it out while he led out the fine sorrel filly.

"She's awfully nice for a packhorse," Anni commented appreciatively.

"For my sister," he admitted. "Payback for leaving her with all the work."

"Has Gwyn seen her yet?"

"Not yet. Pa did, last night. He got that possessive gleam in his eye till I told him who she was for."

He checked and readjusted the packsaddle when Anni finished. She hadn't done badly with equipment he expected was totally alien to her. He handed her the bridle for Buster and tied the lead rope into reins to ride Jester with the halter. Not that he needed even that. The gelding was his old reliable, with him since before he'd left home, just as Buster had been. He used the comm by the barn door to leave Gwyn a message not to pick up Anni, then led Jester and the filly out into the sunlight.

"Ready to go?" he asked. He gave Anni a leg up. She settled lightly, shifting to find her seat without stirrups. He swung up on Jester and brought the filly into line behind him. "Lead the way," he instructed. "I'll follow you."

"Past the apartments, right? I haven't been out to the stead."

"That's the way. I'll let you know when to turn off the main trail."

Seth had to admit that the slender figure ahead of him, moving gracefully with the horse, was a pleasant diversion. She managed to ride the pack saddle better than he had expected. Her clothes and the asymmetrical haircut said Portside or more likely off world. She watched the forest around her with interest, exclaiming about small details, giving Seth a new appreciation of commonplace surroundings.

Normally the ride out to the house took a couple of hours, an hour if he was in a hurry. With no reason to rush, Seth wanted to revisit old haunts. About halfway home he took the lead onto a side trail. The narrow path, overgrown and carpeted with last year's fallen leaves, showed little use in recent days. It wound through the ancient towering palm-pines and the patchy brush, just leafing out in the spring sun, to climb over tumbled rocks up a ridge stretching down from the distant rim. Now, in daylight, that rim was turquoise and green and pale blue with yellow-green fingers of trees climbing the clefts in the rock.

On the crest of the ridge, the forest opened up, giving a clear view of the hollow where the house nestled. He dismounted and tied his two horses.

"Have you been up here?" he asked. She shook her head. He helped her off Buster. "Come on. The view is great."

Seth scrambled onto a boulder where he could sit with his back to warm rock and look out over his old home. He offered Anni a hand up and slid over to give her room.

"That's the stead." He pointed out the house on the edge of a meadow, facing east down a gentle slope to the big barn. Pastures radiated from the barn, taking up most of the surrounding area. Trails separated the pastures, coming from Under Rim to the south and from other steads to the east. "Great place to grow up. My sister and my friend Nick and I rode all over, camped and hunted. As long as our chores got done, we did pretty much what we wanted."

"Sounds kind of wild," Anni said, staring out at the broken expanse of meadows, forest, and rocky ridges.

"I suppose I remember the free time better than the chores and lessons. Pa and Nick's mom and dad kept us well in hand."

"Are the Dunns related to you?"

"Not by blood, but they're family anyway. I pretty much had three parents." He looked down at the stead, thinking back.

"I have a mother ..." Anni broke into his thoughts and then laughed a little at his puzzled expression. "Okay, and a father and brother and uncle but nobody says 'Oh, you're his daughter.' My mother is a lot like your father in some ways, well known and respected. People expect me to be like her, you know?"

He nodded. All the reasons he had left in the first place washed back.

She toyed with a brittle leaf, watching it disintegrate. "Joe comes to the café sometimes for tea, mid-afternoon when things are slow, and he talks about Gwyn and Nick and, sometimes, about you, the son who walks his own path. He's proud of you."

Seth grinned crookedly. "Is that what you're doing? Walking your own path?"

She paused, then nodded. "I am beginning to believe that I may be after all."

. She let her hair fall across her face and studied the rock. He became acutely aware of the warmth of her shoulder against his as they sat.

"Why Under Rim? You haven't been here long."

"I wanted to get away from ... things. I've been here a few weeks. I went to the supply depot in Portside and talked my way onto the first delivery jumper leaving. Under Rim was the last stop, as far out as I could get."

"Seems like you're settled in pretty well."

"The Marshal has been very kind. Mr. Jerdix has tried to be helpful too. He may have a job opening in his office. I'm not sure about working there, but it would pay better, and he's so tech-smart. I could learn a lot."

Curious, he asked, "How old are you?"

She answered, "Older than you were when you left home."

He laughed. "Right! Well, you know a lot more about me from my talkative father than I know about you. A question or two seems fair."

"I have one for you now, Seth. I need to know what's between your father and Mr. Jerdix. They make me nervous sometimes. They are so ..."

"Don't like being the bone between two old dogs?" he asked with an unexpected desire to shock her.

She stammered between embarrassment and outrage, but, when she responded, she did so with cool realism. "That may not be far from the truth. I sometimes think C.T. sets up things like last night just to goad Joe. It's hard, though. I mean, he comes in to eat all the time, and I have to be polite to him."

"I don't know what I can tell you. Jerdix wasn't here when I left."

"Oh, I thought he'd been here a while. He's so well established."

"Really?" Seth recalled his father saying something about Jerdix playing the big man around the district.

Anni crumbled another leaf. "He's hoping for a spot on the District Assembly of Arbiters this election."

Seth looked at her in surprise. "He has settled in fast." The five members of the Assembly were elected by district residents and most Arbiters had lived there all their lives. "When's the vote?"

"In two weeks."

"So he and Pa face off like that a lot?"

"Yes, they do, over lots of things."

"Not very comfortable for you."

"I just wait tables."

"And have dinner at the Reillys'."

"This once." She looked away. "We talk when he comes into the café. That's all."

Seth looked out across the basin, watching increasingly black clouds sailing across the sun. He slid off the rock and reached up to her, tucking the hair away from her face. She stared down at him, something flickering in her eyes.

"Come on, we'd better go before we get rained on." He lifted her down. She was heavier than he expected for someone coming barely to his chin.

Anni brushed the dirt from the back of her duster and pulled her tunic straight, staring reluctantly at the packsaddle.

He took pity on her. She had done well on it this far without complaint. "My turn," he declared. "You ride Jester the rest of the way."

She took his offer quickly enough, letting him adjust the stirrups for her. He knew that portions of his anatomy were going to protest his decision by the time they got to the stead, but he also knew it would not be fair to expect her to stay perched on the pack saddle over the rough trail he had in mind.

She looked down squarely at him for just a moment. "Thank you for letting me ride with you."

"Anytime," he assured her and went to get Buster.

Chapter 5

Seth

The stead's skimmer sat near the house when Seth and Anni rode out of the trees into the meadow. Gwyn had gotten home before them. Seth headed straight up to the house where Joe, Gwyn, and three others waited on the porch. A wiry, dark-haired young man jumped down and came to meet them. Seth reached down to clasp him on the shoulder and found himself spilled unceremoniously to the ground. He managed to take the other down with him, trying to pin him.

"Enough!" Joe roared, laughing. "You two hooligans go put those horses away while the rest of us start the party." He stepped by them, held Anni's horse for her while she dismounted, and gave her his arm to walk her to the house. She grinned at Seth with laughter in her eyes as she passed them.

Seth picked himself up and gave his friend his hand. "Nick, you're still hanging around this trail end? I thought you'd be off in search of brighter lights by now. Just can't get away from Gwyn?"

"Don't get me started on your sister right now." Nick tipped his head toward the porch. "She's all fire over Anni being invited. Now tell me everything. What have you been doing with yourself?"

"Let me save that. I'd rather tell it once."

"Easier to keep your story straight that way."

Seth glanced after Anni and saw Gwyn standing on the porch by herself, stone-faced. He walked over, leading the sorrel. "You'd better come along," he told her.

"Why?"

"Come along and look after your new horse." He held the rope out to her. "I've drug her far enough. It's up to you now."

Gwyn held out a hand to the filly before walking around her with a critical eye. Seth grinned, knowing his sister was hooked. "Hey, she's a gift horse. Take her or leave her."

Gwyn warmed and smiled. "You come to help me out, and you bring gifts. We may be almost even."

Seth threw his sister the lead rope. "You might call her 'Trade Goods'."

"Absolutely not. She's Sunrise, Sunny for short."

With a laugh, Seth caught the two geldings, and headed for the big barn that dominated the lower meadow. Its long side faced south to get the most from the solar roofing that supplied power for the stead. The Marshal's patrol skimmer sat under the shed roof against the north side. Kybr, the stead's stallion, strutted along the corral fence south of the building, announcing his dominance loudly to the strange horses. His companion, an elderly pony gelding, peered between the rails. Everything looked just as it had when Seth had left.

Nick fell in beside Gwyn, and Seth heard him diverting her. "Take your filly to the round pen and check her out. I'll help Seth unsaddle." She wasted no time taking his suggestion, leaving the two men alone.

"That will occupy her for a little while," Seth chuckled. "So, are you two on the same trail or not?"

Nick shook his head. "I've gone off a time or two, but I keep coming back. I can't say you did me any favors when you took off without a word to any of us. That upset her a lot. She was a creek during run-off, rattling over the rocks in all directions, until she got into the communications."

"Elements! Nick, I just had to be gone without any big family discussions and arguments. I'm sorry, but I didn't see any other way."

"Well, mate, you came back and just in time to get me out of having to run things. I do owe you for that."

"Since you owe me, here's another question. What's going on with Pa and Anni?"

Nick looked startled. "Nothing much that I know of. She's alone and young. He's been watching over her a little, making her feel welcome. You know how he hangs out at the café, taking the pulse of the District as he says. Why? Are you staying around long enough to take an interest?"

"I wasn't planning on it, but who knows."

The rain began falling as they finished brushing off the two geldings. Gwyn hurried in with the filly. She helped settle the three horses together in a corral. Sliding in between Seth and Nick, she hooked her arms through their elbows and headed them for the house. As the rain pelted down harder, they broke into a race. Seth lost, as usual.

"Wet coats on the porch." Teri Dunn, Nick's mom, really didn't need to remind them. Seth dutifully hung his hat and jacket. She met him at the door with a pair of moccasins in hand. Rule was: no boots in the house, hers or here.

"Seth Reilly, you are an inconsiderate young man, and I should be very upset with you for staying away so long."

Seth let the moccasins drop to the floor and placed his hands on her shoulders. "Yes, Tia, you should be." She came somewhere near his chin, slender as Anni, with dark, curly hair. He remembered best the warmth in her deep brown eyes and her frequent smiles.

"Oh, get in here." She pulled him down to kiss his cheek. "You might have sent a blip a little more often."

"Yes'm." She had been a mother to him and Gwyn most of their lives.

Inside, Elijah Dunn, known to most as Lije, leaned against a kitchen counter, his collar-length black hair shot with gray that Seth didn't remember. Always a private man, he made no move to come and greet Seth but smiled warmly. "Good to see you, boy."

"You too." Seth returned the smile.

Joe had taken charge of dinner. "Lije, the bar is yours. If I remember right, Seth's old enough now to drink with the adults." Joe continued slicing a roast into steaks. Lije nodded and began taking glasses down.

Anni sat on a stool by the counter, looking out of place in the rustic house. Just as Seth started to cross to her, his father offered her a sample from the dinner pot. Seth went on by the girl. "I'll get cleaned up," he said, leaving the room.

They had barely seated themselves for dinner when the Marshal's comm went off. He excused himself and went into the office to answer it.

"Another call-out?" Teri questioned when he came back to the table. "That's the third time this week."

"Brawl at the Tavern again. Who's on tonight?" Joe asked Lije.

"Hu but she's gone out to Langer's about a break in. I'll take it."

"We're going to have to get some more help if this keeps up," Joe commented acidly.

Lije got up. "Teri, you stay here tonight. I don't want you home alone." He was gone in a moment.

Seth looked around the table in surprise. Things had changed. He couldn't remember the Marshal or Lije responding to calls during dinner. "Crime wave?" he asked.

"For months now," Gwyn answered.

"Lock the doors and watch your back," his father cautioned. "And it's likely to get worse soon."

"What? Why?" Teri asked.

"If Jerdix loses the arbiter election."

"Joe Reilly, it is about time you told us all what's going on." Teri set down her fork, pushed her plate back, and stared at him, waiting. Seth got a sense that this was a long-standing issue.

"Okay, okay, after we eat." Joe hunched his shoulders and focused on his plate.

"This is one time you can't keep work away from home."

He shoved his plate away. "All right, when Jerdix loses the election, he will give up trying to discredit me to ruin my career, and he will take direct action against me or, more likely, people I value."

Seth looked around to see if the others were as confused as he was. Anni looked nervous. No one said anything. "Pa, you're going to have to fill me in. What's been going on around here?"

"That is a long story."

"Hit the high points."

"Okay, for most of the last year, we've had a growing number of crimes — break-ins, thefts, brawls. Nothing big but a constant string of little incidents. I know, but can't prove yet, that C.T. Jerdix is behind it."

Teri leaned forward. "Why would he do that? He's a businessman. He's campaigned hard for the Arbiter position. I won't say people like him, but most respect him."

"They don't know him. I do." Joe stood up. "Let me tell you a story." He began to pace. "It starts over twenty-five years ago, before any of you youngsters came along. My old friend Cris Vawn — Teri's sister — and I helped incarcerate C.T. Jerdix for racketeering, illegal trade in controlled resources, and conspiracy to murder. That was a long ways from Carico. His wife and brother both died when he overtaxed his surface-to-orbit craft trying to escape. We never figured out how he survived. He blamed us, personally, and made plenty of threats during his trial." Joe drew in a long breath. "Now that he has served his time and is free and clear, he's back with his old associates at the Emerging Territories Business Consortium. So he comes here, the middle of nowhere, and involves himself in local politics just when we have an outbreak of criminal activity that makes me look ineffective as marshal. Coincidence? Well, we plan to round up most of the lawbreakers in the next few days and get the evidence we need to link them to Jerdix."

Joe came back and leaned on the back of his chair. "He is a violent, vindictive man. I think he's counting on the arbiter position to give him status and protection from allegations. When things fall apart, he will target you, the people I care about. I want him in custody before that happens."

Teri looked around the table. "What do you need us to do?"

Joe sat down and pulled his plate back in front of him. "For now, take care of business. Just be careful. Lije and I will deal with it."

"Lock the doors and watch our backs," Seth reiterated.

"That's it. Now, this was supposed to be a party. I have my son home, my daughter taking advantage of a great opportunity, and Nick is back to his preferred place as just another rider for Migration. Let's enjoy it."

They ate in silence for a while. Seth studied his family, his father's tension slowly easing, Gwyn shifting restlessly, Nick watching her unhappily, Teri looking composed. Anni sat between him and his father, silent and uneasy. Finally, Seth took it on himself to try and recover some of the evening's good spirits.

"Gwyn, how did you score the training slot? Don't you need years of apprenticeship to qualify?"

She straightened and put down her fork. "Yes, you do, along with a lot of home study. I've been busy here while you were drifting around."

"Don't tell my boss I'm just some wandering rider," Seth protested. "He thinks I've been at his beck and call for the last couple of years. In fact, you owe him for giving me the time off to be here."

"When do you leave, Gwyn?" Teri asked.

"Five days from now. I have a place in student housing. We'll rent one of the Co-op jumpers, and Nick will take me in. I'll be there every other quarter for the next two years."

"And somewhere as an advanced apprentice the alternate quarters?" her father asked.

"Yes." She looked at Nick who reached over to take her hand. "I know this will be tough on you, Dad, if Seth doesn't plan to stay."

Joe leaned back in his chair. "Don't worry about that. He's here now, and that gives us time to figure things out. I could always retire."

"That will be the day." Teri laughed. "Now, if you all will get this table cleared, we can go sit comfortably. Joe, a fire would be nice this evening. I brought a cobbler for dessert."

While Seth helped with the clean-up and dishing up the cobbler, he watched his father escort Anni to the big armchair closest to the fireplace and visit with her while he built and lit a fire. The girl watched the process with a puzzled expression, like she'd never seen such a thing before.

Seth couldn't figure out the older man's attitude toward the girl, whether simply hospitable or paternal or something more personal. Anni stared raptly at the blaze, responding softly and a little shyly to Joe, much less outgoing than she had been with Seth on their ride to the stead. She seemed more at ease as the rest of them settled into the living room. Seth took a seat on the hearth, leaving the chairs and couch to the others. He answered questions about what he'd been doing and asked his own, trying to draw Anni into the conversation when he got a chance.

Teri finally broke up the reminiscing. "Time I headed home," she said.

"Dad wanted you to stay here," Nick reminded her.

"He worries too much sometimes. I'll be fine."

Nick looked at Gwyn and reluctantly said, "I'll come with you then."

"Good idea," Joe agreed. "I'd feel better if you weren't there alone right now."

"All right," Teri gave in. "Gwynni, would you help me with the leftovers? I want to take something with us for Lije when he gets home."

Joe stood up. "Well, Seth, do you still remember how to drive a skimmer, or have you been horseback too long?"

"I think I can figure it out," Seth answered.

"Then give Anni a ride home, please. Make sure she gets safely indoors. We have a rougher element around than when you were growing up."

"Glad to." Seth was surprised but not at all unhappy that his father wasn't driving Anni in himself.

Chapter 6

Anni

A sharp wind whistled around the corners of the house and roared through the trees. Anni stopped at the top of the porch steps and pulled her duster closer around her.

"Wait here," Seth said. "I'll get the skimmer."

"No, that's all right." She stepped out into the full force of the wind.

Once they were securely inside the vehicle, he took a moment to run through the skimmer controls in his head. Truth was that he hadn't driven a vehicle of any kind more than a dozen times since he'd left home. The weather didn't help his confidence. The wind sent the clouds flying across the faces of the two moons, both near half with little Damele chasing Lander across the sky. He took a deep breath and lifted the skimmer away from the meadow.

Anni waited until he had the little craft airborne and a safe margin above the trees before saying anything. "Thank you for the ride."

"Anytime."

"You seem surprised by your father's concerns about safety."

"Things have changed. When I left we never locked a door. Gwyn, Nick, and I wandered all over at all hours, and no one thought anything of it."

"I've heard that a lot at the café. People are unhappy about what's happening."

"Do they blame Joe?" Seth asked. Sometime in his childhood he had begun thinking of his father by name much of the time when the Marshal's position was involved.

"I don't think so, not really. Could Jerdix actually get him removed from office?"

"The Marshal works for Central Services, not for the District, but a request from the Arbiters would carry some weight."

"He seems confident that Jerdix will lose this election."

"This is all news to me," Seth replied. "I haven't paid much attention to Under Rim politics the last few years."

"Seven Wells, isn't that where you said you worked? I think we stopped there when I came from Portside with the delivery driver."

"A big stead southeast from here about four hundred miles, out in the desert."

"And you rode horseback to get home?" She sounded amazed and appalled.

"I live horseback," he answered.

"But you drive a skimmer very well," she said. "And you don't even need to concentrate on it." He could hear a smirk in her voice.

"Lucky for you since you worked so hard at distracting me," he countered, realizing what she had done.

"You were thinking too much."

He laughed. "You could be annoying, you know, playing mind games on a person."

"So I've been told, but it worked."

"It did. Here we are. Which apartment is yours?"

He dropped the skimmer lightly into a parking space near the apartments on the northern promenade.

"Can we go over to the café for a moment first?" Anni asked. "I need to check my schedule."

They walked across the parking lot and around to the front door of Rajir's. At nearly closing time, the place was almost empty. One last patron was just leaving. Seth stood aside to let him through the door and recognized Jerdix.

The man nodded and smiled. "Anni, I missed you tonight. Have you had a pleasant evening?"

"Yes, sir."

"Who's your escort?"

She answered uneasily. "This is Seth Reilly."

Jerdix puffed up and looked Seth over with smug satisfaction. "So the pup has come home. Convenient.

Changes are in the wind, Anni, my sweet. Pick your friends carefully."

"Yes, sir." She let the curtain of hair fall, looking down at the floor. "Good night." She hurried away into the back.

Seth waited by the door, watching Jerdix cross to one of the offices. The man reminded him of a boss tarbh bull eager for any opportunity to show off his dominance. Even without his father's warning, Seth would have distrusted him.

When Anni came back, Seth said, "Jerdix is watching for us."

"That's odd. Why would he do that?"

Seth held the door for her. They were barely outside when he heard someone coming up behind them from the tavern next door. A man staggered into him, nearly knocking him off his feet. He pushed the drunk away in irritation. The man came back at him. Seth glimpsed a knife in his attacker's hand, blocked the blow, and swung the man around him, hoping to bring him up against the wall. Instead, the supposed drunk pulled Seth in to grapple with him, still trying to get the knife into play. Seth smashed the knife hand into a porch post. The man pulled free, turned to run, and collided with Anni, throwing her against the wall, before he disappeared around the corner of the building. Seth was vaguely aware of the lights going on in Jerdix's office as he went over to Anni.

"Are you all right?" He reached out, not quite touching her.

He didn't know the language, but from her tone he didn't think her phrase was acceptable in civilized company. She leaned against the wall, cradling her left arm in her right.

"I hit on my shoulder against the wall. Just give me a second."

"Are you sure? The med center isn't far."

She stretched and rotated the bruised shoulder cautiously. "I'm all right."

"Let's get you home then."

"Seth!" someone called from near the tavern. He turned to see Lije hurrying toward them. "Are you two okay? I saw a knife."

"Anni bruised her shoulder. That's all."

"What happened?"

"Just a drunk, I guess. He ran into me and tried to turn it into a fight."

"Drunk?" Lije sounded skeptical. "Balanced and fast for a drunk. You two get back inside and wait." He disappeared around the corner of the building.

"Come on." Seth led Anni back to the café.

Anni tapped at the locked door. "Tam, it's me."

"Anni, did you forget something?"

"Some trouble outside," Seth told him. "Lije told us to wait here."

"Sure." Tam Rajir opened the door and clapped Seth on the shoulder. "I thought I saw you in here last night but couldn't get away from the kitchen. Welcome home."

"Thanks. Sorry to keep you tonight."

"No problem. I'm just cleaning up. Why don't you finish off the tea so I don't have to throw it out?" He waved toward the pot as he headed back to the kitchen.

Seth led Anni to a seat. He filled two mugs, set one in front of her, and went to watch the street from the door.

"Do you see anything?" she asked.

"Just Jerdix, locking up for the night."

"Why would that man attack you?"

He came over and sat down beside her. "No reason I know of."

"I thought I'd be safe here, at least safer than where I came from. Now I'm not sure."

He took her hand again. "I'm sorry you got hurt."

"Don't say anything to Joe. It's really nothing."

"I won't, but I can't speak for Lije."

"Here he is," she said. Seth got up and opened the door.

Lije slipped in and pulled the door shut. "No sign of him. Now sit. Describe him."

Seth took a seat next to Anni. "A rider, stocky, older. The knife looked like what most of us carry on our belts except he had it out and open. I didn't notice much else about him."

"Anni?" Lije prompted.

"About Seth's height but heavier, dark clothes, hat, blue eyes — I saw that when he pushed by me. I didn't see anything distinguishing. He acted drunk until he ran into Seth. He came from the tavern I think."

"Anything else?"

"Jerdix was watching from his office," Seth said.

Lije nodded. "Okay. Take Anni home and get yourself out to the stead."

"Yes, sir. Oh, Tia wanted to go home, so Nick went with her."

"Thanks." Lije followed them onto the porch. "Watch your backs."

Anni slipped her hand into Seth's. They walked along the promenade around the edge of the plaza and then cut over to the apartments. "On this end," she told him.

A short hallway led back to the apartment door, hers on the left and another on the right. She thumbed the lock and stepped inside, turning to face him. "Come in for a minute?"

"I'd better go," he answered reluctantly.

"I'm glad I rode out with you this afternoon."

"Me too."

"When will you be in town again?"

He relaxed a little and smiled. "I have a Co-op meeting tomorrow night. I'll come by the café when it's done."

"You can walk me home."

He nodded. "Without incident this time."

She laughed softly. "That would be nice."

He wavered, tempted to accept her invitation to come in, more tempted to kiss her. "Well, I'd ... I guess I should go."

"Good night."

The door closed, and he stood alone in the hallway. He listened for the lock to engage, then slowly walked back outside into the wind he had hardly noticed while coming from the café. He hunched his shoulders against the cold and hurried to the skimmer.

Chapter 7

Seth

The house was quiet in the gray light before dawn. Clouds still hung low and heavy. A little snow covered the ground. Seth pulled on his boots and coat and went to check on his horses, glad to be home rather than camped out on the trail.

He walked slowly along the wide aisle of the barn, smelling the wood shavings under foot, the hay in the loft, the sweet pungency of manure. A bunkroom occupied one front corner of the building. Maybe he would move in there rather than cleaning out all the stuff stored in his old room.

He turned on the lights, got a rope and a nose bag with some grain. The stallion, Kybr, hung his head over the door of his double stall and nickered for his breakfast. His companion, Con, stretched hopefully to get his head over the same door.

"Not yet, boys. Pa will be along soon." Seth rubbed both faces.

The two stalls across the aisle were empty. At the far end, three familiar faces waited for him in a line of tie stalls that opened off the big corral. He passed the nosebag from one to another. "Pasture for you three today," he promised. He scrambled up the manger front and swung himself into the loft through the hay drop. He didn't remember it being such a tight squeeze. He threw hay to his horses and used the ladder next to the feed room to come down. He was putting the nosebag away when he heard the sound of hooves out front.

"Hello," he called as he stepped out of the feed room, not wanting to spook the incoming horses.

"Mornin'." Lije was just coming in the door. He continued to the far end and tied his horse to the line of mangers across from the tie stalls. Nick and Teri followed, also leading horses.

Seth laughed. "Tia, I thought you might have outgrown the bareback pony by now." As long as he could remember, she had ridden the mile between their houses bareback on some horse or pony, only using a saddle for longer rides. As kids, they had all done the same. He hadn't been on a horse bareback in years.

They walked up to the house together in the chilly dawn. Fog wisps floated across the meadow and twisted between the trees. No one brought up the incident the night before. Seth suspected Lije had not told his wife and son about it.

Shedding boots and coats at the door, they pushed into the warmth of the house. Joe was in the kitchen, working over something on the stove.

"Tea is ready," Joe said. "Someone set the table, and I'll have you fed in no time. Nick, go up and light a fire under Gwyn. Seth, I hate to send you back outside, but could you throw a couple flakes of hay to the old men? I'll take care of their treats later."

Nick elbowed Seth in the ribs. "Trade you," he whispered.

Seth clapped him on the shoulder. "Good luck, mate. I'll take the horses." His sister didn't always take kindly to being rousted out of bed.

No one lingered over breakfast. Joe and Lije were off to work. Nick went to help Teri with something. Seth found himself alone with his sister to talk about the upcoming migration.

Gwyn came over and bumped him with a hip. "Thanks for doing this for me, Twin."

He laid an arm over her shoulder. "You're welcome, Sis. Now, tell me what I'm taking on."

A printed map of the District and surrounding area hung on the wall by the dining table. Seth ran a finger across it, following the dividing line between the winter and summer ranges. Thirty-some miles south of the stead, an escarpment ran east to west across the countryside, blocking travel and funneling migrating tarbh through a handful of trap sites twice a year. The stead owners had those two chances to check their livestock, separate those to be sold, treat the sick, and insert ID microchips in the calves.

She reached out to point at a symbol on the map. "Tobin Canyon." It was the camp farthest west, the nearest to town, and the last trap Seth had worked at before leaving home.

"Where are the tarbh concentrating?" he asked. With a little encouragement from riders, the animals moved around the winter range and ended up in different areas every spring.

"Eastside, so you shouldn't be too busy."

"Who else is working Tobin?" The Co-op assigned the steads to different traps by a lottery system to balance the workload.

"The Haver and Hu steads are sending two riders each. Nick will be with you, of course, and Tia Teri is your camp tender. Trust me," Gwyn said. "Everything is almost ready. Tia has the food figured out. She and Nick will go down a couple days early and get camp set up."

Seth nodded, leaning over her computer tablet and reading her list. All he had to do was follow through on all the little details that went into supporting eight people and twenty or twenty-five horses for three weeks.

"What about horses?" he asked. His sister hadn't said anything about that critical piece. "I'd like to rest my two if possible. I pushed them a little getting here."

"You'll want six at least plus Tia's pony. You'll have to bring the geldings from winter range and pick what you want. We'll schedule the transport van at tonight's Co-op meeting."

"I'll go get the horses tomorrow."

"Nick and I can help."

"I can handle them, Sis." He tugged her long braid. "Don't you have things to do?"

"I've had my bag packed for days. I'd rather ride than sit around here thinking. We'll come with you to the Co-op meeting tonight too. It's the last planning meeting."

Seth refilled his mug with tea. "Let's have dinner in town, our own little party."

Gwyn crossed her arms. "So you can see Anni again?"

"Maybe — why shouldn't I?"

She walked away from him. "First she has Pa hanging around her and now you. I don't get it. She's such a Central."

He bit back a smart remark and took a breath. "Do you really think there's something going on between her and Pa?"

"Yes," Gwyn shot back and then paused. "I just don't know what."

"We can eat at the tavern if you want," he said, not wanting to spoil the proposed festivity.

"Let's do that but a little early. It'll be packed just before the meeting."

"Sounds good." He didn't mention that he had promised to walk Anni home when she got off work.

Satisfied that preparations for Migration were well underway, Seth took the afternoon to settle into the bunkroom in the barn, sort through his gear, and check the tack room for equipment they would want. He turned his two geldings out with the other saddle horses already at the stead. He cleaned what clothes he had and stood under a hot shower to drive some of the cold from his bones. During his years in the low desert he'd forgotten the damp chill of spring at this elevation. He dressed in the least worn clothes he had, aware that he would see many old friends at the Co-op meeting but thinking more of the few minutes at the end of the evening when he would see Anni again.

"Hey, Seth, aren't you ready yet?" Gwyn pounded on the bunkroom door. "We'll never have time to eat if we don't get moving."

Seth pulled on his rider's jacket, wishing he had something better. "I'm coming."

He and Gwyn got into the skimmer and made the short hop to Dunns' place to pick up Nick. Light was just beginning to fade as they reached Under Rim.

"Busy place," Seth commented as he maneuvered into one of the few open parking spots behind the Gathering Hall. As Gwyn had predicted, most of those coming for the Co-op meeting planned to have dinner first. "Tavern or café?" he asked.

"Tavern," Gwyn said firmly.

The place was packed. Seth got repeatedly pummeled on the back by old friends before they managed to work their way to an empty table. Ila Jones, the proprietor, found her way to them shortly, setting beers in front of them in anticipation of their order.

"Seth, I heard you were back," she greeted. "I suggest you have the steak strips and roasted spike roots if you want to make the meeting on time."

"Good to see you too," Seth laughed. "We'll take your recommendation."

"Be right back. And you three be sure to tell Joe and Lije how much I appreciate all their help the last few weeks."

Seth looked at the other two. Gwyn grinned. "We'll do that, Ila."

"I'm not alone in hoping they can get some trash out of town soon." The woman looked pointedly at a group in the back corner. She patted Seth on the shoulder and hurried off without another word.

Seth tipped a head toward the men Ila had indicated. "Whose riders?" he asked.

"Jerdix," Nick replied. "He bought out three or four steads, mostly small ones, and brought in riders from outside the District. They're a rough bunch."

"Enough," Gwyn said. "This is supposed to be a celebration."

"Oh, right." Nick didn't look very happy. "I'm celebrating because you're leaving?" Gwyn leaned against him and kissed him. He pulled her into his lap.

"Just for a little while," Gwyn assured.

Ila's arrival interrupted them. They applied themselves to the food she brought. People were already beginning to leave for the meeting.

Seth ate hurriedly. "I'd better get over there," he said. "You two take your time."

"The meeting doesn't start for a while yet," Gwyn told him.

"I know, but I want to talk to a couple of people." He left them there and headed for the Hall.

He set his thumb to the check-in at the door and entered the room. Every stead claiming any tarbh was required to participate in the Co-op. Failure to have a "rep," a representative designated to speak and act for the stead, actively involved with the Migration meant a lien being recorded on any tarbh tagged as theirs. Small steaders like the Reillys and Dunns often joined together and appointed a single rep.

"Seth!" someone called. Seth cleared the crowd at the door and saw Flech Haver coming toward him.

"Flech," Seth clapped the young man on the shoulder.

"Welcome home. I hear you're stepping in for Gwyn at Tobin."

"That's the plan. Will you be there?"

Flech laughed and beckoned to someone. "No, I'm staying close to home right now." He held his hand out. Seth turned to see who was coming up behind him.

"Ches ..." He found himself looking into a familiar face. His breakup with the tall, dark-haired girl had been the final push behind his leaving. "Wow, Ches, you look ... great."

She laughed at the double meeting. "I feel great." She ran a hand over her belly. "The baby's due in a few days."

"Wow," Seth said again. He hugged her awkwardly. She kissed him on the cheek.

"Uncle Tam said you had been in the restaurant. When did you get back?" she asked.

"Just a couple of days ago."

"Sorry to keep Flech home, but we'll send a good crew to Tobin." She leaned back against Flech who wrapped his arms around her.

"Thanks, I'll need the help." Seth couldn't help staring. Ches had always been pretty, but now she was stunning. "You cut your hair." He remembered it flowing thick and straight to her waist.

"Last week. It'll be easier with the baby." She turned enough to kiss Flech.

"Congratulations," Seth finally remembered his manners. "I hadn't heard you two were together."

"Two years," Flech said. "Once Migration is over and we're settled in with the baby, you'll have to come for dinner. Dad would love to see you."

"I'd like that. I am really happy for you two."

"Thanks. We'll see you soon."

"I'd better go get signed up for the transport van." Seth backed up a step or two, unwilling to leave.

"I hoped we would see you here, Seth." Ches said. "Now, I'm going to find a seat." She moved away, somehow graceful even now. Flech gave Seth a 'you-lost' grin and followed her.

"That was one piece of news I wanted to let you see for yourself," Gwyn said from behind Seth.

"You could have warned me."

"I'm just glad I got here in time to see some of that reunion, Twin. They're good together, don't you think?"

Seth pulled himself together, trying to focus on the business at hand. "They always were friends," he recalled. "Now, let's get signed up for transport before the meeting starts."

He had trouble keeping his mind on the string of reports about preparations for the various traps. His thoughts tripped between the past and his promise to walk Anni home. He started when Gwyn's elbow caught him in the ribs.

"You're up next," she warned.

Seth's mouth went dry, and his tongue refused to cooperate. Responsibility loomed over him, and the room seemed to fade away. Again Gwyn's elbow brought him back to the moment. Harvey Hu, the moderator, was calling for the report on Tobin Canyon.

Slowly he stood up. He took a deep breath. "Hi. For those who might not know me, I'm Seth Reilly, and I'm repping for the Reilly and Dunn steads. I'll be overseeing the Tobin Canyon Camp." A rustle of whispers ran around the room. Apparently his return wasn't common knowledge yet. "We have almost everything ready," he concluded.

"Welcome home," Harvey said. "Anything you need help with?"

"Just the tagging protocols."

"Come by the Co-op any day, and I'll go over them with you."

"Thanks, Harv. I'm going down to Tobin in a couple of days to check things over. I'll see you after that, and let you know if anything else comes up."

"Glad to have you back, Seth. Now, who's next? Moss Camp?"

Seth sat down, glad to be done with his briefing but wishing he had attracted a little less attention. He didn't want to get held up visiting with people. As Harvey began to wrap up the meeting, Seth whispered to Gwyn, "I'll be back in about fifteen minutes." He stood up the moment others began to rise and slipped out the door. People would linger over tea and cookies, so he had a few minutes.

He hurried across to the café. The lights were dimmed for the night but, when he knocked at the door, Anni opened it. She wore a tunic covered with hot orange and yellow fringe over neon-blue tights, no coat, and a sling strapping her elbow to her side.

"I was afraid you'd left," he said. "The meeting just broke up. Are you okay?"

"The Marshal insisted that I go see Doc Legat this morning. He says I should wear this for a few days. Apparently I strained something in my shoulder."

"I'm sorry you got hurt."

"It's nothing serious."

"Are you ready to go? Where's your coat? It's freezing."

"I didn't bring it. The sun was so warm when I came to work this afternoon."

"Better hurry then. I have to get back, or Gwyn will leave me to walk home." He put his arm around her. She was so slight and tucked in neatly against him, very different from Ches's tall, athletic build. They walked quickly around the café and crossed to the apartments.

"Come in for a minute and get warm before you go back," she invited as she opened the door and turned on the light. "Brrrr — it'll warm up soon."

Seth followed her in. She kicked her shoes off on top of the boots by the door and picked up her coat off the couch to hang on a hook. "Can I get you something?" she asked.

"No, I really have to get back."

"Can you help me get this sling off first? Doc only said I had to wear it to work, or if I was doing something strenuous." She stepped closer so he could reach the fasteners.

He fumbled for a moment; then figured it out. "There, you're free."

"Better." She tossed the sling to the arm of the couch. "Are you sure you can't stay for a little while?" She held out her hand.

He took it and ran a thumb over her palm. "Not tonight. I do have a question to ask you before I go."

"What would that be?"

"When's your next day off? Would you like to do something together?"

"Could we? I mean, do you have time?" She looked up at him eagerly.

"I need to take the skimmer down to the trap camp and check some things. I thought you might like to ride along."

"Day after tomorrow? Could we do it then?"

"I'll pick you up early. Wear something you don't mind getting dirty."

"I'll get a lunch from the café for us." She stood very close to him. Suddenly he didn't feel the slightest bit cold anymore.

"I've got to get back to the Hall," he said reluctantly but made no move to go.

"Okay, I'll see you soon." She stepped away, sliding her hand out of his. He opened the door and backed into the hallway.

"'Night, Anni." He closed the door and stood for a moment before starting for the meeting. Once outside, he let out a little whoop and ran most of the way to the Hall, already thinking about the trip to Tobin.

Seth took several minutes to work his way through the throng of people still in the Gathering Hall. Old friends greeted him warmly with hugs, shoulder slaps, and questions. The sight of Gwyn, impatiently perched on the edge of the stage, kept him moving through the room. Nick sat next to her, silent and glum.

Gwyn stood when Seth approached. Nick stayed close to her.

"Ready to go?" Seth asked. "I think half the people I know are here tonight."

She didn't answer, just walked off toward the door. Nick shrugged and followed, leaving Seth to catch up.

Seth drove the skimmer home while Gwyn and Nick sat in silence. Seth stifled his enthusiasm, realizing that his companions were not in the mood for it. The way Nick constantly sought Gwyn's hand and she leaned against him spoke of what her departure meant to them both. Seth found himself imagining a small, firm hand in his.

Chapter 8

Seth

Seth lay wide awake in the dark of very early morning. His brain jumped from one thought to another, refusing to be quiet and let him sleep. What would Anni think of the rustic trap camp? Would she be bored waiting for him to look at all the things he needed to check? Would the weather be decent? Would ...? Would ...? Would ...?

He tried to focus on the previous day when Gwyn and Nick had helped him bring the horses from the winter pasture — ten horses, six of them experienced saddle horses, two of them young and knowing barely enough to be useful, and two of them waiting to be introduced to the saddle during the coming summer. Which ones should they take to Tobin? Which one would be the best one for Anni to ride sometime? Where would she like to go? Which of his favorite places would she like? Which...? Where ...? When ...?

So much for trying to sleep. He got out of bed and looked out the window. He could almost make out the shapes of the trees. In an hour or so the sun would be coming up. Soon after that he would meet Anni at the café. He saw the lights come on in the house. He got dressed and walked across the frosty yard, shivering in the chill but pleased by the clear sky that gave hope for a sunny day. He whistled cheerfully as he climbed the porch steps.

"Morning," his father greeted. "Hungry?" Without waiting for an answer, he cut off another slice of tarbh ham and neatly slit open the leathery shells of two more spinxi eggs. "You're going down to Tobin Canyon today?"

"I want to check the corrals and everything for myself." Seth poured a mug of tea and sat down at the table. "I wasn't expecting to have to run the show. I need to get my head around it. Getting on the ground will be a good start."

"Good idea." Joe worked at his cooking with his back to Seth. "I hear Anni is going with you." Seth couldn't miss the tightness across his father's shoulders and in his voice.

"She is. Is that a problem?" Seth asked.

"She ... no ... no problem." Joe didn't turn around and his back remained a tight barrier to whatever he was thinking.

Seth studied that broad back. "She's curious, and I'll be too busy once work starts." With a sinking feeling, Seth went on. "She'd probably love to have you bring her down later to see the action." He still hadn't figured out the relationship between his father and Anni.

"Not likely." Joe slid the eggs and ham onto plates and brought them to the table. His expression didn't give any hint to what he was thinking. "Just don't be late tonight. Gwyn leaves tomorrow."

"I'll be here."

Seth got to town a few minutes early and parked behind the Co-op so he could pick up some equipment to take to Tobin. Hoping Anni was early too, he went straight to the café. As he walked in, she came from the kitchen with a box lunch in hand.

"Perfect timing," she said, laughing.

"I thought I was early." He took the box from her.

"I hoped you would be."

A loud voice from the big table interrupted his response. Jerdix was addressing four other steaders sitting with him and whoever else could hear him. "It's time Marshal Reilly put an end to this. Can't he deal with a few petty criminals? I am tired of worrying about thieves and vandals."

Seth didn't respond, well-schooled by his father not to rise to such bait. Anni took his hand and pulled him toward the door. "Come on, Seth, let's go. I can't wait to see the camp."

"Sure," he agreed. He let her lead him outside, shrugging off his irritation. "Come on, the skimmer's at the Co-op." She smiled and put her arm around his waist as they crossed the promenade. All thought of his father's problems vanished. Seth almost forgot to stop for the replacement batteries and other items he needed from the Co-op storage.

He easily caught Anni's enthusiasm as she questioned him about Migration and the country they passed over. Tobin Canyon Camp lay about half an hour by skimmer from Under Rim. The rock rim of a lava escarpment made a natural fence across the countryside. To get through it, animals funneled into Tobin Canyon. The steaders took advantage of that. The camp itself sat on the rim overlooking the trap.

"Wow!" Anni exclaimed. "When you said 'camp', I pictured something more temporary."

Seth landed the skimmer next to the long, low building. The walls were made of the dark lava rock, stacked and mortared into place. Solar-collector panels, ever-present on Carico, covered the south-facing side of the roof.

"Equipment room on the left end; cook's quarters, dining room, shower room, and the bunks on the right,"

Seth identified the line of doors. He picked up the lunch box and climbed out. "Come on."

She followed him up the stone steps, laying a hand on the wall and fingering the texture. "A shame to waste this on a seasonal camp. What a beautiful building."

"Not too bad inside either." He put his thumb on the pad to open the cookhouse door. "It's not really locked," he explained. "Anybody's print will open it, but this way the Co-op can keep track of any off-season use." A long table lined with benches dominated the room. The kitchen lay behind a counter at the back. "We'll leave the lunch here."

Anni wandered around, opening a few cabinets. "What now?" she asked.

"I'll put away the batteries and other things. Then we'll go down to the corrals."

"Can I look at the rest of the place?"

"Sure," Seth said and went to the control panel by the door to release all the locks. "I'll unload the skimmer."

He took the boxes into the equipment room and put away the batteries and various supplies to implant chips, vaccinate animals, and maintain the various equipment. He chuckled at Anni's energetic investigations. She disappeared into the bunkrooms, then the shower room with the enthusiasm of a kid. She met him back in front of the cookhouse.

"What do you think?" Seth asked. "Pretty rustic?"

"Yes, but comfortable," she answered. "It has all the essentials. The quarters look like the berths on a transport ship."

"If the weather is decent, most riders sleep outside. We don't like being closed in, I guess." He started down the steps then turned back and held out his hand to her. "Let's go check the communications vault."

Standing on the step above him, she looked him right in the eye. She leaned forward and kissed him. He pulled her closer, lost his balance when she leaned into him, and scrambled backwards down the steps to keep from falling. She laughed and followed him down. "Someone told me riders were clumsy off their horses."

"Clumsy?" He reached out to grab her, and she dodged past him, running for the communications vault across the yard. She beat him to the small building by half a stride. "You're fast for a cripple." He tugged her coat back over her arm in its sling and leaned down to kiss her.

"Hmmm, the steps were more convenient." She looked up at him.

"I think I've figured out why Pa wasn't happy about you coming with me today."

"Oh?"

"I'm having trouble remembering what I was going to do next."

"Something in here?" She pushed back against the door, but it wouldn't open for her.

"Oh, right." He trapped her there for a moment before thumbing the lock pad. "I'll just make sure everything is working."

She stepped aside, taking his hand. He kissed her again and reluctantly went into the cramped room. "Just give me a minute here."

He checked over each panel, looking for any warning lights or error messages. "This side is the comm equipment. Over here controls the repellers that we use some places where physical fences are tough to build."

"How do those work?" She stood just inside the door, a hand lightly on his back.

"Transmitters ... uh, we put a transmitter out." He turned to face her. "Somewhere we don't want animals to go." He pushed her gently back into the doorway. "It activates their implanted chip. They get a mild shock. It gets stronger, the closer they get. They learn to stay away. Now, wait here. I can't think with you hovering."

"Yes, sir." She leaned against the doorway and watched him silently.

"Okay, looks like everything is working." He resolutely took her by the hand, secured the door, and led her out to the edge of the bench overlooking the corrals in the canyon below. He tucked her in close to his side. "When you come to visit while we're working, you can watch from here."

"It's lusher than I expected. I thought we were coming down to desert."

"It's springtime — it'll dry out in a month."

"I still can't get used to the colors. The yellow tinge makes everything look, well, unhealthy, I guess. Compared to the greens I'm used to."

"That's Carico for you. Gotta be a little different." He got caught up in brown-gold eyes and pulled himself away. "Anyway, the tarbh come up the valley into the big pasture out there. Before we leave today, we'll open the gates so they can start gathering. The crew will work them through the pens, hold any that need doctoring, and move them into this canyon. They'll follow it into the upper pasture. Every couple of days, riders will move those animals out onto the spring range."

"And it works in reverse in the fall?"

"Pretty smart for a city girl."

She pulled back just enough to look up at him better. "I know a little about traffic flow."

"How are you with steep paths through the rocks?"

"We're going down there?" She pointed over the edge.

"Not right here." He took her hand again, enjoying the contact with her. "The trail's this way."

The footpath dropped off and clung to the escarpment, crawling over boulders and along ledges. "Go ahead. Just take your time. It's not far to the bottom." Seth let her go, giving her space to make her own way. She started out uncertainly, testing the footing, gradually moving more surely. Athletic, Seth thought. He took a deep breath and followed. He almost tripped watching the slender, graceful girl before he lost sight of her around a boulder.

He heard a screech, and she retreated around the corner to run squarely into him.

"What is it?" he asked, catching hold of her.

"Things, wiggly things hanging on the cliff. One almost hit me in the face."

"Oh, the ribbon worm colony." Seth laughed. "They're harmless." He took her hand and went ahead of her around the boulder. The sheer rocks on the right side of the trail rippled with movement. Long, thin growths hung from the wall like strips of yellow-green fabric.

"Are they plants?" Anni asked.

"More animal than plant, but they do have some chlorophyll in their skin. See, they're all trying to catch as much sun as possible."

"Harmless?"

"Yes, really."

She stepped closer, studying them carefully. "Odd creatures. Are they permanently attached?"

"They can drop off and slither like a worm to another spot if the colony gets too crowded."

"Carico has its share of surprises. I think I'll let you go first."

He laughed. He found himself doing that a lot. He went ahead, stopping at each of the long steps down the rock ledges to give her a hand. He lifted her down the last drop and set her on flat ground.

They came out next to another stone building by the horse corrals. Snow Creek lay to the right; it chattered over the boulders, careened around a bend, and slowed to wind through the meadows. Tobin Creek flowed down from the left into a ditch around the working pens before it joined the other creek.

She took his hand. "Sorry about that, back there. They took me by surprise."

"A little caution is a good thing," he said, his attention on her brown-gold eyes. "We have our share of hazards."

"I just don't usually scream."

"You are sidetracking me again." He tucked the long side of her hair behind her ear.

"Good." She leaned against him.

"Not yet. Work to do."

"Okay." She looked up at him invitingly.

He stepped back, catching her hand again. "Check the repeller in the mouth of Snow Creek; make sure the pens have all been repaired ..."

"Be sure the tack room is clean?"

"Walk all the way around the outer pasture."

"That must be miles," Anni said in protest.

"Then we'll take the skimmer for that."

She stepped back. "The sooner we get to work, the sooner we'll be done."

Seth tried hard to stay focused on the job at hand but strayed frequently into distraction. Anni climbed on the fences, splashed in the creek, and came back to him, happy to hold his hand or share a quick kiss before going off on another exploration like a puppy. He found himself whistling as he went around the corrals, closed each gate, and turned the water into the pipes that fed the troughs.

"Lunch time?" Anni sat on a fence.

"Sure. Things are set here. We can eat and then open the lower gates before we head back. Pa will have my hide if I don't get home on time tonight."

"Oh," she said with disappointment. "Oh, Gwyn's last night home, isn't it?"

"It is."

"Guess you really can't be late then."

Anni stopped on the way back up the path to study the ribbons again, daring to touch one lightly. She waited at the top to slide in under Seth's arm for the walk across the yard. They brought the lunch out onto the porch in the sun.

Anni started to take her coat off, then stopped. "I don't know if it's quite warm enough to go without this."

Seth took it from her. "Be right back," he said. He stowed the coat in the skimmer and brought back a soft, warm shirt. "I forgot I brought this. I thought you might want something to keep your clothes clean." He helped her get her good arm into the sleeve. He gently pulled the shirt over her sling and buttoned it. It was an old one of his and hung almost to her knees, covering the bright, shimmery blue tunic, hiding its ruffles. "We need to get you some more suitable clothes."

"Look who's talking." She pulled a frayed thread loose from his cuff.

"So, we'll both shop for clothes."

"I can probably afford one change."

"If I buy them, can I pick them out?" Seth stroked the soft flannel that draped over her shoulders. "You look so cute in this."

She moved away. "I can buy my own," she said firmly.

"How about if I scavenge the rag bag at home for something of Gwyn's?"

"Only if you put that shirt you're wearing in to replace it."

"Hey, this is my second best."

"Okay, we'll go shopping when we get back to town if we have time."

"Yeah, time." He put his arms around her.

"Food, then gates, right?" But she didn't move away.

"I know. Be responsible and on time. When's the next day you can distract me?"

"Tomorrow? I'm starting a new job after that, and I don't think I'll be able to get free for a while."

"New job?"

"Twice the pay; what can I say? Let's not talk about that now."

"I can pick you up in the morning, and you can watch me trim horse hooves. We should have the stead to ourselves."

"I like the sound of that."

Seth wished he had much more to do at Tobin. It didn't take nearly long enough to skim around the pasture fences and open those gates so the tarbh could begin drifting in. He took his time around the horse pasture and the upper pasture to be sure those gates were closed.

"Well, that's the last one." Seth sat against a rock so they were eye-level and toyed with the buttons on the shirt she wore as a jacket. "Guess we can head to town now."

"Nothing left to check on?"

"Not a thing."

"No hurry to get back yet though?"

Seth smiled. "Not yet."

"Good." Anni pulled another loose thread from his cuff. "I have had so much fun today."

"Me too." He looked her in the eye. "Why do I feel like we need to rush into this?"

She leaned closer and grinned. "Lust?"

"Well, there's that," he admitted. "Suddenly staying around Under Rim looks a lot more interesting."

"Just enjoy the moment and let tomorrow take care of itself."

"No way. I get to spend the whole evening looking forward to tomorrow."

"That's later. Right now, let's see how long a scenic route we can find back to town."

"Do we have to?"

"Show me what you love about this country."

Chapter 9

Seth

Seth shook the rain from his hat before knocking on Anni's door. She opened it promptly. She wore his old gray shirt and the sling over something sunny yellow and frilly, and she drew him like a magnet.

"I was afraid you wouldn't come," she said, giving him a quick kiss as he came in. "It's raining awfully hard."

"Can't let a little weather get in the way of work. Here, you might want this." He handed her the coat she had left in the skimmer.

"I just need to get my boots on, and we can go."

Seth watched her struggle to pull on her ankle-high boots one-handed. "Sit," he directed, laughing, and slid the boots on for her. "These will never do, you know, not in the mud."

She held up a pair of waterproof boot covers. "I have these."

"Those will get you to the store at least."

"But I can't afford to buy boots right now."

He offered her a hand up and held her coat for her. "I'm not going to have you standing around all day with soaked feet." He couldn't resist kissing her, taking pleasure in the feel of her against him.

"When you put it that way..."

"Come on. My gift to you, and I promise they won't cost more than I'd spend on lunch."

She laughed and skipped out of the door ahead of him. They raced through the puddles to the store. She took him by surprise with her speed. He had to push to keep up.

"You're fast in those city boots." He caught her by the waist and kept her out in the rain.

"Wait until you see me in running shoes." With a quick twist, she dodged away onto the porch.

He showed her the cheap muck boots, designed for nothing but keeping feet dry, and selected a pair of soft, heavy socks to go with them. He took a minute to find himself a new work shirt and pair of pants in the same browns he usually wore. With a glance at the edges of bright yellow showing beneath Anni's coat, he found a second shirt in a deep red silky fabric. He couldn't remember the last time he had bought a good shirt. She came over as he was looking at it and fingered it gently.

"That feels so nice. I love the color."

That decided him. He carried everything to the counter and scanned them, took his receipt and led Anni to the porch. He sat her on the bench.

"Try these." He handed her the socks.

"Oh, those feel marvelous. Warm, soft, ahhh." She rubbed one foot against the other, eyes closed.

"Glad you like them. You want the boots now?"

"If you insist."

They walked through the steady rain to the skimmer. She splashed in every big puddle they passed. "Best present anyone ever gave me," she said before getting in the vehicle.

He drove slowly, using the weather as an excuse to draw out the trip. "I hope you don't get too bored today just sitting around the barn watching me work."

"That sounds good to me. I think I overdid it yesterday. I'm sore this morning."

"Sorry, you should have said something."

She shifted her shoulder a little. "I didn't pay close enough attention."

"It didn't seem like much the other night. What happened?"

"Truthfully, I've hurt it before; it was still weak. Cartilage separation takes forever to heal."

"Okay, sitting and watching is your prescription."

"I'm not good at being a spectator." She reached over, and he took her hand. "But I think I can manage this time. Do we really have the stead to ourselves?"

"Nick volunteered to pick up the year's allotment of microchips for the tarbh so he could take Gwyn to

Portside himself. Of course, you never know what Pa will decide to do, but he said he would be in town all day."

"Just you and me ..."

"And half a dozen horses that need reminding that they are polite so they will stand for their manicures."

He drove the skimmer in under the shed roof on the north side of the barn and helped Anni out. Gathering up his purchases, he led the way to the bunkroom.

He watched Anni as she looked around. It was not even as big as her apartment. Two bunks, one above the other, took up one wall, with two lockers for personal things close by. A basic kitchen and compact bathroom completed the setup. Across from the door from outside, another led into the barn.

"Not much but it's home for now," he said with a grin. He put his new clothes on the top bunk. Picking up one of the two chairs from the kitchen table, he headed for the second door. She followed him into the dry coolness of the barn aisle.

"What now?" she asked.

"You can sit here and watch." He put the chair against the wall. She shut the door behind her and walked over to stand in front of him.

"I can't help?"

"Not yet ... How am I going to get any work done with you looking like that?"

She pulled her coat around her and sat on the edge of the chair. "Sitting. Watching. Trying not to look distracting."

"Can't be done." He leaned over to kiss her. "I'll give you a job to do later. Right now, spectate."

Seth walked the few steps to the pen that took up the end of the barn. He had shut four of the saddle horses there before he left for town. He watched for a minute, concentrating on them, before taking a halter from a hook by the gate and going in with them. He moved slowly among them, using his body language to ask them to pay attention and respect his space. When they relaxed and stood facing him, he walked up to the driest of the four and put the halter on.

"Hey there, Ratchet, I remember you." He talked quietly as he led the animal into the aisle. "Good boy, just come along." He led the horse the length of the barn, turned and came back, asked the horse to back a few steps, then let him stand. Continuing to speak calmly, he ran hands over the dark brown body and down the slender legs until every part of the horse had felt his touch.

"Anni, could you come hold him?" he asked. She stood up and came to him, moving slowly.

"Hi, Ratchet." She let the animal know she was approaching. "Such a good boy. You're a mud ball, aren't you?"

Seth handed her the rope. He brought his tools from the tack room and began the task of preparing the gelding's feet for the work to come. He inspected each foot carefully before he picked up one front hoof. He clipped off the ragged edges and smoothed out the oval shape, rounding the outside edge so it wouldn't chip. As he worked, he explained what he was doing. His unruffled voice reassured the horse. Paying attention to the narrative kept him focused on what he did. He only needed a few minutes to bring the hoof to the point that the horse stood straight and square on it. He picked up a squeeze-bottle and coated the outside and bottom of the hoof with pungent, sticky goo then counted out thirty seconds before putting the hoof down.

"What is that?" Anni asked.

"We call it iron sap. It's left after the sugar is removed from palm-pine sap. Don't touch. It's tough to get off."

"What does it do?"

"It keeps the hoof from chipping and splitting."

"Ingenious." She bent down and looked closely at the treated hoof. "And it's dry already?"

"You have to work fast once you spread it thin."

"Three more feet to go," she said.

"Plus twelve more in the pen." He picked up a back foot and began the whole process again. Anni leaned against the wall, soothing the gelding when needed and watching quietly the rest of the time.

"Okay," Seth said three feet later. "Walk him to the door and back." He watched the horse's feet and the way he traveled. "That'll do. Want another job?"

"Sure."

"He could use a good grooming. You can take him into the stall and brush him while I do the next horse."

Anni did as he suggested, taking the brush he handed her. Seth brought in the next gelding and went to work.

"Seth," Anni whispered urgently. He looked up from the hoof he was bent over. With wide eyes, she pointed at the post anchoring one corner of the stall. "Something's there."

He let down the foot he held and stood up. "What? Oh, that." He walked to the post and reached up to take hold of the creature by its stout prehensile tail. It wrapped the tail around his arm and sprawled there, its body the length of his forearm. It focused four eyes on him and hummed, clacking its stubby pincers and letting its other six legs dangle. "This is a spinxi."

"That's where the eggs come from?" She stared intently, keeping her distance.

"Well, this one's male. Here, he likes to be rubbed between his eyes. Just start from his neck."

She refused to come closer. "With those mandibles, I'm not likely to start from the front."

"He's friendly and don't let the spider-crab-lizard look fool you; spinxi are smart."

"So that is the Carico version of a kitty cat?" She eased a little nearer. "His face just changed color!"

"He's happy." Seth rubbed the smooth gray scales behind the now bright-blue face mask and encouraged the creature to move onto the top of the stall panel. "Off you go and leave the lady alone. She's not sure about you yet." The animal slowly withdrew its tail from Seth's arm, wrapped its pincers and tail around the post, and climbed up to disappear into the loft.

Anni came over and looked up. "I may never eat another egg."

"The next one won't taste any different than the last."

"At least I didn't scream."

"The horses and I appreciate that. How are you doing with Ratchet?"

She took off her coat and hung it over the divider. "He's a big muddy honey." She leaned forward against the boards.

Seth gave in to temptation and kissed her. "I can think of better things to do on a hot date than brushing dirt and hair off shedding horses."

"If you were on a hot date instead of working."

"I'm on a break." The bay gelding behind him shifted restlessly, stomping a foot and switching his tail. Seth drew back. "Maybe not."

She laughed lightly. "Horses first."

Seth worked diligently to finish the second horse. By the time he was ready to pass the third horse off to Anni for grooming, he realized that she was slowing down. He took the brush from her. "What happened to watching me work? Go sit for a while." He turned both geldings loose and brought in the last of the four.

"But the last one didn't get brushed," she protested.

"He's going back out into the mud anyway."

"So I've been wasting my time all morning?" She faced him with irritation.

He pulled her into his arms. "You've been loving on them and getting to know them. Now, save a little for me." He waited for her to soften against him.

"I might manage a little."

"Let me get this last horse done, and we'll break for lunch."

She sat on a bale of straw against the wall, pulled her knees up and wrapped her good arm around them. "Good, then maybe you can warm this date up."

"Patience."

Seth didn't recognize the last horse. The animal acted uneasy about being handled, unusual in those his father raised. "Where'd you come from, Blackie? Why the worried look?" He began a slow dance, moving the gelding around quietly. He watched the ears and the set of the head, looking for little signs of relaxation. He scratched and rubbed and waited. When the horse stood calmly, Seth picked up the first foot. He talked to the horse as he worked and nearly forgot Anni was watching.

"You are an artist," Anni said as he touched up one hoof that wasn't quite the way he wanted it. "I've seen feet trimmed before but never realized how complicated it was to do properly."

"'No foot, no horse' as they say." He lowered the hoof to the floor and retrieved the container of iron sap. Once he finished, he turned all four horses out into the pasture.

"Are you done?" Anni asked.

"I have a couple more to do after lunch. Right now, let's go get warm." He held out his hand to help her up. "Your hand's like ice."

They went into the bunkroom. Seth got a quilt off the bed and wrapped it around her. He pulled a chair over by the heater. "Sit here. How does soup sound for lunch?"

"Perfect."

They ate hot soup and drank hot sweet tea. Anni asked questions about things she had observed. Seth talked about horses, their subtle physical language, how they thought, his awe that they trusted him to confine them and restrain them against all their instincts.

"I think I am warm again," Anni finally said, carrying her bowl and mug to the sink. "What do you need to do this afternoon?"

"I should finish two more, but they'll be wet so no point in trying to brush them."

"I'll clean up here while you get started."

"You don't have to." He pulled the quilt tighter around her. "But you can stay here where you'll be warm."

She leaned against him, and he put his arms around her. She stayed there for a moment. "You're right. All my energy drained out when I warmed up."

"I won't be long."

He brought his own two geldings in, knowing they would be the easiest to work on. He could feel the effects of holding up horse feet in his back and legs. Two more would be all he wanted for one day.

When the horses were done and his tools put away, Seth returned to the bunkroom, looking forward to another mug of tea. Anni lay curled on his bed, sound asleep. He felt guilty about keeping her out in the cold so long. He stood and watched, deciding to take advantage of the chance to get cleaned up. He moved quietly to get a change of clothes and head for the shower, the one thing even better than tea for warming up.

He had to force himself to turn off the hot water; it felt so good after the hours in the cold. Hot showers sat at the top of his luxury list. His hair curled longer than he usually let it grow. He hadn't taken time to get it cut since he got home. He liked the way the new red shirt fit but hadn't thought about how good the smooth fabric would feel. He imagined Anni's hands warming the fabric against him. The rest of the day was theirs.

When he came out, Anni was sitting on the bed, looking half asleep. "Feel better?" he asked.

She nodded. "I'm sorry. I couldn't stay awake."

"The cold will do that. If you'd like, we'll go up to the house and build a fire in the fireplace. I'll start some stew so it can cook a while before dinner."

"Yes, that sounds nice." She stood up and carefully folded the quilt. "Oh, my coat's still in the barn."

"Got it." He retrieved it for her and helped her get it on.

"Thank you." She laid her hand on his arm. "You're all dressed up. Is this the shirt you got this morning?"

"It is."

"I love the feel."

He leaned down to kiss her before stepping back and getting his own coat. He put his arm around her waist as they hurried across the yard through the light, steady rain. She stopped at the top of the porch steps.

"Will Joe be home for dinner?"

Seth shrugged. "No way to know. Want to go back to the bunkroom?"

"You promised a fire."

"I did."

She watched with fascination as he built the fire, selecting each piece of wood and placing one on top of the other with care.

"I don't think I had ever seen a fire inside a house before the other night. Somehow it doesn't feel quite safe," she said. "But it attracts me too."

"I know what you mean. There's something comforting, almost hypnotic about a fire."

"You are so meticulous."

"Pa's training — use the physics to help get it started." He put a lighter to the fine material at the bottom of his construction. He grinned at her look of delight as the flames caught and licked up into the larger sticks above.

"I know enough about fires to know that is weird," she said, staring.

"What?"

"The flames — they're blue and green."

"Yeah." What was she getting at?

"But wood fires burn orange."

"Not on Carico,"

She studied the fire thoughtfully. "Of course, the copper content. I didn't think about that."

"Now orange flames would be weird."

Once the fire crackled vigorously, Seth settled into the big, old armchair closest to the warmth and held out a hand. Anni left the couch and came over. She still wore his old gray shirt over her own clothes.

"You make that worn out shirt look pretty good."

Slowly taking his hand, she let him pull her into his lap. She took a deep breath and let it out, relaxing. "I can't promise not to fall asleep again."

"Is that so?" He tucked her hair behind her ear and looked into her eyes.

"Maybe not for a while," she said softly.

Sometime later, Anni whispered, "Seth, the fire is dying." She tried to slide out of his lap. He held her long enough for one more kiss, then helped her to her feet. He added a couple logs to the fire and sat on the hearth.

"How's your shoulder?" He could see that it bothered her.

"Achy," she admitted.

"While I start dinner, you can go soak in the whirltub for a while."

"Are you offering to help?"

He grinned. "If you need it."

She walked over and stood tantalizingly close. "I can manage."

He pulled her shirt straight. "Then lock the door, just in case Pa comes home."

"Maybe I will." She went to her coat by the door and got something from the pocket, then disappeared down the hallway.

Seth was relieved to find ample leftovers to make into a stew of sorts. He'd intended to start something new but didn't have time to let it cook properly. The gray daylight was fading into night. He mixed a batch of biscuits, put them in the oven, set the stew on to heat, and tapped at the bathroom door.

"Anni, I'm going down to feed horses. I'll be back soon."

"How long until we can eat?"

"Pretty soon. Don't rush."

Seth ambled across the dark yard, thinking about the afternoon. He wasn't looking forward to leaving for Tobin Canyon in a few days. He feared they would lose the fragile new something between them. Then there was the weight of responsibility he did not want to carry. He had no practice bossing a crew.

While he was in the loft, throwing hay down into mangers for the horses, he heard a skimmer pass the barn. So much for a quiet dinner. When he left the barn, the skimmer sat near the house. Seth took that as an indication that his father didn't plan to stay long. As he stepped onto the porch, he saw the Marshal and Anni through the window. Joe held her by the shoulders, standing close, talking urgently, almost angrily. She looked upset, avoiding his eyes, letting that drape of hair fall across her face.

Seth paused at the door, unsure about walking in on them. He clearly heard his father say, "You little fool, if you are going to work for Jerdix, you can't be around me or mine."

Anni murmured something in reply, shaking off his hands.

Joe stepped back from her. "Think this through. You know I'm right."

She lifted her face. "I know what I'm doing," she told him.

Seth opened the door and went inside. "What's this about?" he demanded. "Anni, what's wrong?"

His father stood between Seth and Anni. "I am taking her to town now," he said with an unfamiliar edge to his voice.

"Why?" Seth moved toward her, but his father cut him off. Anni looked from one to the other unhappily.

"For her own good. Anni, get your boots on, now."

She laid a restraining hand on Seth's arm and shook her head very slightly before going to the door. Joe stood, arms crossed, until she was ready, then opened the door and escorted her through. "Your dinner is burning," he told Seth before shutting the door. Abruptly, Seth stood alone in the quiet house, baffled. The smell of scorching biscuits gave him a target. He pulled them from the oven and dropped the pan on the counter. By the time he returned to the door, the skimmer had gone.

Chapter 10

Seth

Seth put things away, made sure the screen was in place on the fireplace, and trudged back across the rain-soaked yard to the bunkroom. His mind scrambled from one idea to another — going to town dominated. He couldn't make any sense out of what had happened. Why was Anni not welcome in his father's house? Even if that was true, why the rush? Why not just let him take her home himself? Town, he definitely had to go to town.

As he approached the bunkroom door, he saw Anni sitting on the step, holding a spinxi and stroking its face. She gently detached its tail from around her arm and put it on the ground.

"You're here," Seth said needlessly. "How?" He dropped down on one knee next to her. Her eyes were red, and her face was wet.

"I told him I wouldn't leave until I explained to you."

"Come inside." He helped her to her feet.

"No, I ... let me say what I need to."

"Okay, what's his problem?"

She dropped her hair across her face and looked at his feet. "My new job — I'll be working for Jerdix. Joe's afraid I'll be right in the middle of the feud between them."

Seth lifted her chin and kissed her gently. "I don't care who you work for."

"Seth ..."

"If you aren't welcome here, am I welcome at your place?"

"Yes, yes, of course." She leaned against him, burying her face, then stepped back and wiped her eyes with her hands. "Take me home, please."

In the darkness of the skimmer, Anni reached out to find his hand. "Thank you, Seth. I have had so much fun the last couple of days."

"Me too." He tightened his hold on her. "When do you start work?"

"Tomorrow ... I won't be able to see you for a while. C.T. warned me he needed me to work long hours for a while to catch up on some things."

"I don't like the sound of that."

"It will keep me busy while you're down at Tobin."

He liked the idea that she would miss him. He'd gone cold inside when his father had essentially thrown her out. "About Pa, I don't know what to say."

"He is so suspicious of Jerdix," she said sadly. "Maybe he hopes his disapproval will keep me from taking the job." She withdrew her hand, and Seth heard her shifting in her seat.

"Will it?"

"No," she answered softly. "Seth, I need this job. I borrowed money for my passage. At the café, I barely pay my bills. C.T. offered me a good salary with responsibility. I can't pass that up."

"Be careful," he found himself saying. Although he was reluctant to admit it just then, Joe Reilly always had good reason when he felt strongly about something.

"I'm an executive assistant for his business. Do you really think he hired me just to get at Joe?" She sighed. "Anyway, maybe it is a good thing you'll be gone for a while so it won't be an issue."

"Maybe Pa will settle the whole thing with Jerdix," Seth said hopefully.

"And I'll be out of a job." She leaned her shoulder against his.

Seth parked by her apartment. "Here, you're home."

"Good." She got out and picked up the pair of ankle boots she'd left in the skimmer when she'd put on the rubber ones that morning. "Are you coming?"

He hurried to catch up with her. She stopped at the door. "I have one stipulation."

"What's that?" he asked, uncertainly.

"You are welcome but only you. We leave Jerdix, your father, work, all of it outside."

"Just you and me, here and now," he promised.

She hung her coat on a hook and kicked her boots off by the door, leaving the woolly socks on. Seth noticed that she didn't have on the tights she always wore. "Did you change clothes?" he asked.

She faced him, unbuttoned the old gray shirt, and slipped it off. "You changed. I thought I should dress for dinner too." She turned slowly to show off the short dress she wore. Its sweeps of red on black accentuated the cling of the light fabric. It was a single wrap, tied behind her neck, leaving her shoulders and back bare.

"Now that leaves just enough to the imagination." He smiled appreciatively.

"I'm glad you like it." She pulled the shirt back on like it was a fancy coat.

"Hey, not fair." He reached out to keep her from closing it.

"Just until it warms up in here."

He ran a hand over the soft fabric of the dress. "That long?" He stepped back and let her button the shirt. He had a sudden thought. "Where did you leave what you were wearing?"

She smirked. "On the floor next to the whirltub." He tried to think of something to say, stopped, and laughed. She joined in. "All my clothes in a pile on the floor in a house where I'm not welcome." She broke out laughing again.

"I'll get them back to you," he promised between chuckles.

"Oh, let him do it himself. Oops — I broke my own rule."

"I'll pretend I didn't hear that."

She backed away and pulled herself together. "I should have enough in the pantry to keep us from starving. One thing I am going to miss about working at Rajir's is having leftovers to bring home."

He wandered around the apartment while she fixed supper. It reminded him of the bunkroom, just one L-shaped room with the kitchen on one wall, the couch in the middle and the bed around the corner. She had no pictures and few belongings except for a scattering of rocks and pieces of wood she must have picked up nearby. He'd noticed she tended to touch things, checking the texture and feel.

"I have part of a bottle of wine, or there's beer if you prefer. Help yourself and pour a glass of the wine for me." She carried a tray with cold steak strips and assorted other finger food to the table by the couch.

He brought her wine with a beer for himself and sat next to her. "Is it warm enough in here yet?" he asked, straightening the collar of her shirt.

"Getting warmer by the moment." She held a bite of steak to his mouth. "Have a little fuel." He took her offering and found that his appetite, so rudely quelled by his father earlier, had returned. He selected a bite for her.

"Am I going to need fuel?" he asked.

"Oh, yes," she assured. He reached over and opened the top button of her shirt. She offered him another piece of food, rewarding him for each button he opened.

"This old shirt has never looked better but ..."

"It doesn't do a thing for my dress." She slid the shirt off her shoulders and let it fall.

He put his arm around her and pulled her onto his lap. "I do like the dress."

"Nice draping, don't you think?" She opened his top button. "Your turn to feed me."

Sometime in the middle of the night he woke up and stretched slightly, reaching out to search for Anni's warmth. She lay on the far edge of the bed with her back to him and stiffened when he touched her.

"What's wrong?" He moved closer.

"Nothing."

"I thought you were okay with this."

She turned over slowly and sat up, pulling the spread around her. "I am. It is just so unfair. The timing is absolutely the worst."

"I thought it was right on."

"Not that!" She relaxed a little. "I don't want to wait weeks to see you again."

"We can find a way."

"No, we can't." She lowered her face.

"Anni," Seth sat up and reached out to pull her close.

She jerked away. "Not Anni."

He pushed the hair off her face. "What does that mean?"

"Anni doesn't exist. She's a fabrication. Seth, you have to remember that. No matter what happens, whatever 'Anni' does, I am not her." She spoke urgently.

He turned the light on. "You are not making any sense. Talk to me."

She took a deep breath. "I'm sorry. I'm being silly."

"Tell me what you mean about Anni not existing."

She twisted a corner of a blanket back and forth, staring at it. "Forget I said that. We've had so much fun, and reality is going to come crashing down in the morning."

He lifted her chin and caressed her jawline. "So you changed your name when you came here. So did more than half the original settlers."

"That's not that." She let the tension out of her shoulders and kissed the palm of his hand. "Just know that 'Anni' is a role, not the real me."

"And the last couple of days?"

"Definitely me." She studied his face a moment before reaching across to turn out the light. He snuggled her against him.

"Morning's not here yet."

It arrived all too soon. The window lightened to a gray block and details of the room became visible. Seth lay quiet with Anni's pleasant weight and warmth against him, not wanting to disturb her. She woke anyway, stretching her full length. She turned far enough to check the clock and turn off the alarm.

"Five minutes," she groaned. "Then I have got to get ready for work."

"Can't be late your first day," he said, pulling her closer.

"No," she agreed, relaxing against him briefly; then she slipped out of his hold. "And I won't let you divert me. Throw something together for breakfast, please, while I shower." She stretched again as she got up and disappeared from his sight.

He stayed where he was, savoring the fading warmth and the spicy smell left on the blankets until he heard the shower running. The deep relaxation stayed with him as he dressed, then scavenged up breakfast for two.

Anni called from the bathroom, "Bring me the dark blue tunic, would you? It's hanging in the closet." She opened the door and looked out.

He found the requested clothing and took it to her. She slipped it over her head and pulled it straight. A ruffle followed a sinuous route from her right shoulder down and around to end up back on the right hem. He began tracing it with a light finger. She backed away, laughing.

"Food; work," she reminded. "Oh, I left the sling at the stead."

He caressed her sore shoulder thoughtfully, then went to his coat and got the scarf he had worn around his neck the day before. "This ought to work. Are you sure you need it?"

"Doc made me promise."

"If that's what Doc wants, better do it." Seth slipped the silvery gray fabric under her arm and tied it the way she wanted it. She finished dressing, nibbled at the food, and watched the clock.

He relented to her unspoken message. "I had better get out of your way."

"I suppose so." She stopped what she was doing. "I wish we had more time."

"Me too."

She came over and kissed him in a way that made him want to stay for another two days or years.

"When will I see you again?" he asked.

"Not soon enough." She slowly stepped back. "Wait right there." She rummaged in her dresser and brought back a piece of light cord. Measuring out two lengths, she cut them off. Taking his hand, she tied one cord around his wrist. She had him tie the other cord around her own.

"There," she said. "Something to hang on to — a knot in the end of our ropes." She sealed it with a kiss.

He fingered the cord. "You're sure I can't just be waiting for you when you come home?"

"Please, Seth, let me have some time. I have to do this. I need this job, and you have responsibilities right now."

"We can find time for both, can't we?"

"I ... stop it. Don't tempt me. Let's ... we'll make a date after Migration, for the day after you get back, at sundown, right here, just the two of us."

"For dinner?"

"For whatever you want."

"You were right before, when you said the timing is lousy." He took a deep breath and opened the door.

They stood there, unwilling to separate. Finally, he straightened her sling and walked away down the hallway, watching over his shoulder until she closed the door.

Chapter 11

Seth

Seth went straight home. He found himself whistling a cheery tune at odds with the gray, windy day. He changed clothes, brought in the horses that still needed their feet trimmed, and began his work. He looked up now and then, half expecting Anni to be sitting, watching him. She'd been so certain they wouldn't be able to see each other for a while, but he knew they would find a way. Meanwhile he had plenty to keep him busy.

The sound of a skimmer served as the light of reality that stripped away his euphoric fog. His father walked into the barn and stopped at Kybr's stall door. Seth continued rasping on the hoof he held between his knees, concentrating on leveling the small irregularities. Whatever conversation his father had in mind, Seth didn't want to have it.

Joe walked over to stand by the bunkroom door. "How are things going with Migration? Anything you need help with?"

Seth looked up. "No," he answered and continued what he was doing.

"About last night..." his father began.

Seth set the horse's foot down gently and straightened up. He didn't try to keep the anger out of his voice. "You threw a guest out of the house — my guest — without any explanation to me."

"Son ..."

"Pa, I don't want to talk about it."

"You don't understand." His father came closer.

"Anni won't be back here. Let it go at that." Seth walked around to the horse's other side and picked up its front foot.

Joe followed. "I wish I could let it go. Now listen."

In the past, Seth would have obeyed the commanding tone. Now he let the hoof down and draped his arm casually across the horse's back. "I don't want to hear it," he replied as calmly as he could. "You have no say about who I see or what Anni does."

"You had better hope that nothing happens to make it my business," the Marshal said softly, worry lining his face.

Seth refused to ask what that meant. "I've got work to do."

"All right, but we'll talk later." Joe turned reluctantly to leave, moving with tight control. Halfway to the barn door, he looked back. "Be at the house for dinner tonight."

Seth wanted to say no, to avoid any further discussion. He ran his hand down the gelding's rough, shedding coat, scratched above its tail. Better to get it over with, he decided. "Okay, I'll be there."

Maybe he could learn something more about the situation with Jerdix, the man that Anni would be working with for long hours. Some niggle of fear squirmed in his belly. He watched his father walk away, hating that he believed the Marshal's judgment more than Anni's assurances. What was the girl involved in? When would he get another chance to see her?

He resolutely went back to work on the gelding's feet. When he finished, he saddled the horse and led him to the round pen. None of the horses had been handled over the winter so needed a refresher on the basics. Seth worked with the bay on the ground until the horse relaxed and paid attention. Next he mounted to walk and trot the horse around. Satisfied, he rode over to open the gate.

Seth could have gone several directions but guided the horse across the meadow into the trees then trotted along the trail leading to the Dunns' cabin a mile to the east. He thought maybe he would stop and visit with Teri for a few minutes, find out when Nick would be home, just talk to someone. But when he actually saw Teri working in her garden, he couldn't face the idea of answering questions. He waved as he went by, took a trail to the south, and circled back to the stead.

He caught the little brown gelding Ratchet next and went through the same routine of groundwork before riding in the pen and then going out. This time, he made a loop to the north. His body read the subtle language of the horse beneath him, leaving his mind too free to run through the last couple of days. He missed Anni's laugh, the magnetic pull he felt to be in contact with her, her insatiable curiosity, and the fun he had sharing his knowledge of the land with her. He couldn't make sense of her insistence that she couldn't see him until after Migration, but he had promised to wait for her to get in touch with him. He shouldn't make promises when he was distracted.

Seth came back into the moment abruptly when the horse shied at a shadow and nearly jumped from under him. Taking the warning, he worked at keeping his mind on his business. Hoping a talk with Teri would help him focus on Migration, he rode the third horse back toward Dunns'.

Teri waved and called him over when she saw him. "How many more horses to tune up?" she asked.

"Five — I want to ride them all before I decide which ones to take to Tobin Canyon. When's Nick getting home?"

"Sometime this afternoon."

"I'd like his help tomorrow if you don't need him. Gwyn suggested moving the horses we aren't going to use to the pasture at Fallen Pine Cabin."

"I have things under control." She studied him for a moment. "Why don't you join me for lunch, and we can talk? I've hardly seen you since you got home."

"Thanks." Seth dismounted and walked with her toward the house. He tied his horse to the hitch rail outside the gate of the carefully tended yard. Teri planted her kitchen garden there, convenient to the house, separate from the expansive plot of medicinal plants she maintained. Still hesitant to face her scrutiny and the questions he expected from her, he took his time loosening the cinch of his saddle before going inside.

The main room served as living room, dining room and kitchen. Work space dominated the room, reflecting its utilitarian nature, with just a small cluster of comfortable chairs in one corner. It hadn't changed that Seth could see.

"Well don't stand in the door," Teri admonished. "Get cleaned up. I'm putting soup on to heat."

"Sounds good. Has it been a cold spring, or have I just been gone too long?"

"We certainly think you've been away too long, but spring is taking its time this year."

Over Teri's thick, well-seasoned soup, they talked about the move to Tobin Canyon Camp and the pending Migration. Teri planned to leave in a couple of days to get her kitchen set up before the crew arrived. Seth had the transport van scheduled for the day after that to pick up their horses. The van would get them in the morning and come back for Havers' crew in the afternoon. Tobin was the last camp on the list.

"I can't tell you how glad I was that you got here before Gwyn left," Teri told Seth. "I'm afraid Nick would rather be out in my garden than dealing with tarbh, much less running a crew. Gwyn was half-afraid to leave, knowing he would have to take her place at Tobin."

"She didn't give me much idea of why she wanted me back. If she had, I'm not sure I would have come. I know exactly how Nick feels."

"You did come, and everything is working out." She smiled warmly.

He sat back and played with his spoon. "Pa doesn't think so."

"Why do you say that?"

"He's acting strange, touchy. Last night he threw Anni off the stead." He looked squarely at her, gauging her reaction.

"He did what?" Teri dropped her spoon and stared at him.

"She has a new job, working for Jerdix. Pa told her she wasn't welcome on his property and was going to haul her back to town. She talked him into letting me take her."

She stood up and crossed behind Seth to look out the window. "I wish he and Lije would deal with that man. They're both about as friendly as bull tarbh these days."

"Tia, what's going on?"

She came back to sit across from him. "Be patient with your father, Seth. They have some kind of plan coming together. People are upset about the rise in thefts and brawls. Joe is feeling that pressure. I think ...

I hope... they'll have things back to normal before Migration is over."

"Anni says she can't see me for a while; she'll be too busy at work." Seth suddenly wanted to hear Teri say everything would be all right, to be reassured.

"You had a good time with her the other day. I could see that when we had Gwyn's dinner."

He grinned. "She's fun." He remembered just how much fun and knew Teri could read it all in his face.

"Did she make another date with you or leave it open?" she asked.

"Dinner, as soon as Migration is over." But would she have another excuse then?

"I think you need to trust her. She must have taken this job before she even met you."

"Is she going to be okay working for Jerdix?" He let his real fear surface.

"No matter what he said, your father will keep an eye on her." She laid a hand on his. "Seth, you came back in the middle of something that has been brewing for years. Your father is doing everything he knows how to keep his family out of what is really going on. We need to stay out of his way."

"So pack up and get to Tobin Canyon?"

"Anni will be here when you get back."

He returned to his horses, concentrating on giving each the attention it deserved. In the morning, he and Nick could make a final selection of which ones to use for Migration before taking the rest up the mountain.

The shadows stretched across the meadow before he finished with the last horse. He washed up and changed his shirt to go to the house. "Order me to come for dinner, then expect me to cook it," he grumbled to himself. He found the stew he had started the night before and put it on to heat.

At full dark, his father still hadn't appeared, not unusual for the Marshal although Seth was a little surprised not to hear from him. He ate alone, put the leftovers away and wandered to his old room. Finding an empty box, he packed away the few things still left on the shelves, miscellaneous treasures from his past. He didn't know how he could have had a better childhood. He missed the fun he, Gwyn, and Nick had had. He had always felt safe, had always had family and friends to depend on, and never worried about his next meal. Well, he hadn't missed many since he'd left either. When he finished with Migration, he had a good job to go back to and friends at Seven Wells. He never planned to stay. He closed up the house and went to the bunkroom to sit in the dark. Brown-gold eyes haunted his thoughts.

Chapter 12

Seth

In the morning, with barely enough light to make out the trees, Seth caught Jester and saddled him. A light showed in the house so his father must be up, but Seth rode away without going to find out. Teri expected him for breakfast.

Lije came out as Seth dismounted in front of Dunns' cabin. "Your pa still at the stead?" Lije asked.

Seth nodded. "Looked like it when I left."

"Good. Check the cabin while you're up at Fallen Pine today. Too many break-ins these days." The older man slapped him on the shoulder and headed for the skimmer.

Seth didn't linger over breakfast. Teri handed him and Nick lunches before they left. By full light, the two of them were bringing the geldings into the corral to sort them. An hour later, he took the lead on the trail to Fallen Pine Cabin, followed by seven loose horses, with Nick bringing up the rear. Most of the horses had been to Fallen Pine before and knew the routine. A lively trot kept them focused on moving and made quick work of the miles. It was barely mid-morning when Seth opened the gate to let the herd into the big pasture.

"You already fixed the fence, right?" he asked Nick hopefully.

"'Fraid not," Nick replied. "That's why we got an early start, isn't it?"

"The tools should be in the shed at the cabin."

They unsaddled their horses and left them hobbled in the meadow while they went to work on the fence. The winter snows left them plenty to do splicing wires and clearing fallen branches. They kept at it long after their stomachs told them to stop for lunch, finishing both the main pasture and the smaller one near to the cabin. Rain started falling as they struggled with the last downed tree, cutting it into small enough pieces to move.

"Hey, a little good luck," Nick laughed. "The wires didn't break."

"True, but I would rather have broken wires and less rain." Seth threw the last branch aside and began tightening the wires. "Got it."

"Good." Nick snatched up tools and ran for the cabin with Seth close behind. They scrambled up the steps onto the porch and shook themselves like wet dogs. "Maybe this will let up before we head home. I think I see a patch of clear sky."

Seth pulled his lunch from his saddle bag, glad he had put his saddle on the porch, and sat down. "What is the weather going to do? Are we going to be working in this down at Tobin?"

"Clearing for a few days. It'll be drier down there anyway. You know how these storms run into the Rim and soak this higher country."

Seth leaned back and put his feet up on the railing. "This was always one of my favorite spots."

Nick pulled over another chair and fished in his shirt pocket. "For lots of reasons. Have a button." He held out a handful of flattened pea-sized seed pods.

"I forgot about that buttonweed patch." Seth took a couple of the pods and put one in his mouth. The seeds contained a mildly euphoric intoxicant. "It doesn't grow down on the desert."

"I hear you came home with the sun bats yesterday." Nick chewed on a pod while he got out his own lunch.

Seth started slightly, wondering who else knew that. "I had breakfast in town," he said as smoothly as he could.

"After dinner in town?"

Seth grinned and raised an eyebrow. "Pa threw her off the stead. I gave her a ride home, and she invited me to stay."

"Is that so? She seems too shy and quiet for you. Or has she been putting on an act for all the riders who have taken to eating at Rajir's since she started work?" Nick ate one of the pods followed by a bite of sandwich.

"They are out of luck."

"Oh, yeah?"

Seth looked at his companion. "She went to work for Jerdix; started yesterday."

"That will hurt the café's business. So she's expecting you tonight?"

"No." Seth tried to sound casual.

"What? No invitation to come back?"

"We have a date the day after Migration is over."

"Ouch — that'll get canceled."

Seth shrugged. "Could be." He stared at his sandwich.

Nick sat forward. "She's more than just good company," he declared. "You're getting snared."

Seth shrugged again. "She's fun."

"I hear you." Nick got suddenly quiet. "Will you keep a secret from the family?"

Seth set his feet back on the floor. "Don't I always?"

"You always did. Well, here's another. Gwyn and I got married in Portside."

"Married?" Seth sat up and let it soak in. He slapped Nick on the shoulder. "And she's not even showing yet?"

"She's not even pregnant, mate. How's that for impulsive?"

"Crazy kids!" Seth laughed. "But why keep it secret? You've only been together forever."

"Oh, we'll do the whole family thing when the time is right. You know what kind of a party that's going to be — after Migration and the election and this mess with Jerdix, when we can give it the attention it deserves."

"Yeah, Jerdix." Seth took a breath and held out another pod. "A toast — to a long and productive pairing." He popped the pod in his mouth, grabbed Nick by the collar and dragged him out into the pouring rain. "And lots of cold showers at Tobin."

"Me and you both." Nick stabbed Seth in the chest with his finger. "Because I think quiet little Anni may not be so shy in private."

Before leaving, they walked through the cabin, making sure nothing was disturbed, and put the tools away in the shed out back. Seth checked the control room, noting the battery packs showed a full charge. Maybe he would bring Anni up for a few days after Migration where they could get away from his family. In their enhanced good moods, he and Nick rode merrily home, sharing stories of old times and joking about their futures.

Seth turned down Teri's invitation to dinner. "I was supposed to have a talk with Pa last night, but he never showed. Better do it tonight," he explained. Good thing buttonweed wore off quickly. He would be better off with a clear head. "I'll be over in the morning to help you load up for Tobin." He exchanged a look with Nick and struggled not to burst out laughing. Teri looked from one to the other but let it go.

When Seth rode out of the trees below the barn, he saw the Marshal's skimmer parked in the shed. His father stood on the porch. Seth acknowledged him with a wave and went into the barn to put away his horse and change out of rain-soaked clothes.

Joe waited on the porch, sitting in a chair with his elbows on his knees. Seth relaxed a little and stopped on the steps, eye level with his father.

Joe straightened in the chair. "Sorry about dinner last night. Something came up."

"Work," Seth said. "I remember how that goes." He climbed the last steps. "I hope you didn't need any of the geldings. We took them up to Fallen Pine today."

"No, that's fine. You're going to Tobin Canyon tomorrow?"

"The day after. Teri and Nick are going down tomorrow."

"Do you need help loading horses?" Joe stood up.

"I can handle it but, if you've got the time, an extra hand wouldn't hurt."

"Come on in." Joe led the way inside. "I'm glad you're here. This place has been echoing like an empty barn since Gwynnie left. Too big for one person."

"She'll be back."

"I doubt that, not to live, no more than you will."

Seth followed his father to the kitchen. "I don't know. She's stayed this long."

"Even if she does, with her telecom work I'll need someone else to run this place." Joe looked hopefully at Seth.

Seth shook his head. "I can give you some names. I know a couple of riders down at Seven Wells that might be interested."

"We can talk about it after Migration." Joe began getting out the ingredients for biscuits. "Do you mind putting together a salad?" he asked.

Seth started to comply, then decided to confront the proverbial tarbh bull in the room. "About Anni ..." he began.

His father tensed and looked at him. "Anni?" His voice raised a little. "Okay, I'm sorry I treated her the way I did. And you too. But you don't understand the situation."

"No, I don't." Seth kept his tone level.

"The thought of that sweet kid working for Jerdix gives me chills but you..." Joe jabbed a finger at Seth. "You need to stay away from her."

Seth stood his ground. "I'll be down at Tobin, remember."

"Good. That'll make it easier. You can't help her right now."

Seth slammed a hand onto the counter in frustration. "It's my choice and my life."

"It is not your life I am concerned with." Joe strode away across the room, running his hand through his hair. Coming back, he sank down on a stool, facing Seth. "Trust me on this. For her sake, stay away. Don't antagonize Jerdix right now."

Seth took a deep breath. "Okay, not because you tell me to but, since I'll be at Tobin, I won't have much choice, will I?"

Joe studied him for a moment. "Good enough. Steak for dinner?"

"Sure," Seth replied and began getting the salad together.

Seth walked to Dunns' for breakfast and stayed to help pack the accumulated supplies into the skimmer. Teri hurried him and Nick, wanting to get to Tobin so she could unload and go into Under Rim for a second load. She had six hard-working riders to feed for the next three weeks or so.

After watching the skimmer glide away, Seth rode Nick's horse home, leading Teri's pony. Both animals would go on the transport with the six left at the Reilly stead. Seth thought about trailing them all down to Tobin. The closest of the camps, it was only about twenty miles from town. But that made it more like thirty from the house, and the Co-op routinely provided transport. Might as well take it.

He found something for lunch and spent the afternoon packing up his personal gear and working with the horses. They rarely rode in a van so getting them to load often took some convincing. The more obedient they were, the smoother things would go. Seth lost touch with everything else when he focused on the dance with a horse, working at it until he led and the horse followed consistently. Suddenly he realized that the sand of the pen was completely in shadow, and he had no more horses to bring in.

The stead's skimmer sat next to the bunkroom door, but there was no sign of the Marshal's. His father hadn't come home. The thought came to him that he should go to town for dinner, his last chance to relax until Migration was over. He acted on the thought before he could talk himself out of it. Just dinner — maybe Anni would still be working, and he could get a glimpse of her from across the street, just to reassure himself that she was all right. He cleaned up and headed for town.

He found a parking spot behind the inn between a couple out-of-town vehicles probably belonging to tarbh buyers there for Migration. If his father believed his seeing Anni was risky, the least he could do was avoid being noticeable. He admitted to himself that he intended to do more than watch the girl from across the street. He came in the back door of the café and made his way to the table in front where he sat his first night back.

Sure enough, the lights were still on in Jerdix's office. He could make out Anni at a desk with Jerdix leaning over her, looking at something. The man's hand rested on her injured shoulder. Seth cringed and forced himself to look away. He'd lost his appetite.

Business was slow. Most of the riders were already out at the camps, and the few buyers didn't make up for them. Tam Rajir came over to take his order. Seth wondered if Tam would even try to find someone to replace Anni until summer.

"Evening, Seth. You're off for Tobin tomorrow I hear."

"Right. I wish Flech was going to be there to help."

Tam laughed. "He has more important things to do. Did you hear Ches had the baby yesterday? A little girl."

"No, I didn't. Good for them."

"The Marshal says you're just here for Migration."

"I left a good job to help out. I'd like to get back to it before they find someone else."

"Well, enjoy your meal, and holler if you need anything. I'll be in the kitchen."

"Thanks. Give Ches and Flech my congratulations."

Seth picked at his food, thinking about changes and family. He kept an eye on the office across the street, hoping they would finish soon and Anni would go home. He had to see her one more time before he left for Tobin, to keep the feel and smell of her fresh but mostly to know she was okay.

He lingered over a mug of tea. Tam came back and filled him in on local affairs until the lights in Jerdix's office finally went out. The man crossed the street with his arm possessively around Anni. Seth thought she moved stiffly, without her usual spark and energy. The two disappeared toward her apartment.

"Guess I'd better get out of here," he told Tam. "Tomorrow will be a long day." He left through the back door and waited, a knot in his stomach, trying to decide what he would do if Jerdix stayed very long. Relief washed over him as the man came from the apartment and strolled back toward the promenade. Seth let him get out of sight around the café before hurrying to Anni's door. He took off his hat and knocked.

She opened it quickly, looking distressed and surprised. "You aren't supposed to be here," she said, looking past him as though she expected someone else to come up behind him.

"Should I leave?" he asked uncertainly.

She shook her head. "No, of course not. Come in." She took his hand and drew him inside, closing the door behind him hurriedly. "I'm sorry. I've had a long day."

"He headed back to the office, I think. He didn't see me." Seth guessed at what worried her.

"Good." She shuddered. "But I thought we agreed not to see each other until after Migration."

"I was in town for dinner and saw you going home. I thought I'd stop by and say good-night." He still stood just inside the door, hat in hand. She took it from him and hung it up.

"Just happened to be here?"

"Pure chance," he said with a grin.

"He's coming to pick me up very early. We're going to Portside for a meeting at their office there."

Seth couldn't quite read her, whether she was setting a time limit or suggesting he should go. He waited, giving her time. She leaned into him and kissed him lightly. He stroked her face, drawing her close. She slipped gently away.

"Let me see if I can shed work with these clothes." The charcoal-gray suit she wore hid her contours, hanging straight and square except where her left shoulder slumped. He saw that he hadn't imagined her lack of energy.

"You've been shopping." He pulled off his boots.

"He wants a city look to his office, even out here."

Seth noticed the harsh emphasis she put on 'he'. "The job's not working out?" he asked.

"Long hours, like I told you it would be for now. Pour me about half a glass of wine, please. I need to unwind a little." Even her voice sounded dull.

He found the wine and a glass and settled down, stretching his legs the length of the couch. She came back, the dark gray stiffness of the suit replaced with the soft light gray of his old shirt.

"One of the best pieces of clothing anyone has ever given me," she said, forcing a smile. She sat on his lap then slid back to lie between him and the back of the couch. "You have no idea how exhausting it is to stare at facts and figures and business stuff that hardly makes sense for fourteen hours."

He shifted down so her head could rest on his shoulder. "He's taking you to Portside?"

"One day turn-around — that's why we're leaving so early. I get to record, carry files, and all the rest of the assistant duties."

"No sling?" He stroked her face and ran a hand along her shoulder, feeling her slight flinch.

"I'm just sitting at a desk; besides the sling gets in my way." Her voice trailed off wearily. She lifted her chin and kissed his throat. "Sorry I'm poor company. He'll be here early."

"So you said. I'll be gone before he comes."

"I'm glad." She snuggled against him. "That you're here, I mean." But she only responded to his caresses drowsily.

"Come on, sleepy." He stood up and pulled her to her feet. "Time for you to go to bed."

She took his hand and followed him across the room. He pulled down the covers. She sat on the edge of the bed. "Don't leave yet."

"I won't. Lay down on your stomach." When she complied, he pulled the shirt down off her shoulders. "Wait right there." He scavenged through the kitchen cabinets for a bottle of bean tree oil. Very gently he spread the oil across her back and worked it in, feeling her tension release. When she slept, slack and peaceful, he tucked the blankets around her and kissed her in the hollow beneath her ear.

"Sleep well," he whispered and left her there, feeling a deep-seated contentment temporarily overriding the impatience he knew would be with him until he saw her again.

Chapter 13

Seth

Seth woke with a start. Someone was knocking. "Coming," he said and rolled off the bunk. He pulled on his pants and crossed to open the door. His father stood there. "What's going on?" Seth asked.

"Another call-out. Looks like you'll have to get by without me this morning."

Seth nodded. "No problem. Something serious?" Even half-asleep, he noticed the unusual tightness in the Marshal's expression.

"Just annoying. You keep that crew in line, hear me? I'll swing by Tobin when I get a chance."

"Sure."

The Marshal turned to go. "Are you taking the skimmer?" he asked.

Seth shook his head. "No, I'll ride down with the van."

"Better if you stay at Tobin anyway — easier to resist temptation."

Seth squared his shoulders, suspecting his father knew where he had been the night before.

Joe chuckled. "Take it easy. I'm not going to lecture. You may not believe this, but I do remember how it feels. Your mother ... well, I had a lot of trouble paying attention to business when I first met her."

Seth stared. He couldn't remember his father ever talking about his mother like that before. Pulling himself back to the moment, he asked, "How did you know?" He thought he had been careful.

"I saw the skimmer, but you weren't in the tavern or the café." Joe looked him in the eye with one hand firmly on his shoulder. "Listen to me. Just stay down at Tobin and take care of Migration. She'll be here when you get back. Now, sorry, but I've got to go."

Seth ate a substantial breakfast, not knowing what lunchtime might bring. By the time the van arrived, he had the horses caught and ready. With unexpected luck, the older animals loaded easily, and the two colts were anxious to join their friends. With all of them on board, the driver helped him throw his gear bag and saddle in, and they were off before mid-morning. An hour later the horses were standing in a corral at Tobin Canyon Camp, and the van was disappearing toward Under Rim.

"Someone left all the upper gates open," Nick said, leaning on the fence next to him, watching the horses.

"What?" Seth stiffened. "Anni and I closed every one when we were here."

"Well, they were open."

"As long as they're closed when we start pushing tarbh that way." Seth made a mental note to have someone check again later. Open gates could foul up the entire grazing management for the summer if animals moved into the wrong pastures early. The weight on his shoulders grew heavier, and Seth didn't like it. He put his saddle in the tack room and shouldered his gear bag for the climb to the bunkhouse.

His mind provided snapshots of Anni climbing the path like a graceful colt, pausing to investigate the ribbon worm colony, laughing. He scrambled up the last rock steps, feeling lighter. He deposited his bag in the separate quarters reserved for the camp boss and came out just as a skimmer stopped in front of the building. A girl climbed out.

"Hey, boss man, going to help unload?" she asked.

"Sure." Seth struggled for the name — Flech Haver's sister, the older one, two years Seth's junior. "Janie, right?"

"Right. Charlie Rajir's coming down with the van. They should be here mid-afternoon."

"Tam's brother," Seth placed the name. "Who else is on the crew?"

"It was supposed to be us and two of Hu's riders, but I hear Jerdix traded with him."

"Jerdix?" Seth's stomach knotted.

"New to the district since you left," Janie said.

"Yeah, I've met him. Pa doesn't think much of some of his help."

"Rough bunch," she agreed.

"Which one's Charlie's bag? He can bunk with Nick. You'll be single, it looks like."

Late in the afternoon, Seth and the three riders lounged on the porch. Teri was inside, getting dinner ready. Seth felt better about things. He had a good crew. Janie might be young, but she knew what she was doing. Charlie was older, experienced and steady. With them and Nick, he could manage. He wished he could just send Jerdix's riders back home, whenever they got there.

Nick stood up. "Riders coming."

He was right. Two men rode along the rim of Tobin Canyon, each leading two horses. They crossed the yard and stopped in front of the cookhouse. The first was young, slightly built, with dark hair and light eyes. He wore a bright shirt and a broad-brimmed hat with copper on the band. His companion looked a lot like the rider who had attacked Seth outside Rajir's.

Seth kept that to himself, determined not to be goaded into something. He stood and came out to the edge of the porch. "You're Jerdix's riders? Just in time for dinner." He came down the steps. "I'll give you a hand with your bedrolls. Then you can take your horses down to the pens."

The younger man looked down at Seth with a smirk and spoke to the other man. "Look who's here, Bull. It's the Marshal's cub."

Seth stepped away from the horses. "Seth Reilly," he said, belatedly taking a firmer stance.

"Well, Seth Reilly, you can call me Whip. Why don't you be a good host and put our horses away for us?"

Seth glanced around. Nick stood at the top of the steps. Charlie had a hand on Janie's arm, keeping her seated. Seth ran his hand through his hair to give himself a moment. How to handle these two? Dougherty, his boss at Seven Wells, would send them packing, but Seth had to take the riders a stead sent. Calmly but firmly he said, "Dinner's in about twenty minutes. Bedrolls here; horses down in the pens."

"Not very hospitable." The man made no move to dismount and pull the bedrolls off the pack horse.

"The horse trail down to the pens is about a quarter mile back the way you came," Seth said, keeping his voice level.

The two men exchanged a look, grinning.

Seth climbed the steps to the porch. "Better hustle. Cook won't wait."

Whip tried to stare him down. Bull jostled their horses together and said, "Better keep the cook happy." He dismounted and dropped their bedrolls to the ground. "The first two rooms look good to me." He pitched the bedrolls onto the porch.

"The far room's empty," Seth said. "Nick, throw their rolls there. Now, are you two planning to eat?"

"Come on, Bull. The pup wants us to carry our own weight." Whip turned his horse and headed back the way they had come. The bigger man waited, watching the group on the porch until Whip was on the trail, then mounted and followed without a word.

"I'll go show them around," Seth said, slipping his hands into his pants pockets to hide their shaking. He hated to give the riders even that much courtesy.

Charlie stood up. "No, Boss. I'll do it. They're not looking to pick a fight with me. But, if you don't mind me saying so, I'd appreciate it if you'd set my door so just Nick and I can get in."

"Sure, Charlie, thanks."

"My door too, please," Janie said. "I've seen Whip around the tavern. He's nasty rude; no respect for anyone. Bull's not much better."

Seth nodded, remembering a knife flashing at him. "I'll set the locks for privacy. Nick, go down with Charlie. Get them settled and show them the footpath." He pulled himself together, thinking how close he had come to letting the men get control of their meeting. He needed to take charge. He looked at his crew. "Nick, Charlie, I want you two to ride with them in the morning to start bringing tarbh in. Janie, I want you to go around and check all the upper gates while they are doing that. I've got a hunch you'll find some gates open, and I don't want animals getting onto the wrong spring range."

He went to the overlook and watched the men unsaddle and put their horses in a corral. Charlie acted friendly enough with them but managed to find something he needed to do so that he avoided helping them. Nick kept his distance, walking through the alleyways and pens that would hold a bunch of half-wild tarbh in the morning. When the four started for the footpath, Seth went back to the cookhouse.

The long table was loaded with food and places set for six. Teri reserved a place at the counter for herself. Seth wished he could do the same. His back itched at the thought of sitting down to eat with the two. He waited for everyone else to sit before nudging Charlie aside to take the place next to Bull himself. Janie sat across from him. Whip had planted himself next to her with a leer. Food disappeared. Nick and Janie ate hurriedly. Seth could barely eat at all.

Custom called for them to remain at their seats until Teri served dessert. The tension seemed to amuse Whip who crowded Janie at every opportunity while watching Seth. The two men delayed clearing their plates and began to talk between themselves, ignoring the rest.

"That little piece from the café is working for the boss now," Bull told his partner. "Too bad."

"Yeah, that'll mean hands off for us." Whip leaned against Janie, reaching for a roll and looking Seth in the eye. "He does have a way of wearing out his women."

Seth gripped his knife, but he managed to return Whip's look without wavering. It was Teri who stepped in, jerking serving plates out from in front of the two. "You want to eat in my cookhouse, then keep it polite at my table," she said coldly.

Bull laughed. "Yes, ma'am. Never pays to make the cook mad, does it, Whip?"

Teri glared. "I'll bring dessert to the porch. Scrape your plates and put them in the sink on your way out."

The days settled into a haze of dust, bellowing tarbh and shouting riders. Seth teamed Charlie and Nick with Whip, leaving himself to ride with Bull and Janie. First thing in the morning one team would sweep the lower pasture, bringing up the animals that had drifted in from the winter range while the other team pushed the tarbh from the upper pasture out the west gates onto the designated spring range.

While the animals just gathered into the pens settled down, the crew ate breakfast. Seth remembered past Migrations when those meals were spiced with discussion of various little contests that went on continually — most "clean catches" by roping both hind legs to drag a calf to the ground crew or most calves roped and drug in a day or, on the other side, most misses. Now meals were mostly silent, uncomfortable affairs. Jerdix's riders were unendingly entertained by the others' silence. Seth slept poorly and ate uneasily. He looked forward to the few minutes each morning when he was alone with Teri, getting the vaccines and implants organized for the day. Somehow her quiet support gave him strength to face the day.

In the pens, two people roped; Seth and one other worked on the ground, implanting chips, vaccinating, and punching the owning stead's mark in the calf's fan; and two stayed horseback, one to scan the mother's chip and call out her number to Seth, and the other keeping angry tarbh mommas away from the ground crew. Nobody escaped close encounters with the powerful animals. Even calves could deliver a damaging kick or butt.

Whip discovered that he could antagonize all of them by eyeing Janie across the table or the corral without ever speaking directly to her. Seth overheard her muttering to her horse about the life expectancy of the strutting cock if he thought he could follow the looks up with action. Bull just bumped into things — the table, a person, or his horse into someone else's.

The two got more than their share of the roping, the preferred job. It was the only task Seth could trust them to carry out reasonably well. Both were too conceited to put on an intentionally poor performance when roping although neither hesitated to drop vaccine injectors in the dirt, have trouble reading the scanner, or fail to divert a charging mother.

The fourth morning, as they began working on the day's gather, a skimmer landed by the corrals. Jerdix climbed out and crossed to lean against the fence. Both his riders broke off roping and rode over to talk with him briefly. Seth tried to ignore him. Steaders were welcome to visit; it didn't require the camp boss to quit working. It made Seth nervous though. He began double checking each cow's fan marks against the number Nick called out from the scan that began with the stead's code. Whip and Bull's roping speed improved dramatically under Jerdix's eye. Seth and Charlie had to hustle to keep up on the ground.

"That's my calf!" Jerdix climbed halfway up the fence to yell across the pen. Charlie stepped back from the animal on the ground. Seth double-checked the code he was programming into the implant, then looked at the cow Janie was blocking. Her fan had an old split that made the mark hard to read. Seth knew her. She was a Reilly cow. He remembered her coming in with that torn fan as a yearling.

"Nick, rescan her." Seth tried unsuccessfully to keep his voice calm.

Nick moved in on the cow. Bull rode over, crowding the already unhappy tarbh. The animal charged at Nick's horse, nearly unseating him, before disappearing into the herd. Bull spurred his horse after the cow, sending the tarbh into flight. Whip's horse panicked and began bucking through the frantic animals. Whip freed the rope; the calf leaped up, bawling for its mother. Seth and Charlie scrambled for the fence where they perched until the motion slowed to a restless milling.

Seth glared at the animals in disgust. He jumped to the ground, snatched up the rope left by the calf, and pitched it at Whip. "Everybody take a break; let them calm down."

"Cut that cow out now!" Jerdix shouted, his big hands gripping the fence.

Seth looked around the corral. "Bull, give your boss your horse. He wants to try and get that cow out of the bunch right now, he can do it himself." Seth caught a glimpse of Charlie's subtle thumbs-up. "Now, Bull. Time's wasting."

Jerdix waved the rider away. "I'll be looking for that pair. They'd better be carrying the same code come fall."

Seth turned his back on the man and cleared the programming on the implant gun. Charlie handed him the water bottle. The noise and dust began to settle. Nick and Janie rode over and dismounted, taking their turns with the water. Without a word, they remounted. Charlie picked up the vaccine gun. Seth nodded.

"Somebody get us a calf," he said. Jerdix scowled at him, then stomped away, climbed into the skimmer, and left.

Two days later, at breakfast, Whip got a comm call from Jerdix. He listened, said "Yes, Boss," and disconnected. He laid a hand on Bull's shoulder, and the two left without a word. Seth started after them, but the comm sounded again. Teri answered it and waved him back.

"It's the Marshal," she said. "The Arbiters want everyone at a District meeting tonight."

"Everybody? That's strange. Did he say why?"

She shook her head. "No, but my sense is that they finally have something concrete on the burglaries."

"That might explain where those two are off to." Seth came back to the table. "The four of us can handle that little bunch we brought in this morning. Everybody gets a chance to rope."

"'Bout time," Janie said with a grin.

"You all can head for town as soon as we're done."

An arriving skimmer interrupted the cheers. They watched Jerdix's two riders load their bedrolls and climb in. The skimmer left, dropping into the canyon.

"Taking their saddles too," Charlie said and returned to his breakfast. "Maybe they won't come back."

"We'd get more work done without them," Nick said.

Seth nodded. "Let's get to it then."

They hurried to finish eating. Seth stayed behind as the rest filed out. "Tia, did Pa say anything else?" he asked.

"He sounded excited."

Seeing the relief on her face, he hugged her. "Things can get back to normal around the steads."

She turned away, fussing with something on the table, and said, "I just want to have Lije and your father home safely at night for a change."

Seth kept his hope to himself that Anni would soon be away from Jerdix. "Come down and watch this morning," he said.

"I'll do better than that. I'll come help."

"I'll catch a horse for you."

"One more thing."

"What's that?" he asked.

"He said to tell you not yet."

Not yet. Stay away from Anni. "I hear you," he replied reluctantly. "I just want to know she's safe too."

"You'll see her at least. Trust him, Seth."

"Yeah." He gave her a quick kiss on the cheek and headed for the corrals.

The morning's work took on the atmosphere of a party. Even so, things went quickly. At one point Nick told Seth, "I haven't seen Mom this relaxed in weeks. You don't know how bad things have been."

Seth conceded that point. "Hopefully she's right about the reason for this meeting."

He tried to get Nick and Teri to go to town with Janie and Charlie right after lunch, but they decided to wait for him. They let the tarbh in the pens drift to the upper pasture on their own, but someone needed to tend to those in the hospital pen. Seth and Nick did that while Teri cleaned up her cookhouse.

Teri objected to going into town for dinner. Seth had to admit that she was right about how busy the café would be, so he accepted the generous leftovers she offered instead. Having made that decision, Seth delayed their start for town until just in time to make the meeting. He badly wanted to see Anni but told himself firmly that he needed to check out the situation first. The less time he was in town, the less tempted he would be.

Under Rim was bursting with vehicles and people. Teri ended up parking behind the Marshal's Office across the plaza from the Gathering Hall. Seth trailed behind Nick and Teri as they pushed through the people into the room.

"Can you see Lije and Joe?" Teri asked.

"Pa's up front," Seth answered. He could make Joe out over the crowd, standing next to a short, sturdy man with very pale skin and near-white hair. Seth recognized Rodahl Vinz, the principal advisor with the Rangers, Central Services' environmental branch. He and Joe had been friends for years. But how were the Rangers involved in the current problems?

Nick led the way to one side where they found an open spot to stand against the wall. Teri kept one hand on Seth's arm and the other on Nick's back. Seth felt her tension and laid his hand over hers. "Looks like Tam's about to call this to order," he said.

The five Arbiters sat in a row across the center of the stage. The Marshal moved to a lectern to the left. He spotted Seth's group and flashed a grin their way. To the right, off the stage, Jerdix stood, talking impatiently with a small cluster of people, mostly his own riders. Whip and Bull were notably missing. Jerdix had Anni's arm tucked under his elbow but otherwise ignored her. She wore the dark suit and looked down passively, taking no part in the conversation. Teri's hand tightened on Seth's arm, just as he was about to cross the room toward the girl.

"Wait," Teri said quietly. "Not now."

Tam Rajir, Chief Arbiter, stood up to thank everyone for coming and promptly turned the meeting over to the Marshal. Seth only half-listened to his father explaining that arrests were being carried out, bringing an end to the crime spree they had been experiencing. He paid more attention to Anni, held in Jerdix's grip as anger flushed the man. When two strangers closed in to put restraints on Jerdix's foreman, Anni nearly collapsed under the pressure Jerdix's heavy hand exerted on her injured shoulder.

Somehow Jerdix regained his control, letting her go and facing the crowd with apparent disbelief. "You hold me responsible? I haven't done anything except try to give some people a chance to get a new start. It is not my fault if they fall back into old ways."

"Sir," Tam Rajir said. "The Marshal's Service has presented enough evidence tying you to the activities to issue an indictment. You will have a chance to defend yourself in court."

"I'm a citizen of this district, a candidate for arbiter."

"Not any longer," Rajir said. "The Planetary Administrative Officer has disqualified you based on the magnitude of the evidence."

Jerdix charged up the steps to confront the Board. "I could make this backwater world important. You, and all those like you, you can't see the opportunities in front of you. I'll beat these allegations, and then you'll see what someone with foresight can accomplish."

"You have five days to report to Portside to answer the charges."

While all the attention was on Jerdix, Seth caught sight of Anni slipping out toward the backstage hallway. He left by the plaza doors and hurried around the hall in time to see her come outside and look around. She saw him, gestured for him to follow, and disappeared into a niche between the Gathering Hall and the building next door. He followed her quickly.

"I was afraid you didn't see me." She pulled him farther into the dark corner. "I had to warn you. He's furious. He'll be vicious now."

He put his arms around her gently, conscious of how her shoulder slumped. "Come to Tobin with me. You'll be safe there."

"No." She raised a hand. "He'll miss me soon. I have to get back."

"Why? And don't say you need the job."

"He has something I need. Please don't ask more."

He kissed her, drawing her tightly against him, letting his body ask for him. For a moment he thought he had the answer he wanted. Then she dropped her chin, let her hair fall across her face, and stepped back.

"I have to go. Be careful, Seth."

"How can you go back in there? Don't you think I see how he hurts you?" He crowded her back to the wall. "I can't let you back in his reach."

She put one hand firmly in the middle of his chest, then let it drift up to rest against his face where her thumb caressed his cheek. "Trust me. I know what I'm doing, and it is necessary. Remember, that's a stranger named Anni, not me. I will see you the day after Migration, just as we planned." She gave him a good measure of the taste of her and the feel of her against him before she stepped past him and went back inside.

He watched her go, unsure why he didn't try to stop her. Not wanting to face the crowd, he wandered toward the plaza to wait for Teri and Nick to come out. As he rounded the corner of the building, a rope dropped over him and tightened around his ankles. Someone jerked, taking his feet out from under him. A boot slammed into his ribs. "I should have knifed him the first time." Seth recognized Bull's voice.

"Maybe the boss will leave you something." Whip bent over him, sprayed a mist in his face, something that smelled bad and tasted worse. Everything went black.

Chapter 14

Anni/Lee

A comm bleeped incessantly. Reluctantly, Lee Vawn-Cory opened bloodshot eyes. Feeble daylight crept between the curtains. She stumbled across the room to activate the device, killing the visual.

"Anni, I need to talk to Seth!" the caller demanded. She recognized the Marshal's voice.

"Seth?" she replied, suddenly wide awake. She was going to have to be 'Anni' for a while yet. "I haven't seen him."

"This is serious."

Her heart rose in her throat. She steadied herself and checked the clock; it was after nine — morning. She thought for a moment, then said with great deliberation, "He is not here. All I want right now is to crawl back under the covers for about twenty-four hours. Maybe then I can help you out." She cut the connection. The Marshal knew she was from Central Services, what she was there to do. And she'd seen Rodahl Vinz, her Ranger contact, with him last night. They'd figure out that cryptic message to give her some time. But if Jerdix had Seth, she couldn't afford to make mistakes.

Slowly, painfully, she hobbled to the bathroom. A shower, just a quick one; that was what she needed. She had showered twice already, but she still felt filthy. Okay, legally maybe it wasn't rape. She had agreed, sort of. She just hadn't anticipated Jerdix's proclivity for inflicting pain.

No, be honest with herself at least; Jerdix had raped her, had raped Anni, and she — Lee — let him for the sake of her cover. She thought she knew him but hadn't understood how brutal he could be.

Gently she washed the damaged areas one more time, flinching at the sting of the hot water. She'd called Doc when she'd gotten home, produced her Central Services credentials, and let him examine her. He hadn't found any serious injuries, just deep bruising and abrasions. With evidence in hand, he had promised not to report it until she wrapped up her investigation.

She dried with caution and reluctantly put on the suit Jerdix insisted she wear to work. The straight-legged pants wouldn't rub abused flesh too much. Part revolt, part comfort, she wore Seth's old shirt under the jacket, concealing it at the collar with the silvery scarf he had left with her. She did, truly, wish she could just crawl back under the covers rather than back undercover. She had gotten so close to the information she came to find, information tying Jerdix to wide-spread smuggling and extortion. Now everything was coming apart.

Then she did the last thing she wanted to do; she went to Jerdix's office like it was any other morning. She would make him believe he had her totally under his control, and she would be where she had some slim chance of finding Seth. If Jerdix was even in the office after last night's revelations.

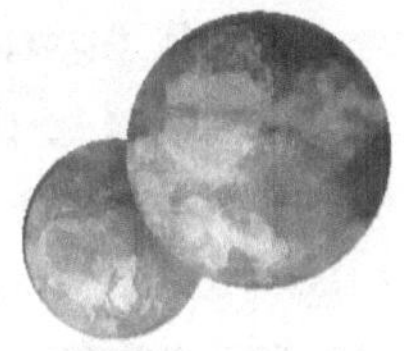

Seth shook his head, tried to move. The world came back slowly, unreal. Cold ... chill, damp air brushing across his body; naked. Pain in his wrists above his head; ache in his shoulders; stretch to keep his feet on the floor to ease the strain. Darkness; faint outline of a small window, high up, with bars. Pungent, musty, sweet; manure and hay; horse barn. Empty, no shuffling feet, no breaths.

Fear knotted his gut. They had hung him like a side of tarbh. He twisted, swung, struggled to get his hobbled feet back on the floor; choked on the gag in his mouth. Helpless.

A crack of light; an open door; sudden bright light, stabbing at his eyes. Solid plank walls, packed dirt floor, then Jerdix filled his view, big and angry and self-satisfied.

"Damage the cub irreparably; destroy the father. I win." The man held a black rod, a hand-span long and the diameter of a finger, in front of Seth's face, then stroked it down his chest. "I enjoyed your sweet Anni but not nearly as much as I am going to enjoy this." He pressed the tip of the rod just under Seth's breastbone, and every nerve in Seth's body seized in exquisite pain.

Gasping for breath, Seth hung from his wrists. His legs refused to hold him. Anni — what had Jerdix done to Anni. The man stood only inches away, smirking, touching the rod over Seth's heart. Seth tried to pull away. Jerdix laughed and extended the rod again — pain again, washing over him, smothering him. Jerdix waited, let him recover enough to look into his eyes, then touched him with the rod again. Agonizing pleasure, more intense than any orgasm, surged through Seth in great ripples, making him curl, swinging. Jerdix waited, caught his eyes, touched him again. Seth flinched away but nothing happened.

Jerdix stepped back, walked around him like a man judging a tarbh for slaughter, casually reached out with the rod; pain. Touched him again; pain. Again; devastating pleasure. Again; pain. Again; nothing. On and on. Always time to recover and anticipate between touches.

And Jerdix talked, ranted about what Joseph Reilly had done to him, gloated about his domination of Anni. Seth lost any sense of time; blanked out Jerdix's words; focused entirely on the rod, the next touch. Pain was horrible; pleasure was worse, every touch a new rape. And they began to blend together in his mind until the only thing that mattered was not being touched.

Jerdix swaggered in close again, flushed with satisfaction. He held the rod in front of Seth's eyes then ran it down toward his crotch. Seth closed his eyes and waited.

Jerdix roared with laughter. "I think I'll go visit sweet Anni. Imagine what I will be doing with her." The light went out, the door closed, and Seth was alone.

He struggled, feeling blood trickle down from his wrists. How long had it been? His pa should be looking for him.

Anni! He had to get loose, get them both free. Before Jerdix came back. He couldn't face that thing again. He couldn't.

But there was no give in his bonds. He even failed to dislodge the gag. In the end, he planted his feet, stretched to take as much weight as he could off his aching shoulders and burning wrists, and endured.

The latch on the door clicked. The light glared in his eyes. He held himself still. He would not show Jerdix his fear. He would not.

The man swaggered in; came to stand in front of him again without speaking. Seth used every bit of strength he had to stand straight and match stares. Jerdix studied him briefly.

"The cub's hackles are up," he said with a laugh, then pulled out the rod and held it up. Seth couldn't help it. He tried to back away and lost his footing. He barely had his feet back under him when Jerdix reached out with the rod. Try as he might, Seth couldn't avoid the touch, or the next or the next. At some point, his brain no longer distinguished between pain and pleasure. He was awash in horror and the sound of laughter. At last the laughter faded, the light died, the latch clicked. Seth hung, his body thrumming like an over-tight wire in an unrelenting wind. Slowly, slowly he went numb, wrapped in safe darkness.

Click; light; touch and touch and touch; overload of sensation; dark; click; absence. Stiffen knees, weight off wrists, wait ...

He lost track of how many times that repeated. He focused on the pain in his wrists, the one constant, the one reality in the insanity. Everything else was nightmare.

Daylight ... high-set, dirty window ... plank walls ... solid door, no latch ... alone. Safely alone ... no man ... no rod.

When Lee, in the guise of her 'Anni' persona, got to the office, by some stroke of luck, Jerdix was there. He didn't even seem surprised to see her. She hid behind her hair, sure he would see her loathing if he saw her eyes. He waited for her to sit down at her desk with her back to him, the hairs on the back of her neck standing up like little antennae, before coming to stand behind her. She dropped her head and hunched her shoulders up, turning revulsion into apparent fear. He laid his hands on her shoulders and literally lifted her to her feet. The feel of those harsh, powerful fingers threatened her control. She fought the temptation to strike him, to plant a foot where it would do the most good.

"Be quiet and come with me," he said softly. With a twist that shot through her injured shoulder, he shoved her toward the back door. "I have something you might be interested in."

He ordered her into his skimmer. She obeyed, huddling as far from him as possible. He had to believe her completely cowed. Her fear was only partly feigned. In his forceful presence, she found it difficult to push aside her role as young, naïve Anni. He did intimidate her. She said nothing, kept her eyes down, and shivered. The rain returned, a fitting cloak for a dark day.

Jerdix drove to his stead and parked next to the barn. When she stayed in her seat, he came around, grabbed her by the back of the neck and pulled her out. He dragged her along the aisle and opened one of the stall doors.

"Don't worry, Sweets, I'll let you go soon enough. You get to carry a message to Joe Reilly for me." He backhanded her across the face, sending her flying into the stall. She collided with something and fell as she heard the latch driven home, locking her in.

Seth sagged, legs no longer holding him, wrists numb to the pain. Creak ... door open ... figure shoved through, stumbled across the floor, smashed into him. He lurched away, breathless, eyes closed, waiting for pleasure-pain.

"Seth?" Soft voice, gentle voice. He opened his eyes. Anni's face, inches from him. Hand reaching out. A dream; his mind making Jerdix over into Anni. He closed his eyes and pulled back, lost his footing, scrambled, hung from his wrists.

The voice again, still dream-soft and female. "Okay, it's me, Anni. Hold still." He wanted the dream to be true. He tried to obey but flinched back from the tugging on the rope around his ankles. Then his feet were loose. He struggled to keep them under him, relieving the drag on his hands.

He looked around. The girl unsnapped a bucket from the wall, turned it over for a stool, and reached up to free his hands. "Stretch!" she commanded, and he did, but it wasn't enough. She got down and pushed the container in front of him. "Up on it." He tried, slipped, tried again, somehow stepped up, and lifted his hands off the hook above his head. He couldn't let her near the knot to try to free his hands. He backed away, into the far corner, pulling at the gag. She let him go and scavenged around the room, looking for something.

The latch rattled, and the door opened. Anni stepped in front of him, her shoulder sagging. "C.T." she pleaded. "Why are you doing this?" So small and helpless in front of the looming man.

Jerdix strutted around her to stand over Seth, leaving his back open to her in glaring disregard. He ran the rod through his hands. Seth curled against the wood, covered his head with his hands and waited, anticipation paralyzing him.

"The cub whines. Do you think his father will want him back like this?"

Seth peeked out and saw Jerdix, holding Anni by her bad shoulder with the rod in front of her face. Her eyes watched the innocent-looking device fearfully. Seth saw recognition in her face. She knew what it was, what it could do. He should do something; save her. He couldn't move. The tip of the rod ran along her jawline. Her whole body arched, and she fell away from her tormentor.

Jerdix laughed and turned back to Seth. "She's a sweet thing, don't you think? A little passive for my taste, but I'll keep her around a while longer. Good for my frustration, if you know what I mean."

Seth struggled to get to his feet but the sight of the rod trapped him. Nothing existed but the rod —

A streak of movement. Jerdix fell forward. Seth scrambled away. The rod flew toward him, bounced off the wall, and landed on the floor next to the man, now lying unmoving. Someone pulled a knife from the man's pocket, opened it and held it out. Not Anni; couldn't be Anni. Strong, forceful woman filling the space with assurance, a woman watching him with familiar brown-gold eyes.

"Take it," she ordered in Anni's voice, dropping the knife next to Seth. "Get your hands free and get out of here." She left him to it, picking up the rope that had been around his feet and using it to tie Jerdix's hands. "Hurry!" she encouraged.

He fumbled with the knife and somehow got the ropes cut. She snatched up the pieces, threw them aside in disgust, and ran out, coming back a moment later with a longer rope to tie Jerdix's feet. Seth pushed himself up, leaning on the wall, struggling with the gag.

"Your clothes, on the floor by the door. Get them on and go," she told him. "I'll be right behind you."

He started toward the door; forgot what he was supposed to do. The door was open. He could leave.

"Seth!" A commanding voice stopped him. "Get dressed." Oh, okay. He pulled on pants and boots, shirt, one sleeve of the jacket then the other. His brain made no sense out of the feel of them against his skin, hot, cold, harsh, soft. But some part of him heard Anni's reassurances, and he did as he was told.

When he looked up, she was holding the rod, pointing it at him, coming toward him. His world narrowed to that small, black menace. His mind flooded with expectation, and he ran from that monstrous promise, losing all awareness of anything else.

Chapter 15

Lee

"Seth, wait!" Lee yelled as she followed him to the door, but he disappeared out of the barn into the rain. Turning back into the stall, she threw the rod at the wall along with a string of curses in several languages. She rushed to finish tying Jerdix's feet, then pulled them up behind him toward his hands, bending him like a bow, making sure he was secure. She picked up the rod to take with her, much as she hated even touching it, and saw Jerdix watching her in disbelief.

Very deliberately she laid the device on the floor close in front of him where he might avoid touching it if he held very still. She turned it on, not bothering to check the setting. "Now I will take your message to the Marshal," she promised. She closed and latched the stall door and ran after Seth. Jerdix's voice followed her, muffled by the solid wood of the walls.

Seth's tracks led across the barnyard and into the woods, straight north toward the Rim rather than northwest to town. He must have run in blind panic, crashing through the brush and kicking up the duff on the ground, leaving her signs she could follow. She had to find him before he was completely lost. She feared he would keep running until he fell exhausted. She plunged into the forest after him.

The rain let up and a cold wind pushed in behind it. With her attention on the tiny traces of his passing, she lost track of where she was. So slow — if she hurried, she lost his trail; time dragged on. Why hadn't she looked for a comm and called the Marshal before leaving Jerdix's stead? The man was a technophile. She'd probably gone right past one in the barn. But she'd expected to catch up to Seth in moments.

She came to a main trail. It had to be the one coming into Under Rim from the southeast. Be smart and go into town. Get help. Then something brown flashed between the trees ahead of her. She followed, sure she had caught up to Seth at last. She found fresh boot prints where she had seen the movement. He had to be close; he somehow remained just ahead, out of sight, drawing her on.

His trail climbed at an angle up the side of a ridge, where the forest opened up into a series of small meadows, giving her a view of the surrounding area. She began to realize that he was not wandering randomly but going straight as a navigated line toward a notch in the Rim. As the forest closed in again, she stayed on his tracks, afraid he would turn aside, and she would miss him. Why wouldn't he just go home?

The nature of the woods changed. Grass replaced brush among slender, closely packed trunks that blocked her view and disoriented her as she wound among them. The cloud cover persisted, so the sun gave her no idea of time or direction. She lost more time, lost Seth's tracks, and finally admitted she was just lost.

Idiot! She was such a fool for not getting help when it was close. She turned around and around, trying to decide which way to go. No one would miss her until the next morning at the earliest, and then would have no idea where to look. Seth needed help. Nobody but herself to blame or to come to the rescue. She had to get herself, get them, out of this mess.

She closed her eyes and pictured the map of the district. She knew where she had started and had some idea of which direction she had been going. Up should take her east toward the ridgeline where she would be able to see landmarks. Down should take her to a stream or a trail. Trouble was that this thicket looked nearly level. How far had she come? She must have passed by the Reilly stead by now. If only she had a gips... but these stubborn, technophobic beyonders didn't want to clutter up their skies with satellites.

She had to find a place where she could see some landmarks. Okay, she had come from that way, past a strangely twisted trunk. So down should be to the left.

She went left, spotting some distinctive tree or rock to aim for, then finding another beyond to keep her going straight. Once she got out of the grove of trees into the more typical forest, the ground began to slope, and she made faster progress. Even so, daylight was fading before she reached an opening that revealed the surrounding ridge tops.

She stopped, staring at the skyline, hoping to find something familiar. The sun broke through the clouds, spotlighting a rock outcropping a long ways to the south, a place where she and Seth had sat once, looking out over the basin. She was north of the stead, still east and above the stream that flowed past it. She kept going down, angling a little to the left.

She stumbled through the low brush and rocks with barely enough light to find her way. The sound of water flowing over rock drew her on until she made out the dark barrier of thicker vegetation that marked the stream channel. Hurrying forward, she tripped in the depression of a well-worn trail. Too tired to think, she turned downstream and let her feet fall into the path. She lost count of the times it crossed the water. Anyway, her feet had been soaked since she'd left Jerdix's barn. Crossing it one more time, she entered an alley between pasture fences. She pushed herself into a staggering run. The massive barn loomed black in the darkness. She climbed the slope to the house, faltered up the steps, and pounded on the door.

No one answered. She tried the door, but it refused to open. In desperation, she shoved her thumb against the lock pad. To her surprise, the lock clicked, and the door opened. She stared at it, blessing Joe Reilly. He'd trusted her, given her a retreat. Now he would take over the search for his son. In a gesture of gratitude, she dropped her muddy boots by the door before going inside.

She went directly to the comm and called him.

"Anni, where are you?" His voice sounded reassuring even at a distance.

"You have to find Seth. I lost his trail; I couldn't catch up to him."

"Where are you?" he repeated.

"Your house. Hurry, please."

He didn't waste time on questions. "You sound exhausted. Get warm. I'll be there in twenty minutes."

Warm sounded impossibly luxurious. She wrapped herself in a blanket, brewed tea, and sat at the table where she could look at the map on the wall, trying to figure out where Seth probably was. She found Jerdix's stead, found the feature on the Rim she thought was the notch Seth seemed to be headed toward. It kept her mind busy while she listened impatiently for the skimmer.

When the Marshal burst through the front door with Lije on his heels, she pushed herself to her feet. He assessed her with stern eyes. "Where is Seth? What happened?"

"He's somewhere up toward the Rim. We got away from Jerdix. He ran into the forest. I couldn't catch him." She knew that wasn't enough explanation, but it was all she could manage at the moment.

The two men looked at each other, sharing their puzzlement. Joe came forward. "Sit," he ordered and pulled up a chair across the table from her, putting on his Marshal's face. "Help me. What do I need to know to find my son?"

She took a deep breath, pulling the blanket tighter around her and looking at him directly. "Do you know what a P&P rod is?" she asked flatly.

"I know."

"Jerdix has one. He used it."

"On Seth?" The hard, fierce look on his face frightened her.

"I didn't see him do it but, yes, I'm sure he did. I got Seth loose, but he saw the rod and ran."

Stiff armed, Joe pushed himself up from the table and strode to the map, tight with control. "From where?" he asked.

"Jerdix's stead."

Lije crossed to the table. "Fallen Pine, Joe."

The Marshal nodded. "Right, he'll go to Fallen Pine. He always went there to get away from things." He spun and headed for the door.

Lije blocked his path. "I'll find him. You get Jerdix."

Joe started to push him aside. Lije refused to move. "Marshal, go get that belly-crawler. I'll see that Seth is safe."

Joe stepped back sharply. "Don't let the boy see you. Don't spook him. Just make sure he gets safely to the cabin and watch over him."

"He'll never see me."

"Wait. Is Teri home?"

Lije nodded. "I'll send her here before I go."

"Take care of my son."

"And you finish what should have been done years ago." None of them had any doubt what Lije meant.

"I'm not laying aside my badge."

"No, I don't guess you should."

"I'll get him, Lije, and the rod guarantees he'll never walk free again. Now find my son."

Anni watched the exchange silently. When the door shut behind Lije, she stood slowly. "Marshal, there's more."

"More?"

"You know I'm from Central Services, investigating Jerdix. You need to confiscate all his files before he can destroy them."

He went back to the table and sat down, waving her into her chair. "Where is Jerdix?"

"I left him tied up in a stall in his horse barn. He might still be there unless one of his riders found him." She dropped her eyes, remembering how badly she had wanted to use the rod on him.

"What about the rod?" the Marshal asked.

"I left it lying next to him." She shuddered.

"Anni, what did he do to you?" He enclosed her hand in his own.

Slowly she pulled away. "Not Anni."

"No, of course. Anni is your cover."

"My name is Annalee Vawn-Cory. I go by Lee. You know my parents."

He nodded. "Your mother, Cris Vawn, the one I helped to capture Jerdix twenty-five years ago. Does he know?"

"I didn't think so but, after last night, I wonder. You go find that …" She couldn't find words to describe what she felt.

"Lee, where are your parents? Cris must be as much his target as I am."

"She's on a two-year survey assignment."

"With your father?"

"No, he's working out of Oasis but could be anywhere. But Rodahl Vinz, the Ranger principal in Portside, can do that. He's my contact here, my oversight."

"Okay, I know Ro. He was here for last night's meeting and stayed over I think. I'll get word to him. Will you be all right?" He reached out to lightly touch the bruise on her face. "Teri, your Aunt Teri, your mother's sister, should be here soon. How did I miss the resemblance before? You carried off your role very well."

"I'll be okay."

"Good, I'll go then. You can tell me the rest in the morning."

"What about Seth?"

"He'll feel safe at the cabin. Tomorrow, when he's had a chance to pull himself together, we'll go up with Doc. Don't you worry about him right now. Lije will watch over him."

"Yes, sir." She watched him start for the door. "Marshal, did Vinz leave a gear bag for me?"

"He did. It's in my room where I knew no one would get curious about it." He hurried upstairs and came back with bag in hand. "Here you go."

"Thank you."

He came over and helped her to her feet, guiding her to the couch. Wrapping a second blanket around her, he kissed her forehead. "You tell Teri everything and do what she says." Then he was gone.

She sat as the silence wrapped around her. She had done everything she could. Lije would find Seth and make sure he was safe. Joe would find Jerdix so none of them had to worry again. She had done it.

Suddenly she was crying. She buried her face in the blankets; felt the smoothness of the jacket sleeve on her cheek, the suit Jerdix insisted she wear. She shuddered at the thought. She saw the gear bag sitting where Joe had dropped it. She, Lee, was in that bag. She disengaged herself from the blankets and began stripping off the jacket and pants, flinging them across the room. She snatched up the bag and ran for the bathroom, half-blinded by tears, driven to wash away even the thought of the man's hands on her, to strip Anni away and be someone who hadn't lived through the last day.

The first thing she saw in the mirror was Anni, damp strings of hair trailing across one side of her face. She pulled open the bag, dug down under her Ranger issue pants and shirt, boots, and other clothes to find her multi-tool. Opening the knife blade, she began to slash at the hair. Anni had to go. She would not be Anni anymore. Anni was the one Jerdix had violated, not Lee.

"Hello!" a voice called. "It's Teri."

Lee sawed harder at the offending hair.

Someone took the knife from her hand. "Let me help with that," said a gentle, firm voice. Lee turned, wiping away her tears. Teri handed her a towel. "You wait right here. We'll get your hair looking just fine in no time."

"Could you?"

"I've been cutting family hair for years, sweetie."

Lee recoiled. "Please don't call me that!" Jerdix and his "my sweet" rang in her ears.

Teri nodded. "All right."

"I'm Lee. I'm Cris's daughter."

Teri held the hair back from her face. "Now how did I miss that? But I'd say it's your father you take after. Does Joe know?"

"He does now."

"We can talk about it later. Right now, I'll get your hair trimmed, and you can get cleaned up. You look like you've been rode hard and put up wet."

Lee grinned weakly at the old phrase. "Thank you."

"Better call me 'Tia' like the kids do. Just wait here."

Teri came back in a moment, sat Lee down in the chair she brought from the kitchen, and produced scissors from a cabinet. In a matter of minutes, she turned Lee's chop job into a tidy, short haircut. "There, dear. Now you soak for a while. Then I'll come back with something for the scrapes and bruises. I don't know how you can walk on those blisters. I have something for those too."

"Tia, thank you." When Lee stood up, blisters she hadn't noticed earlier made their presence known.

Miles of walking and running in the mud in boots designed for casual strolls in town left huge blisters and raw spots. She sank into the whirltub, feeling empty of emotion, focusing on the heat and the sting, the physical, letting everything else fade away.

Chapter 16

Seth

Seth fled from the barn. His ragged run slowed to a walk as the mass of rods around him gradually reshaped into normal tree branches. He kept going until he found an opening where he could see the skyline. He couldn't — wouldn't — remember where he came from. He just knew something terrifying was back there. Safety, where was safety?

A notch in the distant rim caught his eye. Below that break, tucked into a hollow under the sheer cliff faces ... a cabin, quiet, solitary ... a haven. Nothing would threaten him there. Get there; everything would be all right. He walked, ignoring the rain soaking his boots, his clothes, fighting his way through thickets and rock piles to hold his line. The forest wouldn't hurt him. As long as he kept away from the man, got to the cabin, stayed alone.

Rain stopped; breeze made him shiver; clothes protected him — he'd been naked; no — don't think about that. Look ahead; Rim closer; stay away from trails; sneak to the cabin. Getting dark; so tired ...

The cabin, at last. He stumbled up the steps, pulled wet boots off at the door, dropped the jacket too. No wet boots or coats in the house. Cold and empty inside; silent; no one there. He was alone and safe. He pulled a blanket off a chair, climbed the ladder to the loft, and curled up in the dormer where he could see if anyone followed him.

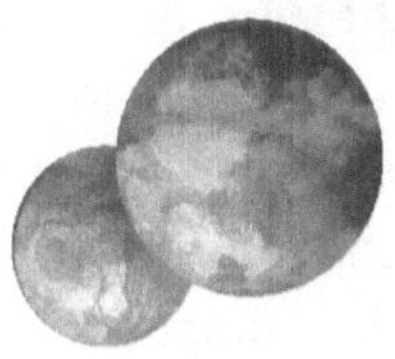

Seth woke from a nightmare of darkness where Anni screamed, and he ran but, no matter which way he went, found himself back in the same place. Moonlight came through a window, showing him enough to recognize the sleeping loft at Fallen Pine. He found his way downstairs, trying to remember how he had gotten there. The cabin was warm; hot water came from the tap when he turned it on; something simmered on the stove, something that smelled wonderful. When had he done all that? Who had done all that?

He ate, made tea, lit the fire that was laid in the fireplace. It felt good, and the bright flickering comforted him. Outside, a night flyer called its mournful, wavering whistle. Another answered from up behind the cabin. The hunter sailed over the roof on silent, leathery wings, casting a shadow across the window. A host of tiny creatures buzzed and croaked and glurped in the spring night. He wrapped himself in the blanket and lay on the couch where he fell asleep again.

Lee curled in a chair in the living room at the Reilly stead. She could hear soft, slow breathing from the other chair. She and Teri Dunn had talked for a while, waiting for the Marshal, until Teri had fallen asleep. Lee wished she could. The analgesic Teri had given her had worn off. She ached. And she had too much to think about.

A skimmer stopped outside. She sat up with a groan. Three days, she told herself. Teri had promised the worst of the aches and pains would subside after the first three days.

"Tia, someone's here," she said quietly as she got to her feet and limped to the door to look out, her heart pounding unexpectedly. Anticipation of good news? Or fear that it was Jerdix and not the Marshal? She told herself not to be silly. She opened the door, and the Marshal came in.

He opened an arm to hug her. She stepped in and accepted the gesture. "Did Lije find Seth?" she asked, looking up at him.

"He did. Seth went to Fallen Pine, just as we thought. Lije will keep an eye on him." He walked her to the couch and sat down, facing Teri. "Bad news is Jerdix disappeared."

Lee slumped back. "Someone discovered him and set him free."

"Looks that way. He was nowhere to be found. That's what took me so long."

"Portside!" Lee said with certainty. "He'll want to get off world before you can stop him, so he can regroup."

"First thing I did was put a block on him. Don't worry. We will catch up to him."

Teri leaned forward. "Are you sure he's gone?"

"As much as we can be. He packed a bag, took everything from his safe — left it wide open — scattered things all over at the office. A couple of people in town saw him leave in his skimmer."

"So what now?"

He took his arm from around Lee and rested his elbows on his knees. "We're still in the middle of Migration. Teri, I think you need to go back to Tobin Canyon in the morning. They need their camp tender."

"No, not until I see Seth for myself." She glared at him. "Migration can just wait for a day or two."

"I'm worried about him too, but I've got to get to Portside or risk losing Jerdix."

"I know that. That's why I have to go to Fallen Pine. Seth needs family right now."

He shook his head. "I wish it was that simple. Teri, I don't thank you enough for being a mother to my kids when they're no blood of yours. Right now, all of us may need to give him some room."

"Will he be okay?" she asked.

Joe sighed. "I wish I could answer that, but we don't know enough yet. It's more than just the trauma. The rod messes with the brain physiology. He'll need some specialized help. At least he was thinking clearly enough to go somewhere he feels safe."

Lee listened silently, suppressing her fear. She knew from her Ranger training what the rod was and how it functioned. She had seen Seth's reactions, so different from the man she knew. She refused to consider how the information might apply to her.

Teri stood up. "I still want to see him. I'll take him a change of clothes and some other things until I can send his gear from Tobin. Don't worry. I won't crowd him."

Joe stood too, leaving Lee alone on the couch. "Trust you to think of the details." He walked over to hug Teri. "Would you pick Doc up in the morning when you go to the cabin?"

"Of course."

"Lee." The Marshal turned back to her. "We need to talk to you. Vinz is waiting outside. Can we talk on the porch while Teri brews some tea?"

"Official?" she asked.

He nodded. "We need your statement before I leave for Portside."

She nodded, recognizing the inevitability. "Let's get it over with."

"Joe," Teri said, blocking his path. "You go easy with her."

"Don't worry." He laid a reassuring hand on Teri's shoulder. "We'll be back in a few minutes."

Lee followed him out onto the dark porch. Vinz rose from a chair. "Are you okay?" he asked.

"Yeah." She didn't know the man, had only met him once, off world, before she had come to Carico.

"Here, put this on the skin behind your ear," he said, holding out a chip the size of his fingertip. "Deconditioning."

She did as she was told, eager to do whatever she could to shed the 'Anni' persona for good. "I'm ready."

"Okay," Joe said. "Ro, you're welcome to listen in. I'm sure you'll want to debrief her yourself later."

"Yes, about her undercover op." Vinz sat down. "Beyond what you need to get into tonight."

Joe pulled a recorder out of his pocket and set it on a low table. He motioned her to a chair, but she shook her head and leaned back against the railing. Somehow she couldn't sit through this no matter how sore she was. He settled into a chair and opened the interview with the usual date, time, and place information.

"Identify yourself, please," he directed.

"Annalee Vawn-Cory, CS Ranger attached to the investigations branch, currently on undercover assignment at Under Rim on Carico." The formal procedure helped her focus.

"You are investigating Charles Thomas Jerdix, commonly known as C.T.?"

"Correct," she said. "My task was to document his connection to illegal trade in resources and interplanetary racketeering."

His eyebrows raised. "Were you successful?"

"No," she answered. "Not yet."

"You went to work for Jerdix to get access."

"I did." She took a deep breath, anticipating his next question, expecting him to somehow see the magnitude of her miscalculations about the man.

He looked her in the eye. "Yesterday morning I called you, looking for Seth Reilly. What happened next?"

Not the question she expected. Didn't he know about the rape? She looked down. "I went to work. I got dressed and went to Jerdix's office as I normally would. When I got there, he took me to his stead, to the barn, and locked me in a stall where he had Seth prisoner."

"Describe Seth's condition." Something in his voice drew her eyes.

"He was hanging by his hands in the middle of the stall with his feet barely touching the floor. He tried to pull away when I touched him. I managed to untie the rope around his ankles. I found a bucket and used it as a stool for Seth so he could lift his hands free of the hook." She walked away, along the porch, remembering the terror she'd felt when she'd heard the latch opening. "That's when Jerdix came back. He had the rod with him. I recognized it, knew what it was. I ... I played up the role I had taken — submissive, frightened — and waited until he turned his back. Then I took him down. I tied his hands and feet and left him there."

"You saw Jerdix with the rod?"

"Yes." She shuddered. "Seth ... Seth was terrified. When he saw it, he ... I had to order him to get dressed. Then I told him to go; that I would meet him outside. When he finished dressing, he looked up. I had the rod in my hand. He saw it and ran out." She turned her back to the Marshal and looked out into the night. He had to know it all, and she didn't know if she could say the words.

"Did you actually see Jerdix use the rod?" The Marshal's voice chilled her.

"Yes."

"On Seth."

She turned back to face him. "No."

He looked puzzled, then shocked. "Who did you see him use the rod on?" he asked very softly.

"He used it on me ... twice, no, three times."

"When did he do that?" He leaned forward, one hand half-reaching toward her.

"Once in the stall, in front of Seth. Pain setting." She straightened. "And twice the night before when he raped me."

Joe got to his feet abruptly, anger on his face, then consciously lowered his shoulders and walked away from her, slapping his hand against a post. Slowly, he turned back to her, keeping his distance. "Can you prove that?"

"Doc has the evidence that I was raped and that a rod had been used on me. I don't know if it will clearly implicate Jerdix. He's arrogant and was angry so he may not have been concerned about leaving evidence."

"When?" Joe maintained his distance, shifting restlessly. Vinz sat motionless, silent.

Lee drew in a deep breath. "He took me to his house when we left the meeting. He was off base after you destroyed his plans. I hoped that would give me an opportunity at the information I was sent to get."

"Your cover, as Anni — he didn't expect her to fight back?"

She found it easier to speak as if it had been someone else. "No, Anni did what she was told. She knew he would use her injured shoulder to punish her if she did anything he didn't like. He said to take off clothes; Anni took them off. But he didn't want compliance. He wanted to hurt someone, to use someone so he could feel powerful, he wanted ..." She stopped, took a breath and held it, let it out slowly. "How much detail do you need?" she asked with a clenched jaw.

Joe released his fists, opened his hands wide and closed them again. "He forced you. Doc can support that?" She nodded, and he went on, "And he actually used the rod on you?"

"Yes." She could barely speak. Her control threatened to shatter.

"Take a minute. Do you need a break?" His professional voice lay thinly over some emotion she couldn't decipher.

Another breath. "No, I'm all right." She walked the length of the porch and back, rolling her shoulders. "He used the pleasure setting. The pain he provided physically. I ... Anni ... let him do what he wanted, refused to fight, refused to beg or cry either. That irritated him. It wasn't what he wanted. He lost interest."

With infinite control, he came closer. "What happened next?"

"He gave me a dress to put on, loose, too big for me. He picked up my clothes, dragged me out to the skimmer, drove me home. Took me inside, stripped the dress off. I thought ... he ... I thought he was going to do it again. That's when he used the rod on me the second time. I gave him what he wanted then. I begged. I'm not sure what for. He picked up the dress, and he left."

"Ranger," Joe used his Marshal's voice. "Finish it. He left you at your apartment. What did you do?"

She returned to where she had started, leaning back against the porch rail facing the table with the recorder. "I called the med center. Doc came, checked me over and collected evidence. I got him to promise not to report it until I told him it was all right. I ... well, that's all. Until you called in the morning."

"And you told Doc about the rod."

"Yes, and he scanned to confirm it."

"And the last time you saw Jerdix?" Joe asked.

"Was after Seth ran out. I left Jerdix tied up on the floor of a stall in his barn."

"What did you do with the rod?"

She remembered the fury and hatred she'd felt at that moment. With a tight voice, she answered, "I left it on the floor next to him."

"Why didn't you call me before you left Jerdix's stead?"

Why hadn't she? Looking back, that seemed odd. "I thought Seth would be waiting outside or just into the trees, and we would contact you once I found him. Then he kept running. I was so afraid I would lose his trail, and he would get completely lost."

"Okay." He came over slowly. "What makes you think that Jerdix used the rod on Seth?"

She stared at the recorder and made an effort to sound professional, detached. "Marshal, Seth panicked at the sight of it. He had no marks to indicate he had been beaten, but he couldn't bear to be touched. He was barely coherent. I had to tell him what to do. Then he turned, saw me coming toward him with it in my hand, and ran from it."

It took him time to process that. His face was bleak when he finally asked, "Can you think of anything else I should know?"

"No, sir."

"Make note of things as they come to you. We can talk more later." He switched off the recorder and put it back in his pocket. "Truth now — how badly are you hurt?"

"Nothing that won't heal," she said with a weak laugh.

"You stayed in character," Vinz said. "That conditioning is intended to be hard to break, to protect an agent." He looked at her directly. "You showed remarkable strength when you overcame that to confront him to free Seth."

"But I let him get away. I didn't finish the job."

"Teamwork, girl." Joe smiled encouragingly. "You leave the next step to me. Do you feel up to some activity in the morning?"

"What do you have in mind?" she asked.

"Doc will be going up to Fallen Pine to see Seth. I briefed him as well as I could on what to expect and, if I know Doc, he'll be up all night studying. Anyway, will you go with him and Teri, maybe stay if Seth will let you? I think you might be less threatening to him than anybody else right now."

"Me?" The last time Seth had seen her, she had seemed threatening enough.

Apparently misunderstanding her concern, Joe said, "I'm just asking. I don't know if what was going on between you two was part of your cover or not."

"It was not. And Ranger Vinz, here, will probably write me up on it, but my relationship with your son had nothing to do with my assignment. Of course I'll go."

"We can talk about that later," Vinz said. "With your cover broken and Jerdix running, your debriefing can wait."

"Okay," Joe said. "Are you ready to go back inside? Teri will have guessed the generalities if she doesn't know the specifics."

"She does have some fine ointments." Lee let him open the door for her. Vinz stayed behind in the dark.

Chapter 17

Seth

Seth sat on the cabin porch, looking out over the sloping meadow of wildflowers. Rowdy-fowl, dull black until the sunlight made them flash in wild colors, whistled and shrieked as they sailed and dove overhead. Suddenly they vanished. Seth heard the faint purr of a skimmer growing louder. His heart thudded. He rose from his chair to hide inside. Not sure what he was afraid of, he stopped in the doorway to watch.

A battered, antiquated skimmer settled to the ground at the far edge of the meadow. Through the fog in his brain he caught a mental picture of an older man, a comfortable, reassuring figure — Doc, who had patched up those things beyond Teri's ability since he was a child. Sure enough, the person who climbed from the driver's seat matched that image. Then Teri got out of the other side.

Someone came out of the trees and joined them, kissing Teri. Lije! Seth realized who had turned on the heat and power, laid the fire, and left him food — his second dad, looking after him from a distance. Seth felt safer, and his haze cleared a little more.

A stranger got out of the skimmer, a slight figure in Ranger brown. Seth gulped back the panic. Just people, not threatening — none of them held the ... what was it that was so terrifying? He hovered in the doorway; the nearness of a safe retreat gave him the courage to stand his ground.

Doc and the stranger slowly walked across the meadow toward him. Teri waited with Lije by the skimmer. The Ranger, a girl, looked familiar. She carried a gear bag over her shoulder, moving stiffly like she hurt. As they came closer, he shifted uneasily, edging back into the cabin. They stopped, and the girl put the bag down.

"Morning, Seth." Doc kept his hands low and held them out to his sides, palms forward. "Is it all right if we visit with you for a few minutes? Your pa asked me to check on you. We can stay right here if you like."

The girl gestured to the bag. "We brought you some things." He knew the voice, but it didn't belong with Ranger brown. The voice continued. "Teri cut my hair. Do you like it?" She ran a hand through the short, dark crop.

He saw the knotted cord around her wrist. "Anni?" He fingered the cord around his own wrist, remembered something about a knot to hang onto at the end of his rope.

"Yes, it's me," the familiar voice said gently.

He recognized her eyes, more brown than gold now, but he looked away from the bruise on her cheekbone. He knew how she had gotten that. Anxiety rose in his throat.

She lowered her eyes and stepped back. Her voice soothed him. "You're safe here, Seth. Can we come up and sit?"

He thought about that. "Okay." He could still escape inside.

She retrieved the bag and slowly climbed the steps. She set the bag down and moved to the side, turned one of the chairs to face him and sat down. Doc followed her.

"Seth, what you're feeling is normal," Doc said quietly. "Don't worry about it. Just relax."

Doc knew what had happened to him. Everyone must know. He had cried and screamed and cowered. He ...

"Seth," Doc's firm, calm voice cut across his shame. "You're okay here. You did fine, and you can rest."

"Fine?"

"Right and tight, boy. "

"I'm supposed to be ..." somewhere, he should be doing something ... Migration, Tobin Canyon. "I have to go work; they're counting on me." But he couldn't move his feet.

"Easy, it's all taken care of. You can take a few days off and relax." Doc remained seated, leaning back in his chair with his legs stretched out. "Sit down and join us."

Seth looked at the two on his left, at an empty chair to his right. He sidled over to it, keeping his eyes on his visitors, and lowered himself to perch on the edge of the seat.

"You're Anni?" he asked the girl. "You don't look right."

"I told you once that Anni was just a role I was playing. Do you remember that?" She leaned back in her chair, but he could see she was tense.

He nodded. "I think so. When you gave me this." He fingered the knots around his wrist.

"That's right. Well, now I don't have to pretend to be Anni anymore."

"Now you're a Ranger? If you're not Anni, who are you?"

"My name is Lee. But, Seth, I'm the same person you took to Tobin Canyon Camp and showed how you take care of horses' feet."

"And ..." He shivered. There was more, but those feelings scared him.

"Never mind now. We're friends. That's the important thing."

"Yes." Important that they were friends.

"Seth," Doc leaned forward a little. "Is there anything you need me to do for you? Do you have any injuries?"

He thought about it; let his mind run over his body. "No, don't think so. Just my wrists." He held them up, staring at the grooves. "But they feel okay."

"That's good. You've eaten? Slept okay?"

"Yes." Well, he'd had nightmares, but he had slept.

"Very good. Now listen to me. Do a couple things for me."

"Okay."

"Stay here for a few days. Don't worry about Migration. Just rest and maybe work around the cabin, but go easy."

"I should stay here and rest." He nodded and eased back in the chair a little.

Slowly Doc reached into his shirt pocket and brought out a small flat square that fit neatly on the end of his finger. Seth processed the imminent panic, decided the chip wasn't a threat. Doc leaned forward and gently set it on the porch rail near Seth.

"That is a post-trauma debriefing chip. Stick it on your skin right behind your ear. When you sleep, it will help you process things. It's not going to fix everything, but it'll give you a start."

"Okay, behind my ear."

"Do it now," Doc insisted and waited while Seth picked up the chip cautiously. "Twist the two halves until they click and press it to your skin. Now, one more thing."

"What, Doc?"

"Find some buttonweed if you can."

Seth nodded. "I know a patch."

"It'll help the anxiety. One button at a time, no more than six a day. Are we clear on that?"

"Yes, sir, one and six." Seth sat back in his chair. Buttonweed would help.

"Good, good. Seth, I've got an expert coming, someone who understands all the implications of what happened to you. Until then, I think you should stay here. Pay attention to what triggers anxiety. Use the buttonweed. Sitting here talking with me is a good sign, so try not to worry."

"Okay."

"All right — now I have sick people to attend to."

Seth couldn't make himself stay sitting when Doc stood up. He got up and moved behind his chair.

Doc spoke again. "Seth, would you do something to help Lee?"

"What? Who?" Seth asked uncertainly.

"This young lady needs a place to wait until the Rangers are ready to debrief her. I would like her to stay here where it's quiet."

No, Seth wanted to shout. No, he couldn't have her around. But she said they were friends. She looked so beat up and tired.

He couldn't make himself say yes. He didn't think they would hear him over his pounding heart. But he nodded.

"Thank you," she said softly. She seemed relieved, losing some tension in her jaw and hands.

He watched Doc walk across the meadow, speak for a moment with Lije and Teri, and climb into the skimmer. Lije pulled something from the cargo compartment, two saddles, and handed a bag to Teri. The two climbed the slope, stopping when they got a few steps from the porch.

"I'll put these in the shed for you," Lije said and continued past the cabin.

Teri came to the foot of the steps. "Hi, Seth." Her knowing eyes scanned him. She seemed satisfied with what she saw. "I brought the only clothes I could find in the bunkroom."

Seth wanted to say something. Tobin — he should go there. "What about Migration?" he asked.

"Ches agreed that Flech could take over. I talked to them this morning, explained that a couple of Jerdix's riders roughed you up." She stopped when he began to back away and added soothingly, "Everything is all right, Seth. You can stay here as long as you want."

He focused on that — he could stay right here where he was safe. Everything else was taken care of. "I will stay," he said, holding the back of the chair.

"Seth, some of your things are in this bag. I put in some ointment you can use on your wrists. I'll leave it here." Teri set it on the bottom step. "We'll be waiting for you to come home when you're ready."

Seth started as Lije came back around the cabin.

"You two should be set for a little while," the older man said calmly.

Seth wasn't sure what to say. Anni, no — she said her name was Lee — Lee answered for him. "Thanks, we'll be fine."

"Call the office if you need anything."

Lee got up and slowly went to them. "Let me know if ... well, what the Marshal finds out."

Lije nodded.

Teri hugged her. "You take care," she admonished. "We'll see you both soon." She took Lije's arm and led him away toward the skimmer.

What was the Marshal trying to find out? Something about ... about the things he didn't want to remember. He tried to shut his mind down, to pay attention to the way the blue flowers bobbed in the light breeze.

Lee's voice surprised him. He had almost forgotten she was there. "Seth, you can get cleaned up. Change clothes. I'll just sit here."

She was right. He could, now that she was there to keep ... to keep the danger away. He got the bag Teri had brought and went inside.

The hot water sheeted over him. He closed his eyes and felt the cold melt away. He heard clattering in the kitchen. His stomach grumbled. Normal things. Everything had changed, but he still wanted food, sleep, and hot showers.

As he dried off, he realized the fog was clearing from his head. The anxiety lay sleeping in his gut, ready to jump to life at the slightest thing, but he could think again, even if he still consciously pushed aside the details. He looked himself over. A few bruises but nothing notable, no visible sign of the damage he knew he suffered.

He ran a finger down the old scar on his shoulder and recalled the feeling. When a colt had slammed him into a tree, the gash had gotten infected and had to be cleaned out. Now he felt like he had after the sedative and pain killer for that, catching glimpses of reality through a haze. He had hated the feeling then. He hated it now but wasn't ready for clear memories to return.

He dressed in the ragged old shirt and pants Teri had brought. He had left those in the bunkroom when he had gone to Tobin Canyon. They would have to do until he got back to Migration. Maybe tomorrow he could go.

Anni — no, Lee — curled in a chair at the far corner of the front room, cradling a steaming mug of tea. A plate of food and another mug sat on the counter. He picked them up and walked toward the door.

She said quietly, "You could sit at the table."

He looked from her to the table at the other side of the room. Whatever within him was judging safety decided that would be all right. He made his way over without turning his back to her. "Thanks, I'm hungry."

"Teri made sure we wouldn't starve." She eyed him cautiously with a look he had seen on colts wondering what the human would do next.

He sat and picked up the sandwich. One taste was enough. He found himself wolfing it down.

A chair creaked. He tensed, then realized the girl had just shifted a little. He paused and began eating again, slower now, finishing the last crumbs. He leaned back, relaxing a little, holding the warm mug between his hands. The aroma of one of Teri's herbal teas took him back to the days before he had left home. Tea made things better.

"Seth." A quiet voice jerked him back to the present. Lee said, "Better put that down before you drop it."

"What?"

"You were falling asleep. Why don't you come and lie on the couch?"

She was right. Clean and fed, now he was drowsy. Leaving the tea half-finished on the table, he moved to the couch and stretched out.

Next thing he knew the daylight was failing, and the front door clicked shut.

"Sorry," Lee said. "I didn't mean to wake you."

He sat up slowly, running his hand through his hair. "It's okay."

"Are you feeling better?" she asked.

"Some," he said. His head was clearer, and the panic farther away.

She stayed by the door. "I went outside — I didn't want to disturb you — but it's cooling off now. I'll just sit in the big chair, all right?"

"Sure," he nodded. He found himself looking away as if seeing her move would threaten him. He remembered Doc telling him buttonweed would help. He should go get some before it got dark.

"It feels so nice just to sit here with nothing that has to be done." Lee spoke quietly but with a trace of the zest Seth recalled Anni having.

He looked around. The wood box was partly full, enough for the evening but not for the morning. He wanted to see flames, feel the heat, hear the crackling. Beds needed making up. And he didn't have time to be sitting around here. They were in the middle of Migration. He started to get up, but he had no way to go anywhere unless he walked. "I should be at Tobin," he said, hearing an unfamiliar whine in his own voice. He coughed to cover it.

"No," she said, "Teri said they don't expect you back for a few days."

He'd forgotten. "It doesn't feel right." He sat back, fumbling with the worn cuff of his shirt.

"Give yourself a day or two at least. I know I need it." She pulled her knees up, tucking her slung arm against her chest. "I walked my feet raw in the mud yesterday."

"You did? What happened?" His heart began to pound. He held up a hand. "No, I don't want to hear it now. But you … Anni … Lee … who are you?"

"I am sorry, Seth. I hated lying to you. As it was, I told you more than I was supposed to."

"Who are you really?"

"This is me, a CS Ranger. And that was me you spent two very enjoyable days with. Working at Rajir's and the rest — that was Anni, a character I was playing."

"Why?"

"An assignment." She stopped, chewed on her lip and continued. "I would rather not go into detail. Someday I'll tell you everything." She got up and turned away from him, looking out the window. She shifted slightly, like her feet hurt. He could see the bruise on her face.

"You were there. You cut me loose." He found himself gripping the edge of the couch until his hands hurt. His heart pounded. He stood up abruptly and paced to relieve the tension.

"Breathe." Lee's voice cut through the panic. He leaned against the wall and struggled to draw in air. She kept talking. "Look where you are. You know this cabin. You came here because it's safe."

He let her voice pull him back to the here and now, feeling his heart rate slow to normal. Don't think; don't remember. He went to the table, picked up his plate and took it to the sink, focusing on something normal.

"What's buttonweed?" she asked. "Didn't Doc say that would help?"

He loosened his shoulders, let his breath out slowly, and turned to look at her. He half-expected the sight of her to set off another panic, but it didn't. "Buttonweed." He pulled himself together. "It makes you feel happy. There's a patch a little ways above the cabin."

"I can go pick some for you," she offered, setting her feet down to stand.

"No, I can do it." He raised a hand to stop her. It was something he could do to help himself. "I'll do it. It'll only take a few minutes."

"Are you sure?"

"Out the back door, across the pasture and about five posts up from the corner," he mapped it out in his mind. "I'll be right back."

"You'd better be." She clutched her knees with her good arm. "You have no idea how badly you scared me yesterday. I couldn't catch up with you and didn't know where you were going."

Heart pounding. Why had he done that? He didn't want to remember. He wouldn't ...

"Seth, sorry. It's fine now. You go find the buttonweed. I'll stay here, all right?" She was making herself small in the chair, unthreatening. "Bring some back for me too. I'm a little nervous, I guess."

He nodded, carefully shoved aside everything except his mental map to the buttonweed, retrieved his boots from the porch, and went out the back of the cabin. He couldn't let his mind wander to all the questions he knew hovered in the wings. If he stayed in the here and now, he would be okay.

Chapter 18

Lee

Lee watched Seth go, resisting the urge not to let him out of her sight. What if he ran again? What if?

When she heard the back door close, she followed, stopping on the back steps where she could see him. He walked calmly and surely across the pasture, but she worried. Panic, irrational anger, depression, withdrawal — the list of behaviors Doc had warned her about ran through her mind. So she waited uneasily as Seth disappeared into the trees. She wanted to chase after him; she stood cautiously on her tender feet. Teri's ointment and a pair of soft, thick socks worked wonders, but a gentle throbbing pointed out that she had been on them too much. She sank down on the porch, leaned against the wall and propped the offended extremities up on a chunk of firewood to wait. He should be back soon.

She watched the tree line where he had gone into the forest past a big, twisted palm-pine. Evening shadows stretching; bushes swaying slightly in the light breeze; all the small sounds of the spring day, chirps, hums, distant squawks; peaceful, restful.

A body warm against her; strong, gentle hands caressing, soothing; suddenly harsher, holding her down, brutal on her injured shoulder; a florid, conquering face inches from her. She twisted, struck her elbow on a wooden floor, and woke up, gasping for breath. She heard footsteps behind her and scrambled to her feet.

"There you are," Seth said from the doorway. "I found the buttonweed and some greens for dinner."

"Good." Her heart still pounded from her dream. She straightened her sling, avoiding Seth's eyes.

"I came out to get some firewood," he said slowly, shifting uneasily.

"Oh." She looked around, then stepped out of his way. "I'll be inside." The sun had gone down. She shivered and went in.

"So, that's buttonweed," she said, understanding where the name came from. The seed pods did look like small, thick buttons. She sat on a stool at the kitchen counter where he had left a handful of them.

"Last year's," Seth replied. He sat on the bench at the table with his cleaned plate and empty mug in front of him.

"May I try one?" She picked up the smallest pod.

"Go ahead."

"Did you have one?"

"When I picked them."

She touched her tongue to the husk. It felt coarse and tasted like nothing much. "The whole thing or do I peel it?"

"All of it. Just chew on it enough to break it up; then leave it under your tongue for a while."

She followed his directions and would have been sure he was teasing if Doc hadn't suggested the herb. It crumbled and lay under her tongue like the dried weed it was, slowly softening as it moistened. Not sure what to expect, she continued cleaning up the kitchen. As she sat on her stool, washing the few dishes from dinner, she was aware that Seth wandered aimlessly around the room. Soothing warmth crept through her, smothering her distress and her assorted aches.

"Oh, wow." She stopped what she was doing and absorbed the feeling. "So that's what Doc prescribed."

Seth stopped his rambles for a moment. "Nice buzz," he commented. He started to move again, then looked around in confusion. "What was I going to do?"

"You could light a fire," she said. Maybe the mood set by a fire could give her some of the comfort she sought. Given a task to focus on, he moved with assurance to carry it out. She finished the dishes, put things away, and wondered what came next.

She walked across the room to sit in her preferred chair by the fireplace. Seth jumped when she approached, dropped the chunk of wood he was putting on the fire and perched on the hearth like a bird about to take flight. She curled into the chair, making herself small. "Tell me about this place. It doesn't look like a riders' camp."

The diversion worked. He straightened and moved over to the couch. "It isn't. It belongs to friends of my Pa — Teri Dunn's sister and brother-in-law. They've been off world for years."

Lee leaned her chin on her knees. "Ran Cory and Cris Vawn — they're my parents."

He stared. "You're *her* daughter? Pa told a lot of stories about Cris."

"See, just like everybody — I'm her daughter, not theirs, or his."

He stared in surprise. "She was the one Pa talked about."

"I know. She's the fire, the blazing light; like Joe Reilly, she's the one people remember."

"But ..." His voice hardened. "Why are you here?"

"Here on Carico?"

"Here with me, now."

She thought about it. Why was she here? "Because I want to be. I need some quiet time with someone I like being with."

"I'm bad company."

"You are not the only one wounded by Jerdix," she said quietly, risking pushing him into a panic attack. "You and I are damaged goods, thanks to him. No one else understands as well as you do what I need right now."

He gulped deep breaths and closed his eyes, fighting for control. She wanted to reach out and touch him, hold his hand, put an arm around him. She stayed where she was. "Seth, we are safe here, just you and me. Look around. This is your safe place."

She sat, unmoving, until he regained some composure. "Try the buttonweed," she suggested.

He looked uncertainly from her to the counter where the seed pods lay. "Right. Buttonweed will help."

She remained quiet while he got a pod. He paced until the effects set in. When he finally sat down, she relaxed a little. "Seth, why don't you go to the bedroom and get some sleep? We'll talk about it in the morning."

"You won't leave?"

"I'll be here."

"I, uh, thanks." He shrugged and gave her a weak grin. "Good night."

"'Night."

Lee sat up long after Seth went to bed, feeding wood to the fire, soaking in the radiant heat and staring into the bluish-green flames characteristic of the local wood. She felt like this attraction to flames came from deep in her genes. The cabin was so quiet that she could hear the crackles, pops, and hisses of the combustion song. She had nothing that she needed to do or could do at the moment.

It gave her too much time to think about all the mistakes she had made in the last few days and the things she had failed to accomplish or prevent. She'd be held accountable. She only had a few days, maybe less, before she would have to leave Under Rim. She did not want to go. Rejecting that line of thought, she found spare blankets in the drawers under the couch, wrapped herself in them, and lay where she could watch the embers die.

Much later she struggled out of sleep. It felt like early morning, but it wasn't light yet. Rain fell, not hard but steadily, a constant patter on the skylight. She'd been dreaming of someplace warm with sunshine. She snuggled into her blankets against the damp chill. Had the rain awakened her? Then she heard it again, a low moan punctuated with indecipherable words, a haunting, spine-tingling sound. Seth?

She started toward the hall, trailing the blankets. The moaning tapered off, and the door of the bedroom burst open. Seth came out, wild-eyed, and headed for the front door. He came toward her like she wasn't there. She stood in his way, backing up until she blocked the door. She didn't want to have to actually touch him, but she was determined to stop him.

"Seth," she said softly, "Seth, it's me, Lee … Anni." Probably still Anni to him, in this state. Some part of him realized his path was blocked. He stopped, puzzled. "Seth, everything is fine. You're safe. Seth, it's okay." She kept repeating reassurances, hoping he heard her. "Just sit down," she encouraged. "Sit on the couch."

Slowly he complied, following her directions, sitting, then lying down on the couch, and drifting back into sleep. She covered him with a blanket, careful not to touch him directly. Her heart ached to see him flinch from even the contact with the blanket. She built up the fire, pulled one of the armchairs over in front of the door, wrapped in the other blanket, and settled down where she could keep an eye on her companion.

Chapter 19

Seth

Seth struggled free of the blanket he was tangled in. Nasty dreams! Might as well get up. He could see the first beginnings of dawn through the front windows. Front windows? What was he doing on the couch? In the faint light, he made out Anni, no, Lee, in a chair in front of the door. She was curled tightly with her head against the back and her knees drawn up.

He got up quietly and pulled the blanket around him, aware that he hadn't exactly been sleeping fully clothed. Trying not to wake her, he checked the fire. She must have added wood not too long ago. Softly he tiptoed to the bedroom for some clothes. Maybe a shower would wash away some more of the fuzz in his mind. He was sure he had gone to sleep in the bedroom.

He turned on the water to let it get hot and rubbed at his scruffy face. Sound erupted from the front room, followed by hurried footsteps and doors opening and closing. The bathroom door burst open, and Lee appeared. "Seth! Scorch it — I thought you'd gone. I thought ..."

"Gone?!" He shut off the water. "Where? Why?"

"Out there! Running! You were sleepwalking earlier."

"That's how I got on the couch?"

She nodded. "I'm sorry I rushed in on you."

With a vestige of his former humor, he said, "At least you know I am really here and in one piece."

"Oh, yeah," she smiled weakly.

"Go start breakfast or something."

Her back was turned before the memory of them in her bed, of the pleasure they had shared, set off a debilitating expectation of pain that brought him to his knees. He didn't even recognize where it came from. But no pain materialized. The anticipation faded and settled deep in his gut as a fear that he would never be able to touch or be touched again. He sat back on his heels and groaned. He could deal with the anxiety, but he didn't know how he could live with this. Hugs, hands on shoulders, everybody always touched. And Anni, Lee, the feel of her.

"Seth," Lee called, pounding on the door. "What's that? There's something loud and unfriendly outside."

"Be there in a minute," he answered, glad for the distraction. He got to his feet, pulled on his pants, and opened the door. Lee stood at the end of the hallway, looking toward the front door. She moved out of his way when he came out.

"Sounds like a whole pack of something big," she said.

He crossed to the front door and opened it slowly. A grunting roar echoed off the Rim and was repeated along a ridge to the east. Suddenly annoyed, he grumbled, "Just notalions. Fierce predators, if you're a spinxi."

She sank down on the loft steps. "False advertising?"

"The kits are just starting to come out of the dens. They like to hear themselves at that age." He closed the door, shutting out most of the noise.

"Sorry I bothered you."

"Can I take a shower now?" he asked. "Without interruption?"

"Give it another try."

He snatched up a buttonweed pod as he passed the kitchen. Shower, food, maintenance on the cabin — he mapped his morning in his mind. He had to keep busy, keep focused.

Dust from several years covered the contents of the cabin. Determined to concentrate, Seth finished the food Lee put in front of him and started in the front room. He cleaned and scrubbed, swept and hammered. He kept his mind on searching out dirt. He was clumsy. He managed to bang and bruise himself a dozen times. Pain was okay. Pain wasn't followed by more pain. Pain was followed by ... He plunged into more work.

He tried to ignore Lee sitting in the chair in the corner doing nothing. She watched him silently. It distracted him.

Without stopping his efforts to scrub a stain off the floor, he said, "If you aren't going to be useful, go somewhere."

She didn't move. "You could slow down a little."

"Can't," he replied.

"Ease up," she said firmly.

He stopped and stared at the spot on the floor. "I've got to keep busy. Now help or go away."

"Stop it."

He looked at her, startled. She glared at him, wrapping one arm around her knees. She reached down and stripped off one of her socks.

"There!" She held her foot out, sole toward him. "Take a look at why I am sitting. Look!"

Under the sheen of "temporary skin" ointment, Seth saw the mottling of blisters and near-blisters. "Ouch," he said, coming closer.

"I got those trying to catch up to you." She brushed her hand lightly over her bruised face. "You saw how I got this. And Doc says I need to go to Portside to have my shoulder treated. So keep busy if you need to, but I'm not going anywhere." She worked the sock back on clumsily with one hand and clasped her knees again, turning away to look out the window.

Seth got up from the floor, shaken from his self-absorption. He vividly saw in his mind the silhouettes in the stall door, the man striking the girl, sending her stumbling across the floor, slamming the door and leaving them alone. Awareness that he hadn't given a thought to what had happened to her stilled his rising anxiety like cold water in his face. Only two, or was it three, days ago he had been concerned about her safety and eager to see her. Now he balanced on a knife edge between heart-pounding panic and reality that threatened to fuel that panic. Unable to cope with the turmoil, he fled to the porch.

He leaned against a post, holding on like a drowning man. He felt like he had fallen into a spring-wild river, tumbled and rolled and frantic for air. The roar filled his ears. He closed his eyes and got lost.

"Seth." A voice penetrated. "Please, come inside."

He opened his eyes and saw the peaceful meadow of flowers stretching to the woods. No whirling; no chaos. Sunshine, a light breeze, sweet smells and quiet.

"Seth, please."

He pushed away from his anchor post and turned back to the cabin. Lee stood in the door. "In a minute," he said. "Give me a minute."

She nodded and went back in. He saw her move the kitchen stool to a spot where she could see him. He walked along the porch, trying to find enough balance to have a simple conversation. Focus on one thing, one step. Walk inside, talk to Lee, do more cleaning. He could do that. What to say? What would he have said before? She hurt. He didn't want her to hurt. He went to the door.

"I'm sorry," he said, fingering the knotted cord on his wrist. "I get lost."

"I know. Can you sit down for a few minutes?"

He stepped inside and sat on the bench by the table. "It's all confused. I think I want to keep it that way."

"I am not asking you to talk about what happened. Just remember you aren't alone."

"What happened to you?" He had to ask.

She shook her head. "Someday I'll tell you. You aren't the only one not ready to talk."

"What do we do now?"

She stood and shuffled across the room to her favorite chair. "I need to rest and let some superficial damage heal. What do you need?"

"To be here. Quiet, time, room." To wrap the familiar peace around him.

"I need the same. I want to make a deal with you — to stick together and help each other through this, kind of nudge each other back on track when we need it, and help keep the demons at bay."

He studied her, waiting to see if panic set in. His heart behaved. "Knots at the end of ropes? I'll do my best, but I can't promise much right now."

"Can you fix lunch?" she asked.

He chuckled, surprising himself. "Lunch I can do. Then I want to catch a couple of horses from the pasture."

"Good," she said, sounding halfhearted. "Although personally, I don't feel like riding just yet." She drew her knees up.

"I'll just feel better with a horse handy."

"You're right. You should bring a couple horses here."

He went to the kitchen and gathered together makings for lunch. The simple act of taking a plate across the room to her took all the control he could muster. He backed away hurriedly after setting the plate down. Embarrassed, he retreated to the kitchen to eat his own sandwich.

"How does a horse react to unexpected things when it's nervous?" she asked.

How would a horse react? A horse escaped from what threatened it. He did feel like a horse in a strange situation where it was sure everything was dangerous.

Gently she said, "Be as easy on yourself as you would be with that horse."

Seth thought a lot about that as he walked through the forest, halters in hand. The world felt almost normal except his shirt rubbed uncomfortably. He couldn't make sense of the sensation. It shifted from smooth to harsh, gentle to heavy. Frustrated and disgusted, he took the irritating garment off and carried it.

When he got to the big pasture where he and Nick had left the horses, he rubbed and scratched his geldings but caught the two untrained colts. The horses didn't startle him, didn't cause his heart to pound. He could deal with horses. So he took the two that gave him a job to do.

Chapter 20

Lee

Lee let Seth go, resisting the urge to watch him, to reassure herself that he was in control. His nightmares and difficulty interacting with her haunted her. Unexpectedly tears welled up. She ached at the thought of his assurance, his innate calm, so shattered. With luck, he would feel comfortable around the animals when he didn't with people.

It was a person, a fellow human being, who had tormented him. She knew beyond doubt that Jerdix had used the rod on Seth repeatedly. She guessed the setting had been random so that Seth couldn't predict what to expect, pain or pleasure, instilling an aversion to being touched at all. Different for her with only a few widely separated uses. After the first, she'd known exactly what to expect. Still, she wasn't feeling much like being around other people just then either.

She remembered the couple of days she and Seth had spent together. She'd felt a connection between them that she had never felt with anyone before. Events hadn't changed that. Looking for a distraction, she went in and applied Teri's herbal concoctions to bruises, scrapes, and blisters. Already the discomfort was fading. She'd be back in good shape soon, hopefully before she had to account to Vinz, before the Rangers would expect her to leave Carico for reassignment. Something she had no intention of doing.

That thought came as a surprise to her. She hadn't consciously considered staying on Carico, but she had already made that decision. She put down the jar of ointment. She had enough time in service to resign but had always considered the Rangers her career. Of course, staying with Seth meant she would stay on Carico. She just hadn't thought through all the implications.

Then there was Jerdix. She firmly reminded herself that now he was someone else's responsibility. She needed to trust Joe Reilly and look forward to a day in court to finish what had started here. That was where she would face Jerdix, place the rod undeniably in his hand, and watch judgment fall. Today she had other things to concentrate on.

She went out on the porch to sit. From there she could see across the field to the trees. To the east, a promontory of the Rim jutted south in tiered verdigris cliffs. A light breeze made waves in the tall grass and flowers of the meadow. Insects flitted among the plants. A larger flyer soared on the thermals, dipping and circling with mesmerizing flow. She put her feet up and dozed, willing to leave everything until later.

When Seth came back leading two young horses, the soft sound of hooves on dirt woke her. Seth waved to her and headed toward the corrals. Lee went through the cabin and sat on the back steps where she could watch. Seth tied one colt and led the other into the round pen. He'd taken off his shirt even though it was not hot. Did he usually do that?

Lee soon quit being distracted by dust-frosted skin. As she observed his quiet, intricate dance with the horse, she was seeing into his soul. Here was the man she had only begun to know, the one she feared had been irrevocably damaged. She could almost see the invisible connection between the man and the horse. He guided its movements, reading subtle signs she couldn't distinguish, putting pressure on the animal with slight changes in posture or more assertive repositioning. Fascinated, she moved to sit at the base of a tree where she could get comfortable. If she could just decipher what he looked for and the timing of his reactions. The timing would be the key. She leaned against the rough bark of the tree, ignored the dampness of the ground, and knew she wanted to spend the rest of her life watching Seth Reilly work this magic.

When he finished with the second horse, he led both to the pasture and turned them loose. She'd been so engrossed in what he was doing, she had barely moved in all the time she had sat there. She struggled to her feet, stiff and chilled, and sought a sunny spot against the wall of the cabin.

Seth came over carrying the halters and his shirt. "I'm going to go get saddle horses."

"Now?" she asked. Afternoon was progressing into evening.

"Why not? Shouldn't take too long."

"All right." She felt a little in awe of him at the moment. "I'll see what we have for dinner."

"Stay off those feet." He grinned and ambled off.

They spent a quiet evening sitting on the porch. He had his shirt on when he came in although he shifted his shoulders as though it made him uncomfortable. Did his touch avoidance extend to something as simple as clothing?

She got him to talk about the country around them, the plants and animals, the weather. Full dark settled in. She saw him nodding off in his chair, but he made no move to go to bed.

"I don't know about you, but I've had a long day," she said at last. "I'll get a couple things from the bedroom and get out of your way."

He took his feet down from the railing and ran his hand through his hair. "I should let you have the bed tonight."

"The couch is fine, for now. Anyway, it's a little short for you." She didn't want to say out loud that she was afraid he would sleepwalk again. She went inside, stifling a complex of emotions she couldn't begin to sort out.

She slept well enough until his nightmares disturbed her from the other side of the wall. He didn't walk, but his moans and cries kept her awake long after he was quiet.

In the morning, Lee couldn't feel discouraged with a bright sun, fresh breeze, and most of the tenderness gone from her feet. A sharp stab from her shoulder squelched her temptation to leave the sling off. Otherwise, she felt good.

Seth came out of the bedroom shortly after she started moving around. Had he been listening for her? He mumbled a greeting and began to fix breakfast. He was irritable, an aftermath of the nightmares maybe. The only thing she could do for him was to stay out of his way. He ate silently and headed out to the horses. She let him get started with the colts before going out to watch.

She couldn't get as enthralled with the process as she had the day before. She stayed for a while, determined to learn what she could, but she was restless. As she walked toward the cabin, she noticed that he stopped for a moment to hang his shirt on a post. Her mood sank. Inside she tackled the cleaning, something she could control.

Limited by her sling, she took her time, exploring the dwelling in the process. Not only was the cabin comfortably laid out, the furnishings had been beautifully crafted. Who was the woodworker? Her parents' home ... she climbed into the loft and stared around at what might have been her room. Why hadn't they come back to Carico?

She guessed that answer. Her mother probably loved the wildness but couldn't confine herself to one little frontier planet. Cris never stayed in one place long. Lee had grown up living with her uncle, her mother's brother, most of the time while her parents shuffled around from one Central Services assignment to another. Not that she minded. Uncle Nyle was great. She'd always had someone there when she needed them. Still, she could imagine growing up in this space, sung to sleep by notalions with the wind keeping time around the eaves.

From one of the dormers, she saw the Marshal's skimmer coming into the meadow. Reluctantly, she left the loft and went out to meet him. Maybe he'd have some news about Jerdix. Maybe it was time for more questions, more explanations.

Joe walked slowly from the skimmer to the steps, "Jerdix — looks like he got off world," he said bluntly. "We haven't found his trail yet."

She stopped on the bottom step. "How?"

"We haven't found that out either." He reached out and tugged her sling. "How are you doing?"

"Right and tight, Marshal, well, soon enough anyway."

"Seth?"

"Out back with a colt."

He grinned. "That sounds good. Keep my friend company." He nodded toward the skimmer and jogged off around the side of the cabin.

Lee looked back at the vehicle. A man got out of the passenger side. She stared at her father. He must be the specialist Doc had talked about. "When did you get here?" she asked.

"Hey, tough stuff, word is you needed a little help."

She met him halfway, eager for his hug. "Oh, Da. You're here."

"Come on, kiddo. Let's sit down, and you can tell me why you're wearing that fancy scarf." Ran Cory laid his hand lightly on her bruised face. "Just a father-daughter chat, nothing official."

"I'm okay, Da. Nothing that won't heal."

"I know. Now, inside. We'll fix some tea."

She took her perch on the tall kitchen stool. "Have you spoken to Cris — Mom?"

He put the kettle on the stove. "I sent her a message, but she's out on the edge. It may not reach her for weeks."

"How did you know to come?"

"Joe, of course. Although he didn't foresee how far Jerdix would go." He opened the cupboard. "Look at that. Everything is right where we used to keep it. All this time …"

"Will Seth be all right?" Lee stood and got mugs from the dish drainer.

"You told Joe he was working with a colt? That sounds promising. But he'll need help he can't get here to fully recover. You know that the rod affects how the brain processes the sense of touch among other things. That needs to be treated."

She nodded, fumbled with tea, afraid to look at her father. She wasn't ready to tell him what had been done to her.

He laid a hand gently on her good shoulder. "I'll spend some time with him and do what I can. Now get off those feet. I hear you wore them out."

"Yes, sir." She let him finish getting water on the herbs.

While the tea steeped, he wandered around the cabin. "Lije made the furniture," he said, running a hand over the silky-smooth stone set into the surface of the table. "He's quite the woodworker. Is any of the garden left? Teri planted herbs for the kitchen."

"You never said a word about this place. Why not?" She couldn't keep the edge off her voice. She felt a little cheated somehow.

He looked at her in surprise. "I'm not sure. You like it here?"

"I do."

"What do you plan to do?" he asked.

"Stay here, with Seth." She answered promptly and firmly. Might as well get it on the table now.

"It's like that, is it? You're sure; not just wrapped up in the moment?"

"I'm staying."

"Okay, we won't argue about it. You know I trust your judgment." He came to her and kissed her forehead.

The back door banged, and Joe strode into the room. "Well, did we take good care of the cabin?"

Ran Cory laughed. "Looks fine. I can't say the same for my daughter, but she volunteered for this assignment and wouldn't listen to advice."

"That doesn't surprise me." Joe clapped his old friend on the shoulder. "I'll take your daughter with me now and leave you with Seth."

Lee stood up to protest. He held up a hand. "Girl, you come. You have an appointment with Doc. You can bring back the stead skimmer. You can drive one, can't you?"

"My pilot credentials are current, so I think I can manage a skimmer."

"Fine, now give your father a chance with Seth. He knows more about rod effects than almost anyone."

The aftermath of trauma in many forms was an area her father had studied in detail over the years. He volunteered to counsel victims sometimes. She knew that but, like most children, hadn't given it much thought. "Okay, I'll see Doc."

Chapter 21

Lee

"Now listen to me, Ranger." Doc faced Lee down. "That collarbone separation has worsened. Do I need to confine you to bed? Or can I just ship you to Portside and get it properly treated?"

"You know why it hasn't healed," Lee said, remembering Jerdix's heavy hand on her shoulder. "I can take care of it now. Nothing to do but sit around."

"You?"

She grinned. "Honestly, Doc. Don't make me go yet."

"Worried about Seth?"

"I stand by my partners."

"Okay, get out of here. It'll stay weak until you get that cartilage welded together. I'll get a brace for you so you can use your arm a little. Until then, take it easy."

"I'll do my best." Lee left the med building and walked along the promenade to the store for a few things they needed. Then, instead of leaving, she crossed the plaza and entered the Marshal's Office. To her relief, Joe hadn't said much on the way from Fallen Pine. He'd simply dropped her off at the stead and left again. Still, she wanted to see him for a minute before leaving. Something was left unfinished.

At her call on the intercom, Joe came to the front. "Doc let you go, did he?" He forced a smile.

"He did, for now," she replied. "I got supplies. Anything else I should do while I'm here?"

"Not that I can think of. Ro Vinz went back to Portside for now."

"I'll stay with Seth."

"I know that."

"I'd better get back; find out what Da has to say."

He leaned against the counter, avoiding her eyes. "I wish you two would come to the stead," he said.

She carefully lightened her tone. "Don't you trust us to get by on our own for a few days?"

He answered in kind. "Hey, it's lonesome at the house."

"Is that really all?"

"I'd feel better if I had proof of where Jerdix went. And where all his people are."

"I'll keep my eyes open." She shrugged with her good shoulder. "See you soon," she said with an encouraging grin and left him there, trying to pretend he hadn't just scared her silly.

She had an hour of skimmer travel to think. She tried to focus on her surroundings, what plants to ask Seth about, the topography, anything except what came next. Just get through today and close her mind to debriefings, recovery, and missing bad guys.

No one met her at the cabin. She put away the groceries before going out back. She found the two men rolling a log onto a stack that hadn't been there earlier. Nearby two saddled horses stood with cocked hips.

"Firewood," her father said over his shoulder. "Seth put me to work."

"I see. Do you want dinner?"

"Starved," he answered. "How about you, Seth?"

Seth shoved the log into place and straightened up. "Me, too."

Lee went back inside. She found something unsettling about Seth and her father side by side doing chores. She wasn't accustomed to seeing Ran Cory in this setting at all. Their home was her Uncle Nyle's penthouse in the heart of the city of Kasba on the Center world of Oasis, a long way from a cabin in the woods. She'd spent time in unsettled areas during Ranger training and, more recently, on assignment, but she hadn't been out like this with her father since she'd been a child. And all that time they'd had this cabin and hadn't come back to it.

"I am well fed." Cory pushed back his chair and carried his dishes to the sink. "You've settled into Carico nicely."

"Thanks," Lee answered, suspicious of his motives. "And?"

"And?" he echoed. "All right, and now it's time to wrap up some business."

"You're debriefing me?" she asked with disbelief.

"You know better. You'll have to deal with Vinz for that. I'm just tasked with delivering you Portside for that interview. I'll pick you up here day after tomorrow as soon as it's light enough to land my surf-or. Assuming you'll take me back to Joe's stead now."

He rated a surface-orbit transit craft to check up on her? She must be in trouble. Or was he tied in with the bigger Jerdix operation? Of course he must be.

"You aren't staying here?" After what Joe had said about Jerdix and his people, she thought he would.

"Not tonight. Joe and I have some talking to do." He went to the door and pulled on his boots. Flashing a warm smile, he added, "Don't worry, Seth, she'll be coming back here when she's done Portside."

Seth let out a deep breath and nodded.

"Why don't you just take the skimmer tonight?" Lee asked.

"I'd feel better if you two had it. Now get me back to the stead, daughter."

She let him drive. She sat in the dark, uneasy about the debriefing and about leaving, even for a little while. "Da, you're sure I'll be back? I promised Joe I'd stay with Seth."

"Seth will be fine alone for a day or so. His problem is going to be around people." He reached out and rubbed his hand lightly down her slung arm. "We'll keep an eye on him."

"How long will you be on Carico?"

"Just a few days this time."

She looked away into the dark forest below them. "I'm not leaving."

"You have time to make that decision."

"How can you be sure?" Lee wondered aloud.

"Because your extended post-assignment leave is already approved. You have six months standard after your debriefing before you have to report back."

A knot of worry loosened deep inside. She had that much time to work out her future. She didn't have to have answers in two days. "What about Jerdix?" she asked. "Won't he come back after us or Joe?"

"Let us worry about Jerdix. This didn't work out the way he planned. He'll change his strategy, like he always does."

"And go after Mom or Uncle Nyle?"

"If so, someone will be waiting for him. It's out of your hands."

"I can't help worrying."

"Just don't let it plague you. He left Carico. You have more important things to work on right now."

He set the skimmer down next to the Marshal's vehicle in front of the house. When she refused to come in, he hugged her close for a moment. "You had me worried, A'lee."

She accepted the comfort as she had when she was little, wishing those arms could block out all the aftermath yet to come.

Then he stepped away. "I'll see you day after tomorrow — early." He brushed a hand over the yellowing bruise on her face and left her standing alone in the dark. Slowly she climbed into the skimmer and started back to Fallen Pine.

Seth was cleaning the kitchen when she got there. She saw him shrug into his shirt as she came in the door. He looked up but didn't say anything. She sat down at the table and rubbed at her aching shoulder. "Doc is ordering a brace for me," she told him. "I'll be so glad when I can use this arm again."

"Will you really come back from Portside?" he asked, looking steadily at the plate he was washing.

"Yes," she assured. "Da promised, and he always keeps his word."

"I like him."

"You put him to work," she said with a laugh. "Bet he'll be sore in the morning."

"He did his share."

She wanted to ask what they had talked about but bit back the question. She knew she wasn't going to want to give him all the details of her debriefing, so she hesitated to set up any expectation. "I think I could handle a little riding if you'd like to show me around tomorrow."

He put down what he held and faced her. "I want to go to Tobin Canyon," he said. "I ... your father, he gave me some exercises to cope with ... to manage my symptoms. I need to see how things are going, with Migration, you know." He looked down, fingering the knotted cord on his wrist.

She breathed slowly and studied his face. "If you think you should, we'll go." She swallowed all her arguments about not pushing things. "Can we just watch for a while until I understand what's happening? From the overlook you showed me?"

He nodded, the quick jerk of his head showing his tension. "From the overlook, for a while." He turned to the sink and continued washing dishes. Finishing the skillet, he wiped it dry. Without looking at her, he said, "I moved my things upstairs." He hung the skillet on the wall and began wiping down counters, carefully not facing her.

She looked at the steep steps and thought of the big, comfortable bed down the hall. She didn't think she would sleep in it. "I like the loft," she said, unable to think of anything else to say. She wanted to hold him and kiss away the hurts, to sleep easy in his arms. When he was ready.

She went over and curled into her chair by the fireplace. She stared at the unlit fire and consciously focused her thoughts on what she would say in her debriefing, what emotionless language she could use to sort fact from visceral memory. When Seth said good night and climbed the steps to the loft, she made up her bed on the couch and lay in the stillness for a long time before drifting into an uneasy sleep.

In the morning, Lee waited restlessly to leave for Tobin Canyon. Seth caught both colts for their daily training. She could see him trying to keep his attention on them and recognized his need to center himself before facing the people and the work of Migration. When he was ready, she let him take the controls of the skimmer.

When they reached Tobin Canyon, he parked halfway between the cookhouse and the overlook. Teri waited for them on the porch.

"I'll go talk to her," Lee offered.

"I'll come," he said, climbing slowly out of the vehicle. Lee let him lead the way, stopping a few feet from the steps.

Teri smiled warmly, taking a slow step forward. "I am so glad to see you. The crew just went down to the pens. Will you join me for sweet rolls?"

Seth shook his head. "I don't think ..."

"I'll bring them out to you. We can sit here." She gestured to the row of chairs along the porch.

He relaxed a little. "Sure, Tia."

"I'll be right back."

"I'll help." Lee gave Seth an encouraging smile and hurried inside.

Teri was pouring tea into mugs. She quietly asked, "How are you doing? Is he going to try to work?"

Lee shook her head. "I don't think so. Da spent yesterday with him and gave him some exercises to help him deal with things. He agreed to watch for a while today. I doubt he'll try to join in."

"Your father's here? That is the best news." Teri handed her a plate of massive rolls dripping frosting. "What about Cris?"

"Out on the edge. She probably hasn't gotten word about any of this."

"You tell Cory to hustle himself down here and see me."

"I will, but tomorrow he's taking me to Portside for my debriefing."

Teri stopped. "Does that mean you're leaving?"

"No." Lee shook her head. "I have some personal time coming. We'll be back in a couple of days."

"I am glad to hear that."

They found Seth still standing on the steps, watching the dust rising from the canyon along with the rumbling growls of tarbh and shouts of riders. Teri grinned and shook her head. "Take your mug and go," she told him. "Lee can sit and keep me company for a few minutes."

Lee watched Seth walk to the overlook, quickly at first then uncertainly as he got closer. He found a place where he could sit against a rock.

Teri took a roll from the plate. "How is he doing?"

Lee sat down with a sigh. "Not good, but better than I expected. He does fine when he's working with the colts but around people ..." She picked at her food, trying to find the right words. "He's not there," she finally said. "He's out of reach, to me at least. He and Da did okay."

Teri nodded. "If anyone can help, it's Ran Cory. Now, what about you?"

Lee stared into her mug. "I'm okay. Not looking forward to tomorrow." She kept thoughts of Jerdix to herself. No need to worry Teri more than she already was.

"The debriefing or the travel time with your so insightful father?"

"Both."

They sat quietly, watching the still figure in the shadow of the rock. Lee finished her tea in a gulp. "Maybe he'll talk to me about what the crew is doing," she said, getting up.

"Let me know if I can help." Teri said.

"I will." Lee took her mug back inside before walking to the overlook. She scuffed her feet a little in the gravel so Seth would hear her coming. He looked up and scrambled to his feet. Giving him plenty of room, she found a spot where she could look down into the pens. Through the haze of dust thrown up by milling feet, she could see twenty or thirty mottled gray-brown backs and flashes of the blue neck fans. Three riders kept the tarbh to one side of the corral. The animals settled down, mothers seeking out babies, nosing them in under their necks.

"They just brought this group in from the bigger pen." Seth came closer. "They need to let the mommas and babies get back together so they know who the calves belong to. Once the tarbh have paired up, the real work begins."

One rider, carrying a scanner, moved slowly into the bunched animals and separated out a cow and calf. He called out something to the camp boss who stood behind a barricade in one corner. Another rider moved in and neatly dropped a loop to catch the calf's hind feet. With a quick jerk, like a fisherman setting a hook, he tightened the rope and dragged the calf from under its mother's nose. The third rider cut off the cow, her horse dancing between the anxious tarbh and the whining calf while two people on the ground ran in to vaccinate and fan-mark the calf and insert the microchip under the skin. One of them reached down and loosened the rope. The calf jumped up and ran to its mother as the riders drove the cow out the gate into another pen.

"That's it?" Lee asked in surprise. The whole sequence took only a couple of minutes.

"When everything goes right," Seth answered. "See the cow in the corner with the cuts on her haunches? They'll leave her for last. She needs to be doctored. They'll rope her by the front and back feet to stretch her down. Catching those front feet isn't always easy."

The work went on with good-natured teasing all around. The ground crew traded with the riders every few animals. Only the camp boss stayed in place, keeping track of the chips and the vaccine.

One cow got by the rider holding her and charged toward the ground crew to defend her calf. Another rider intercepted her, the big bay horse ignoring the bright blue fan waving in its face to shoulder the cow aside. The horse staggered at the contact, and the rider nearly lost his seat. The first rider moved in on the cow, forcing her to retreat, flapping her fan with irritation. One of the ground crew called for the rider who had let the cow by to give up his horse in penance for the mistake. Laughing taunts supported the exchange.

Seth abruptly stepped away from the edge. "I can't do this," he said, wide-eyed and breathing fast.

"Not yet," Lee agreed. "But you can train a horse."

He shook his head. "I should be down with them."

"You will be, just not today." She started to extend a hand to him, withdrew it, and stood awkwardly unsure of how to help.

He squared his shoulders. "Let's go," he said, striding determinedly toward the cookhouse. He went inside and came out with his bedroll and bag. He loaded his gear into the skimmer and climbed in. Helplessly, Lee waved to Teri and hurried to get in with him.

Climbing from Tobin Canyon to Under Rim, they left the sunshine behind. By the time they got to Fallen Pine, rain beat down steadily. Seth snatched his things from the skimmer, carried them in, threw them at the foot of the stairs and stalked out the backdoor, slamming it behind him.

Lee told herself anger was a change, an improvement. She gave him a few minutes and followed him out, sitting on the top step under the eaves just out of the rain. He was chopping wood, the ax swinging up and dropping, the pieces of wood falling to the wet ground, him reaching for another piece. He moved smoothly and steadily, rain slick on his bare shoulders, all rhythm and anger and pain.

She wished she could get to the anger stage. She couldn't get past her own denial, refusing to admit what had happened to her, what it might mean to her life. Maybe if she stood out in the rain, it would wash her clean of everything.

It was nearly dark when he came inside, packing a prodigious stack of firewood. She filled a plate for him, and he ate in silence. The anger had faded, poured out into the rhythm of the ax. She wasn't sure what had replaced it.

When he finished, he started a fire and stood watching the flames. Without looking at her, he said, "I don't think I will ever be normal again."

She went to sit on the hearth, not getting too close but wanting to see his face. "Neither of us will be the same, but what's normal?"

He turned away. "When you get to Portside, you should just keep going."

"Seth, what's this about? I thought we agreed to get through this together."

"I can't be together with you or anyone right now." He sounded so calm, like he was at peace with the idea.

Frightened by his serenity, such an abrupt change from the earlier anger, panic squirmed in her gut. "Did you listen to my father? Did he tell you the only way was to have help?"

"Maybe he's right but not now."

She searched for something to say to convince him. "He knows what he's talking about, Seth. He has a friend, someone he used to work with, who lives in a force bubble. That man will never be able to tolerate a human touch without heavy sedation first. When they found him, got him free, it was weeks before he came back to reality at all, months before he regained memories of who he was. He will never remember exactly what happened to him. The doctors have blocked that. He was captive for five days."

"Five days!" Seth shuddered.

"You've come a long ways already. Give yourself a chance."

He stared at her. "He used it on you. You said he did."

She choked on her reaction. Oh, please, don't go there! Don't make me go there! Her fragile control slipped. "You saw him ..." she answered very softly.

"When?" he asked. "I ... in the stall. I remember. Just once?"

"No ..." Suddenly she was back there, trapped and molested. Her control nearly snapped. She pulled herself off the hearth, turned her back to him, leaned against the wall. Wanted arms around her to keep her safe; wasn't sure she could stand to be touched; knew he couldn't touch her, and he would suffer for that. "I'm all right!" she insisted. "I'm all right!"

"Anni?" He was close. Out of reach but close.

"My name is Lee!" She shouted that to him, herself, the Elements themselves. Lee had never let herself be raped. Lee was clean. "I am Lee."

"Lee," he repeated. "Please."

She struggled to breathe slowly and evenly. She turned to face him. "Sorry."

He reached out from across the floor. "What did he do to you?"

She held still, not moving toward him, her control still marginal. "Not what he did to you," she said. He took a step toward her. She backed off slowly, giving them both room. "I'll be okay soon enough."

His eyes reflected the thoughts she knew were running through his mind. She saw the realization take shape in outrage and sympathy. "He ..." Seth began.

She held up her hand. "Not now. I can't talk about it now," she pleaded. "When I come back from Portside, I promise I'll tell you."

He withdrew, crossing his arms. "Maybe you shouldn't," he said without meeting her eyes. "I have enough to deal with."

She understood. She really did. She didn't want to hear the details of what had been done to him. She didn't want to see his reactions to her story. Still, her heart sank. They weren't together in this after all.

She dreamed that night of making love with Seth with innocence and abandon, but suddenly Jerdix was there with the rod. She woke screaming in her mind.

Chapter 22

Seth

An hour after Lee and her father lifted off from the meadow in the sleek, graceful surface-to-orbit craft, Seth rode Jester onto the trail toward the Rim. He needed the time by himself. He couldn't go back, couldn't make it all go away. He had to choose to stumble ahead, but he was entering strange territory with little to guide him to an unknown destination. His mind whirled with the information Ran Cory had given him. Somewhere in all of that, he hoped to find some direction.

He let his horse pick the way along the path through the forest until the ground rose sharply into the rock debris that skirted the foot of the cliffs. Although sunlight swept across the lower country, the trail lay in the shadow of the promontory that jutted out to the east. He shivered a little in the cool morning air and tried to focus on the narrow track twisting through the boulders and scraggly fern trees clinging in pockets of soil. The ground was wet from the rain the day before. Jester set each foot carefully, moving calmly with sure balance. Seth recognized that the animal had no concern for what lay out of sight, worrying only about the next step.

"Smarter than me, huh, old boy," Seth said to the horse. "One step at a time." Jester stopped, rubbed his nose against his knee, and continued on the way.

They reached the base of cliffs that topped the Rim and found a persistent snowbank blocking their way. Seth dismounted, led Jester to a relatively flat spot against the rock face, and tied him firmly to a tree. He loosened the cinch and scratched the horse's neck.

"You wait here. I'll be back in a while," Seth said. He climbed over the snow and scrambled up the last couple hundred yards of steep zigzag between fractured slabs of rock to reach the top. The trail came out of a deep niche between boulders into open sunshine. Seth turned to follow the edge to a point looking down on Jester only a stone's throw below. He found a place a few feet back from the drop-off where he could sit in the sun with his back to a boulder and look out across the forested basin all the way to the desert in the hazy distance.

"Sure do hope you know what you're talking about, Ranger Cory," he muttered to himself. "This self-hypnosis is supposed to let me explore memories without reliving them. We'll see." He closed his eyes and took himself back to the night at the Gathering Hall and the moment Anni left him to go inside to Jerdix.

In his mind, he watched the events unfold as if he watched a movie — Whip and Bull grabbing him; waking up in the dark stall; the light coming on to reveal Jerdix and the rod; the horrific time that followed; pale daylight; Anni being pushed in and the door shutting behind her; her freeing him and transforming into Lee; and his flight to the cabin.

Even as an observer, Seth's guts twisted and his skin crawled. The montage was a thing of nightmares — the victim so totally helpless; the torturer dispassionate at the beginning but becoming more and more enthralled in drawing forth intense responses. All so unreal — not something he could ever explain to someone who hadn't been there.

What a sham his tough independence had been. And overwhelming everything else, the image of that simple little rod loomed. Anxiety struck him sharply. Alone with the rocks and trees, he managed to swallow the panic and hold himself still.

Ran Cory said that he suffered from more than a response to the trauma. The rod changed something in his brain, affecting his ability to respond correctly to stimuli, particularly touch. With specialized treatment, he could recover. But that meant leaving Carico and its relative wilderness for a medical facility crowded with people. He could barely tolerate being in a room with a couple of people he knew and trusted. How could he go somewhere so alien without breaking down completely?

No, he needed to be somewhere he felt safe, where he was in control. He could not surrender himself to anyone right now, even for the best of reasons. He needed time and isolation and an intimate connection with horses to find himself again. Kieron Dougherty would give him a place at Seven Wells, at one of the lonely camps where he wouldn't have to explain anything to well-meaning people who couldn't understand.

His fingers found the cord tied around his wrist. Lee had placed that there when she was Anni, and he had been falling in love with her. With whom, though? She said the time they had spent together had been real, not part of her role, but how could he know? Lee had saved him, gotten him free from Jerdix; Lee didn't ask questions; her brown-gold eyes were Anni's eyes. He shoved away the memories of intimacy that got tangled up with the effects of the rod. He barely knew Lee. Better for both of them if he never did. He would go to Seven Wells alone and let the horses work their magic. Maybe then he would feel strong enough to get that professional help he was supposed to need.

He stood up and took in the sunlit vista. He was at home in that wildness. With horses, he never lacked for company. He slid and scrambled back to Jester and rode to the cabin, methodically planning what he needed to do to be far on the trail to Seven Wells before Lee got back from Portside. He laid it out in his mind, step by step, so he could stay focused. Even routine things took some planning, or he got distracted.

He took the two colts back to the big pasture. He packed his things. He put the second saddle Lije had brought on Buster and tied on his gear. He laid a fire in the fireplace, ready for Lee to light when she got back. The scarf she had used as a sling hung over the back of a chair. He put it in his pocket. Finally, he found the old gray shirt he had given to her, folded it, and left it in the middle of the counter. He hoped she would see it as the offering it was. He couldn't bring himself not to leave anything for her. He ignored the whispering voice that told him she was still the knot he held onto at the end of his rope.

He reached his father's stead late in the afternoon and wasted no time collecting his trail outfit from the tack room. Good thing his horses had had a rest. In the morning they were going back to work. Just before dinnertime, when he knew Dougherty would be in the office at Seven Wells, he went to the house and sent a blip saying he was on his way back and asking for a job at one of the isolated camps for the summer. He got an immediate response assuring him they could work something out.

That left only one more thing he had to do. He wouldn't leave without talking to his father. He had caused enough worry already. He made a mug of tea and settled down on the porch to wait. He refused to listen to his internal debate about paying attention to the experts and taking help when it was offered, about the support of family.

Dark settled over the stead, softening edges of the buildings and fading fences into the background. Stars brightened. Spinxi chirruped from the barn in an evening chorus Seth had known all his life. He felt so normal, sitting there enjoying a fine spring evening.

The Marshal's skimmer hummed in and settled under the shed roof, home for the night. Joe walked up the easy slope to the house, moving slowly, shoulders slumped. Seth shifted in his chair.

Joe's head came up, and he stopped. "Seth, I didn't expect you," he said, continuing onto the porch. "Let me get cleaned up, and we'll have some dinner."

"I just need to talk to you for a minute," Seth said without standing.

"Son, have dinner. Then we'll talk as long as you like. I am glad to see you home."

"I'm not staying," he said.

Joe stiffened. "That's it, is it? All the more reason to spend a little time with your old man."

"Pa, please." Seth wanted to get it over quickly and be gone.

"Steaks are waiting."

Seth gave in, knowing his father's persistence. "Okay, I suppose you want me to cook while you wash up?"

"I trained you well."

Seth hadn't anticipated how difficult it would be to stick to his decision to leave when he was going through a familiar routine in his childhood home. The surroundings stole reality from the recent events. He ate his dinner quietly while his father talked about trivial happenings around the stead, when the mares were due to foal, whether the wet spring would delay Teri's garden crops, a leak in the barn roof, things impossibly far from Jerdix and a black rod.

The plates were cleared and fresh tea made. Seth sat at one end of the long table, watching his father restlessly putter around the kitchen. Joe finally sat down at the other end of the table with a sigh.

"Don't misunderstand," Joe said, "but I'm glad you're leaving. Staying here would make it too easy for you to avoid getting help. Are you going with Cory?"

"With Cory?" Seth asked with surprise. "No."

"Son ... I'd hoped that was it."

"Pa, I can't," Seth blurted out. "Ships and hospitals, all those walls and people. I'd go crazy."

"It's the only way. I know Cory explained that. What do we need to do to help you through it?"

"Give me some time. I'm going back to Seven Wells."

Joe got up and paced the length of the room. "Seven Wells? Why not stay here or up at Fallen Pine?"

"It's too close, too many reminders. I need to spend the summer at the Wells where I can sort some things out. I know what Cory says I have to do but I'm ... Pa, I'm not strong enough, not right now."

His father sank onto the arm of the couch. "You do know I would give anything to change what happened? I wish I had dealt with Jerdix a long time ago."

Seth took his mug to the sink and rinsed it. "Leave the blame on Jerdix where it belongs. You taught us that.

Look, I promise I will send you blips regularly once I'm back at the Wells."

"It's a trap, Seth, hiding someplace where you can avoid doing the hard work that's needed."

Seth leaned on the counter, back hunched against advice he didn't want to hear. "I'll keep that in mind," he said with gritted teeth. "Right now, I need to go. I need to be gone before Lee gets back."

His father studied him for a moment. "So you do care what happens to her?"

Seth straightened sharply. "Sure I do. She saved me. But don't let her ruin her life trying to fix me."

"Is that what she's doing?" Joe asked.

"She's better off going back to her life, like I'm doing."

Joe stared at him in silence for a minute. When Seth refused to be drawn into saying more, Joe shrugged. "I can see you're determined to be a fool for now, so there's the door, son." He moved toward the fireplace, clearing Seth's path. When Seth reached the door, Joe followed him. "Just promise me you'll stay in touch and come back when you're ready."

"I promise," Seth said with the best of intentions.

"Anything we can do, anytime, Seth. Just call."

"I know; I will. And tell Lee, just tell her to get on with her life."

As soon as it was light enough in the morning, Seth was on the trail, just him and his horses, the way he had arrived in Under Rim short weeks before. His father had watched him from the porch, waving as he rode away.

Darkness settled in to obscure the pocket of meadow within a black hedge of trees. Seth fed another branch to his tiny fire and looked over at his horses in the brief flare of light. They dozed where they were tied. They were sleek and well-fed in spite of the days on the trail. He stopped early each day so they could graze before nightfall and let them fill themselves up again in the morning before starting out. Some days they took a long lunch too.

Once away from Under Rim, Seth couldn't find the drive to hurry. He had trouble going to sleep at night, woke unrested, and stumbled through camp chores. Some mornings he was tempted to linger all day in one place. Packing up to move a few miles down the trail seemed like too much trouble, but he always managed to do it anyway.

His route kept him in the forest, winding up and down over a series of ridges. In a few more days, he would turn south to a valley where he could cross the Glas River even in the spring runoff. Or maybe sit and watch the water run for a while.

The horses shifted restlessly, staring intently across the meadow. Seth looked too but saw nothing in the moonless night. As quickly as they had alerted, the two geldings lost interest. Seth stretched out on his bedroll and stared at the sky. Maybe if he counted stars, he could keep his mind from wandering, keep from seeing brown-gold eyes in the embers of the fire or a half-burned branch turn into a slender black rod.

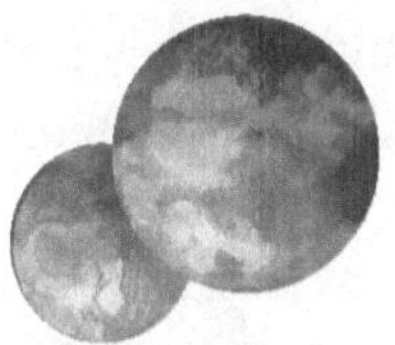

Day eighteen or was it nineteen? He had lost track and didn't really care. Seth sat on Jester at the top of the winding grade leading to Wide Ford, a village nestled at the edge of the valley where the trail crossed the Glas River. The river burst from a narrow canyon and, in spring flood, scattered into a dozen channels across the width of the valley. A cautious rider could get across without having to swim his horse.

At mid-morning Wide Ford's short street was nearly deserted. He had avoided every town and stead he had passed so far. He needed supplies. He should send his father a blip. He could take care of both at the store, one of a dozen buildings in town. He had to go right by it to reach the ford anyway. The nagging little voice in his head urged him to cut off the trail and go around — not to take the risk of meeting people.

"Shut up," he said. Jester cocked an ear at him. Seth rubbed his neck. "Not you, horse. Let's go."

The trail wound along the hillside into a ravine that spit him out at the edge of the village. He was stunned to see a group of riders crowding the street. Seth stopped. He couldn't see a way of reaching the store without going through them. His heart pounded as he turned his horse to ride around behind the buildings. Past the village, he swung onto the trail and urged his horses across the first of the multiple stream channels. He told himself he didn't really need to stop. He would be at Seven Wells in a few more days.

Seth planned the last couple of days of his ride carefully so he would reach the Seven Wells headquarters the middle of the morning when the riders would all be gone. Kieron Dougherty could almost always be found close to the office that time of day. With a little luck, Seth could check in, find out where Dougherty was assigning him, resupply, and be gone without seeing anyone else that he knew. Weeks of riding time to think, and he still hadn't figured out what he could tell them. Better not to have to explain anything.

His plan worked as far as it went. He rode into the headquarters on a less-used trail past the house and cabins, reaching the office without going near the barns and corrals. Dougherty came out of the office as Seth rode up.

"Reilly, is that you?" The stead manager stared at him.

Seth took stock of his unshaven face, shoulder-length hair, and generally unwashed state. He hadn't thought much about what he looked like. "Morning, Boss," he answered. "I'm here."

"So I see. I expected you about a week ago."

Seth rubbed self-consciously at his beard. "Tell me what you want me to do, and I'll be gone before anyone else sees me."

Dougherty leaned against a porch post. "Are you planning to tell me what's going on?"

"I'd rather not talk about it. Just give me horses to train someplace I can be alone."

"Tell you what — you go to the cottage by the house garden; you can get yourself cleaned up without having to use the shower house. I'll be there in half an hour to talk."

Unconsciously Seth backed his horse away. "But..."

Dougherty straightened up. "I don't want the whole story, but I need to understand a little if I'm going to help. I'll bring you some lunch when I come."

"Then let's do it now." Seth found himself reluctant to break off the exchange. He hadn't heard another voice in weeks.

"Later, when I can stand the smell of you." Dougherty grinned. "I'm amazed your horses let you near them. Now off with you."

Seth managed a weak laugh. "Okay, Boss. I'll see you in a little while." He rode off, weighed down by the thought of Dougherty's questions. He shouldn't have expected to get by with no explanation at all, but he had hoped.

Chapter 23

Seth

Unlike the riders' cabins with a shared shower house and cook house, the cottage was self-contained. Seth recognized that Dougherty had made a big concession by letting him use it. Normally it was reserved for guests.

Seth threw his packs on the porch and turned his horses into a nearby corral. Irritated one moment, anxious the next, depressed, angry — he took a deep breath, leaning on Jester's shoulder, drawing on the horse's calm. He missed the sound of a human voice; he hadn't realized how much until he had spoken with Dougherty.

Get cleaned up. Focus on that and worry about the rest later.

He'd never been in the cottage before. Its neat comfort halted him on the threshold. He dropped boots, hat, even his shirt, outside. He was surprised to find he had a clean change of clothes in his pack. He must have worn the same tattered shirt for days. If he laundered it, it would probably fall apart. He tip-toed through the spotless quarters to the shower, afraid to contaminate the place with his grime.

Hot water carried swirls of dirt down the drain, stung his newly shaven face, brought his attention to minor scratches and bruises he had collected during his travels. Little things like ducking out of the way of a branch didn't seem very important these days. "Careless," he muttered to himself. He would have to pay more attention around untrained colts.

Scrubbed and dressed, he almost dared sit on the furniture, but the walls closed in. He bundled up his filthy clothes and headed back to the porch. In the repair kit he carried, he had a leather thong he could use to tie back his hair until he could get it cut. How could he get a haircut? A heavy dose of buttonweed? He only had a few pods left. It didn't grow around Seven Wells.

He picked up the shirt he had shed, added it to the roll of dirty clothes, and opened one of the pack bags to shove them in. When he looked up, he realized someone was sitting on the swing at the end of the porch. He froze, trying to control his rising panic.

"Hi, Seth." Brown-gold eyes under close-cropped dark hair, a slender, firm figure sitting stiffly. "I hardly recognized you when you rode in."

He must be imagining things. Lee's voice echoed oddly in his brain. "What are you doing here?"

"Working," she replied. "I got my shoulder fixed. See, no more sling."

"No, you were supposed to leave, go back to the Rangers."

"I don't recall ever saying that."

"Are you real?" He'd seen her face in so many campfires over the weeks.

"You look a wreck, love, but you're not hallucinating."

He sank onto the top step. She had come after him. He didn't have to be alone. He'd been so lonely. "Pa's right; I'm a stubborn fool."

"Makes two of us; I told you we're a good team." She leaned forward anxiously. "We are partners now, aren't we?"

He closed his eyes, surprised by the intensity of his relief. "Yes," he answered. "We're partners."

She eased out of the swing and came over to sit just out of his reach on the step. "Kieron'll be here shortly. While you two talk, I'll go get my things."

"Wait; stay."

"Okay."

He looked her in the eye; she smiled crookedly. They sat very still for a moment. "How much does Dougherty know?" Seth dreaded the answer. If she had told Dougherty everything, he wasn't sure he could face his boss.

"He knows we're suffering from a traumatic event but no details. He'll do everything he can to accommodate us. If you're willing to work with me, everything's arranged."

"How long have you been here?"

"A couple of weeks. Here he comes. I'll be back in a little while. You will be here?"

"Right here." He watched as she walked away, exchanging a few words with Dougherty as they passed on the path. Dougherty laid a hand on her shoulder, the ever-present gesture, before they separated. Seth knew to the moment the last time anyone had touched him; the memory made his skin crawl.

Dougherty casually lifted a chair from a patio area along the path, set it below the steps, and settled onto it with his arms crossed on the top of the back. "Glad to have you back, Seth."

"Thanks," Seth replied. "I'll do my best not to let you down."

Dougherty shifted, wobbling the chair, and sat straighter. "I've talked with both Lee and your father, enough to get a hint of what you're going through."

"I can still train a horse," Seth assured. "I'm not much good around people right now."

Dougherty smiled. "You aren't the first to deal with a trauma-induced stress reaction, not even the first on this crew. I still have a firm rule against putting anyone out in a camp alone."

"I know, Boss. Lee will go with me. If that's all right."

"Right and tight. I hoped you would say that. How's Trego Flat sound? There are a couple dozen colts up there now. Once you finish with them, I'll get you some older horses that need tune-ups. Should be able to keep you busy all summer."

"I ... that sounds good."

"And look after the girl. She's tough, but she's still new to Carico. She'll need some help learning to ride herd on the tarbh and tending camp. Up to you to make sure she's okay."

Seth looked away and caught sight of Lee in front of one of the riders' cabins, talking to his old friend Kiri. "We'll be fine," he said distractedly. Lee and Kiri?

"One more thing."

"What?" Seth asked, anticipating some requirement he would have a hard time living with.

"Remember the roan colt you helped doctor when you first came here?"

Seth nodded. "A yearling? No, two-year-old, the one that was attacked by a wolf-lizard?"

"That's the one. He's running up in the Trego country with a couple others that we haven't been able to catch."

"It took a lot of work to clean up the infection in those bites, and he wasn't very grateful. I remember he didn't want much to do with people after all that."

"See if you can bring him in and get him started. He's four now and doing me no good running wild."

"Sure, Boss."

Dougherty stood up. "Then get out of here. I'll make excuses to the crew, just enough to keep them from showing up on your doorstep to see how you're doing."

"Thanks."

"You are welcome." Dougherty set the chair back where he had gotten it.

Seth cleared his throat and shifted uneasily. "Uh, you said something about lunch?"

Dougherty laughed. "Lee's bringing it. And don't forget to send a blip to your father before you leave here."

"Yes, sir."

"Good." The man nodded with a grin, then walked away without another look.

Seth took a deep breath and let it out slowly. A flutter of fear in his gut calmed. Dougherty had taken him back with no impossible explanations and still trusted him to do his job without someone watching over him. It was going to be all right.

Trego Flat was the better part of a day's ride up in the higher country, out of the worst of the summer heat. He began to think about what they would need to take, but Lee had said everything was arranged. Did that mean the cabin had been stocked, and they could leave the headquarters right away?

His stomach rumbled again. Lee still stood talking to Kiri, the last person Seth wanted to see. She was too aware; she would see too much and have too many questions. He stood up, fumbled with his packs, started inside, and changed his mind.

"Stop," he told himself, annoyed that he was so indecisive. Catch his horses; he could do that while he waited. What had Lee told Kiri? What had Kiri said about him? Maybe he wasn't hungry after all. The sooner he was away from here, the better.

The two women parted. Kiri strode toward the barns while Lee headed his way. She carried a box, and Seth's stomach grumbled. Okay, lunch first.

Lee stopped a few steps away. "Everything worked out with Kieron?" she asked.

He nodded. "We can leave now."

"I brought food." She held up the box. She was waiting for him to give her room. He stepped out of the way. She sat on the top step and put the lunch down. "Help yourself. You look starved."

One smell was all it took to take his mind off everything else. He sat on the other end of the step from her and grabbed a hefty sandwich.

She let him eat until he took the edge off his hunger. With a determinedly light tone, she said, "I sent a blip to Joe for you, and Kiri went to get my horse. Do you need anything from the store?"

"I'm good," he mumbled around a mouthful. He did need a change of clothes and some other items but not enough to risk running into old friends.

"Finish eating. I'll get my pack and horse."

"What do we need to take?"

"Just personal gear. Everything's set at Trego. I knew you wouldn't want to stay here long."

She left him alone again. He finished a second sandwich and set aside the fruit and cookies to eat while they rode. By the time she came back, he was settling the pack saddle on Buster's back.

"Where did you get that horse?" he laughed, staring in surprise at a gelding he would have sworn was not a Seven Wells horse. The animal was a lightly built, athletic bay with jagged white splotches on each side and a white mask from nostrils to above its eyes. He would remember a horse like that.

She shrugged and dropped her pack next to his. "Kieron got him in some trade. Just look past the flash. He's a great ride."

"Easy to find in the dark."

"Who has to look? He's in my hip pocket."

She was right about that. The horse stood two steps from her, its nose like a compass needle, following her every move as she handed Seth the pack bags and her compact bedroll. Something caught Seth's attention; he recognized the saddle on her horse.

"Pa gave you that?" he said in surprise.

"What? The saddle? He did. He said it had been hanging in the tack room for years. Gwyn didn't like it for some reason?"

He remembered. It had been too big for Gwyn when their father had put her up on it. She'd been about six and had never ridden it again. It had gone back in the tack room, carefully covered and unused.

"It was my mother's," he said. Why had his father given it to Lee?

She stopped what she was doing. "He didn't tell me that. I suppose I am family in a way."

"I guess." He puzzled over it while he secured the gear on Buster with the efficiency of long practice. He wanted to be gone before any riders came in for the midday meal.

"Ready?" he asked Lee as he swung up on Jester. "We'll go past the main house." That would keep them away from the barns and bunkhouse, away from people.

She laid a hand on his horse's face. "You're not going to see Kieron again before we go?"

"No need."

"And Kiri?"

"What about her?" he snapped, taking himself by surprise.

"She's worried about you, and she's been a great help to me. Let's just ride out past the barns and say good-bye to her."

Reasonable but ... Seth shook his head. "You can go and catch up to me. You do know how to get to Trego?"

Lee mounted her horse. "Never mind. Let's just go." She went past him to take the lead on the trail away from the barns.

He followed, wondering again what the two women had shared about him. Kiri had been a good friend, always ready to listen, fun to party with but a steadying influence. She knew — had known — him as well as anyone. He tried to focus on the tail of the horse in front of him and not think.

They went back the way he had come for a couple of miles before turning off the main trail toward a range of hills. The normally dry brush took advantage of the spring rains and sported waxy yellow leaves that would drop off in the heat of summer. Bright yellow-green foliage and wildly colored flowers painted the gravelly blue-green ground. Tall trees traced the lines of distant streams coming off the hills to vanish into the lower desert.

They followed a chattering creek to the foot of the hills where it emerged from a narrow, overgrown canyon. The trail crossed the water and entered the rift to hug the base of a rock wall. Seth could see where someone had recently cut back branches to make the way passable. Lee's horse nimbly picked its way through the rocks and logs that cluttered the path, scrambling through the creek again and again as the trail crisscrossed the water. The girl called out warnings occasionally when her passage sent a limber branch springing back at him. Other than that, they rode without speaking.

Seth tried not to watch Lee as she rode, her body moving easily with the horse, stirring up responses that threatened to topple him into darkness. The first time an opportunity presented itself, he took the lead so he couldn't see her. He hadn't done well alone, but he began to doubt he could share a camp with her and stay sane.

They climbed steadily until the enclosing walls fell away, and they came out into a basin encircled by high, steep hills. The trail wound up and down over the broken ground. The vegetation changed, reflecting the increased rainfall the higher country received. Sparse grass replaced the spring flush of wildflowers. Grayish trees grew persistently on the north slopes and gave way to grass on the south. Palm-pines and other trees appeared. The sun had set when they finally crossed a grassy meadow and reached a pocket of ancient vine trees sheltering the cabin at Trego Flat.

Chapter 24

Seth

Seth sat on his horse and stared at the rock house that would be their home for the summer. So small — barely room inside for two people. It had a long arbor running along the south side, thickly roofed with living branches from the vine trees. A rock outcrop loomed at the west end of the little cabin, blocking the afternoon sun. A spring bubbled from under the rocks to supply the cabin before joining the larger stream that fed the cluster of corrals beyond it. Plenty of space, he told himself. Besides, Lee understood. She wouldn't crowd him.

Lee swung easily off her horse and tied it to the hitch rail. "Welcome home," she said with a grin. She tugged the pack horse's lead away from him and began to unload. He got off and went to help from the other side of the horse. They only needed a minute to pull the bedrolls and pack bags off and set them under the arbor.

"I'll unsaddle," he said, catching up her horse's reins along with his two.

"Thanks."

He took his time with the animals, considering what he had gotten himself into. He'd jumped at the chance to partner with the one person who needed no explanations. Now he just had to toughen up and get past the other part of their history. He'd find a place outside, set up his camp, tread a fine line between having the companionship he craved and avoiding feelings he couldn't handle.

Lee had dinner heating when he came in. Bunks with storage lockers occupied two walls; the kitchen lined the back wall; a door led to the shower room. She'd already curtained off one of the bunks with a couple of the wraps she sometimes wore as dresses. He carried his personal gear to the other one and opened the locker to put things away. He found some clothes already folded on the shelves. When he looked around, she was watching him with a satisfied expression.

"I picked up a few things for you," she said with a smile. "You never got a chance to get much at Under Rim, so I knew you'd be in tatters by now."

He wanted to be angry that she thought he couldn't take care of himself. He wanted to hug her for bailing him out. "I ... thanks," he said, looking to see just what she'd gotten him. A couple shirts and pairs of pants, several pairs of socks, underwear — he blushed at the thought of her buying him underwear — a set of loose camp clothes to relax in. On the bottom shelf he found a bag he had left at Seven Wells when he had gone to Under Rim. "My braiding!" He opened it and pulled out a bundle of horsehair.

"Kiri said you'd want that. There's a bag of buttonweed for you too. Teri sent that along. Now, better come eat while it's hot," she said. "Gloomy in here. I think this is the first cabin I've seen on Carico without windows everywhere."

"Keeps it cool in the summer heat. We'll move the kitchen out to the arbor and live outdoors most of the time."

"Work early and late with a long break in the midday heat?"

"You have it all figured out." He helped himself to the stew she set on the table. "Nice and quiet here. It'll be fine."

Later he lay in the dark, planning out the morning in his head. He'd have to take Lee out and show her where to ride to locate tarbh and move them around according to the grazing plan. Then he could come back and get started with the colts. Across the room, she slept, her slow, regular breathing stroking his nerves, keeping him on the edge of things he didn't want to feel. He got up, bundled up his bedroll, and left the cabin for the shelter of the arbor where the light breeze sang an arrhythmic song in the leaves.

Seth got up in the morning with more enthusiasm than he had felt in a very long time. He ambled down the trail, crossed the single log that bridged the stream, and climbed onto the corral fence. From that perch he could see the horses in the pasture, feeding in the pre-dawn light. He jumped down and walked around a point of rock to the round pen and holding corrals. A clump of scrubby copper trees topped the rocks, promising evening shade. He'd spent a couple months the previous summer at Trego and liked the setup. He would have plenty of time morning and evening, when it was cooler, for the colts.

He wandered back toward the cabin, taking time to clamber along the stream bank to the cool, deep pool sheltered by vine trees that lay around a curve below the camp. That was going to feel fine during the midday heat. He danced across the steppingstones at the bottom edge of the pool and found his way through the trees to the main trail and back to the cabin.

Lee watched him from the doorway of the cabin, jacket on against the slight chill of the morning. "Ready for breakfast?" she asked when he reached the arbor.

"Sure. Then we can saddle up. Where are you riding today?" He was eager to get her started so he could come back and bring in the first group of colts.

"Aren't you ambitious," she said. "It's a rest day. Besides, you just got here."

"I'm good. I took it easy."

"It didn't show yesterday. I wasn't sure you'd be able to ride up here from headquarters."

"I'm fine," he insisted. "But if you don't need to ride, I'll just get to work."

She studied him until he shifted uncomfortably. "No," she said finally. "Let's ride up the Ridgeline Trail to the crest. You can help me figure out how to cover the west basin most effectively. I need to ride there tomorrow."

"Okay," he replied. That would work. He could start with the colts first thing in the morning if he got her set today.

"I'll get breakfast going out here." She stepped out of the door, clearing his way inside. "Oh, and there's a set of clippers in the shower room if you want to tackle your hair. Might not be pretty, but it'll be cooler if you shorten it."

The girl thought of everything. He freed his shoulder-length hair from the thong that held it back and headed inside with a grin. He set the clippers to the longest setting and buzzed off inches, leaving it much shorter than he usually wore it. It was the best he could manage by himself; it felt light, like he had shed a weight with the hair.

They ate quickly, caught two of the Wells horses Lee had brought to ride her circles, and headed out. The Mainline Trail ran past Trego Flat and followed the stream up the canyon. Not far above the cabin, the Ridgeline Trail turned off and wound back and forth up onto the ridge where it followed the crest between two drainages. The basin to the west was a jumble of rock miles wide, cut by a web of stream channels.

From an overlook, Lee stared at the confusing labyrinth. "Why don't you people use gips?" she moaned in frustration. "I'll get lost down there in an hour."

He laughed. "No, you won't. You can read a map, can't you?"

"Of course."

"If you get turned around, you can always follow the streams down to get out. You'll end up about ten miles below Trego where you hit the Mainline, but you won't be lost."

"Thank you so much!"

"Relax. Get your map out and let me show you how to work this country."

They spent a while talking about how the tarbh used the basin and how she could break it down into day-length rides. He made sure she understood the grazing pattern. Someone, Kiri or Dougherty, had explained it to her, but she would make more sense out of it looking at the ground. Her job was two-fold, keeping the animals in the designated grazing areas and watching for any that were sick or injured. She would deal with the latter herself if she could, or he would come back with her later.

As she asked questions, Seth began to realize how much of a rider's job he took for granted. Raised with it, he gave little thought to how much knowledge it took.

He let her puzzle out a lot of answers for herself; she'd have to do that when he wasn't with her.

He took her on to other overlooks until she seemed comfortable that she wouldn't disappear forever into the wilds. He showed her several places where trails dropped off east back to the Mainline. As the day began to heat up, he led the way down one of those into the shady relief of a canyon bottom. By lunchtime, they were back at Trego. He left her unsaddling her horse and rode out to bring in his first batch of colts.

Seth stood in the center of the pen, watching the bay gelding by the gate looking at its companions in a nearby corral. Unexpectedly, his pulse pounded in his throat. He clenched his fists and rubbed the sweat from his palms. It was just a horse.

He turned away, walked to the far side of the pen and leaned on the fence with his back to the animal. He'd worked with the colts at Fallen Pine but that had been something to keep himself occupied. This was business. Dougherty counted on him to do a good job. He had to be calm and focused.

He tried to visualize what he needed to do. The colt was not wild. It had been handled and halter-trained as a baby. The basic groundwork had been reinforced and expanded as a yearling. Now Seth's job was to refresh the past work and add some new lessons but, as a two-year-old, that ended with a few easy rides to introduce the idea. At the Wells, horses were not expected to join the work force until they were four.

Right now, he did not even need to make contact with the animal. Today was a dance to reestablish that when the man pushed with subtle body language the horse gave way. That was enough for the first lesson. He took a deep breath, let it out slowly, and went back to the center of the pen. He raised his arm and encouraged the colt to move. He'd been right to come back here to the horses.

Chapter 25

Lee

When Seth left to start working with the colts for the first time, Lee followed, turning aside to climb onto the rock outcrop overlooking the round pen. She took a seat against one of the copper trees. The bark was smooth under her hand, bright as its namesake in contrast to the bluish-green of the sandpaper rock. Sitting there, she could see down into the corral without being noticed.

She practiced a breathing exercise to steady herself. Since Seth had found her on the porch at Seven Wells — was it just a day ago? — she hadn't had much time to think. He'd looked so ragged and unkempt and had been unbelievably relieved to see her. It was a little frightening. She'd half-convinced herself he would just send her away or leave himself. His instant acceptance had startled her.

When he brought the first colt into the pen, she observed his struggle to gather his confidence with a sinking feeling. If he couldn't connect with the horses ... well, maybe that would be best. It might force him into submitting to outside help sooner. But, when he pulled himself together and showed much of his old skill and assurance, she was relieved. While he concentrated on the horse, she slipped away, back to the cabin.

Time to get focused herself. She felt like she had done nothing but wait for weeks — for her shoulder to heal; for some word about Jerdix who she was told was no longer her concern; for Seth to reach a point where he would accept her presence if not actual help. Two out of three. With Jerdix apparently off world — if she could just believe that — she had things here and now to deal with.

She set up the outdoor kitchen, covering things on the open shelves with cloths to keep the dust off. She found a sheltered place under the drooping branches of a vine tree a little ways away from the cabin and laid out her bedroll. The broad, overlapping leaves would keep off all but the heaviest rain, if this desert got such a thing. Finally, she got out the map showing the different grazing areas. Once she understood the job, she would be free to decide where she most needed to ride each day. Until then, she trusted the suggestions Dougherty and Kiri had made about the best way to cover the country.

She and Kiri had already spent a few days at Trego. The older woman had shown her what she was expected to do, and they had ridden much of the country east of the Ridgeline Trail. Now she was on her own to figure out the west side. The Ridgeline marked a change in geology and in the terrain. She and Kiri had ridden in steep-walled canyons with few places a horse or a tarbh could climb out onto the flat ridge tops. To the west the rock was softer, and the canyon walls sloped from narrow crests. She had much less chance of getting trapped by a rim but had many more little draws and gulches to explore.

Something whistled at her from the rocks next to the arbor. A little creature about the size and shape of a teapot sat on its haunches, dangling powerful front paws on its rotund belly. A slender, snakelike tail wrapped around the boulder it perched on. It was covered with blue and green scales with softly fringed edges. It looked at her with four large, dark eyes, tipping its rounded head to one side and rippling a bright blue frill across the back of its neck. Those eyes, two toward the front and two toward the sides, characterized Carico's fauna. The animal whistled again and yawned, displaying a narrow muzzle and very long tongue. A moment later the tongue snapped out to draw an insect into the waiting mouth.

"Hello," Lee said softly. The frill stood up, then slowly folded again. The creature chirped. "You are a little beggar, aren't you? Glad to have a crew back here?"

The animal hopped down and waddled under the bench where it settled into the shade and imitated a rock. She laughed. "I guess I have someone to talk to. Well, what do you think? Should I see if Seth will ride with me tomorrow or just accept the inevitable?" She knew the answer and traced out what she hoped would be a fairly easy ride for her first day.

Late in the afternoon, she went to the swimming hole to cool off. When the shadows began to lengthen, she returned to start dinner, getting things prepared so she could finish cooking when Seth came in. She resisted an urge to go back and watch him. While she waited, she cleared the rocks from an area of ground in the shade and began to run through the martial arts forms she had practiced since she was sixteen; she had let them go as 'Anni' and not done them routinely since. Time to reestablish the drills. She suspected she would need the meditative aspect in the days to come.

Kiri had asked her why she had followed Seth, putting her career on hold and risking an unfamiliar job. She'd shrugged then and not answered. Dougherty hadn't asked, letting her actions speak for her. In her heart, the answer was simple. When she had tied the cords around their wrists that morning before he'd left for Migration, she had meant it as a commitment even though she couldn't tell him so at the time, not until he could know who she really was. Nothing that had happened had changed the way she felt. She would stand by him, be his friend, his crutch, do whatever was necessary to help him even if it meant getting lost in the wild brakes of this technophobic frontier.

A rock resolved into her little camp pet and whistled. She looked around and saw Seth crossing the log bridge.

She completed the last couple of moves in the form and pulled on a loose, long-sleeved shirt over her tank top. Better not cook until she knew if he wanted to shower first. The little animal disappeared into a rock pile, leaving her alone. Lee went inside and brought out a couple of cold brews. Seth took one from her with a grin.

"Food?" he asked.

"Did you want to get cleaned up first?"

"Do I have time?"

"How long do you need?"

He went in and showered while she finished getting dinner ready. He ate hungrily, dropped his dishes in the sink, and collected his bedroll. He started around the rock outcrop to the west, then turned around. She suspected he saw her tracks. He headed toward the grove of trees along the stream. She had the handful of dishes washed and put away when he reappeared. He got out his braiding bag and turned his attention to some project. She was going to need some activity to occupy herself if she didn't want to spend her evenings doing chores.

Lee heard Seth clattering around the kitchen before it was light enough to be called day. She crawled out of her comfortable bed and joined him under the arbor. He grinned. "Tea water's started. I'll bring the horses in. Who do you want to ride today? Rocky?"

She tried to get her brain to wake up. They'd ridden Creamy and Bo the day before. "Sure, Rocky will do." She liked the chunky sorrel the least of the four horses in her string. He was short and stout, built to rope off of, but Kiri said he'd shown no aptitude for it. So he was a circle horse with a choppy walk and a tendency to spook at shadows. Since she had to use him some time, she might as well keep him for shorter days.

Seth strode off toward the corrals. Lee went into the cabin to trade camp clothes for her work clothes. Then she went about getting breakfast and putting together a lunch to take with her. She didn't expect to be back until sometime in the afternoon. While she waited for Seth to return, she did her best to clean the kitchen of the inevitable dust.

Seth wasted no time downing a sausage and biscuit sandwich. "Just right!" he said. "I don't usually eat much now. I'll take a break mid-morning and have something then. Show me where you're going today."

She brought out the map and explained the loop she had in mind. He pointed out a couple places where she needed to look for tarbh and a likely spot for lunch. "You'll have a good day," he said. "I'll probably be working colts when you get in, so I'll see you at dinner." He scooped up a crisp roundfruit and hurried off. His enthusiasm was so different than his attitude two days before that it made her uneasy. One more reason to keep her ride short.

Even Rocky's slow walk didn't spoil her enjoyment once she was on the trail. The morning was still cool with shadows gradually growing shorter. The movement of the horse beneath her, the light breeze running up the slope as the sun heated the ridgetops, and the quiet soothed her. As she got higher on the Ridgeline Trail, she felt the promise of heat later in the day, presaging what summer would bring when it truly arrived.

She found the head of the draw she planned to follow down into the basin and turned the gelding onto the faint trail. The tarbh should be to the east. Today her job was to be sure none had drifted over where they didn't belong. The lack of use on the trail suggested she wouldn't find any.

She dismounted and led the gelding down the first steep drop until she reached the bottom where water trickled out of a bank and between the stones to form a tiny creek. She reset the saddle that had slipped forward on the round-backed horse and remounted to wind through the brush along the stream. She saw no sign of tarbh although something else left tri-split prints in the mud. Rocky stepped forward stiffly and danced sideways at imagined wolf-lizards in the shadows. Lee was grateful when the path climbed out of the brushy bottom to meander across an open bench.

A second canyon met the one she rode down. According to the map, a couple of miles up it she would find a draw that she could follow back to the Ridgeline Trail. She turned onto the barely visible trail and urged Rocky into another jungle of brush.

Seth had promised her a good spot to stop for lunch where Rocky could graze. Lee found the place not too far from the junction of the two canyons. It was early yet, but she stopped anyway. A draw came in from one side, creating a small flat. She pulled the saddle off her horse's sweaty back and hobbled his forefeet so he could move around the meadow. She found a tiny spring seeping from the rocks. Someone had built a basin below it, big enough to serve as a bathtub. A copper tree clung to the bank, shading a grassy niche by the basin. Lee got her lunch and stretched out on the inviting little lawn.

She stayed long enough to eat and to wash her feet in the cold water but was restless. She would need to bring something to occupy her when she began waiting out hot afternoons in places like this. This job gave her far too much time to think. She dredged up mental exercises she'd learned in counseling while she had waited out the treatment on her shoulder in Portside. Vinz had seen to it that she went through the required deconditioning after an undercover assignment. Thanks to that, she could separate herself a little from her actions as Anni. Now she had to concentrate on not getting herself lost or hurt in this wilderness. At least she was a long way from any place Jerdix might be.

She caught Rocky and gave him the core from her fruit as a treat. A little bribery went a long way sometimes when your partner was a horse. She rubbed the sweat off his back and put her saddle on, a saddle that Seth said had belonged to his mother, dead twenty-some years now. Joe hadn't mentioned that when he had insisted she take it. Good saddle, well-cared for; it gave her an eerie feeling.

She rubbed Rocky's face. "Come on, silly. I'll lead the way for a while. Will that make you braver?" Truth was she had ridden more in the last couple of weeks than she ever had in her life, and, although she would never admit it to Seth, parts of her hurt. Walking now and then helped. She took a quick look at the map to find landmarks for the draw that would lead her back to the Ridgeline Trail and started walking along the path through the brush. Rocky tagged along behind her, trusting her to spot the big bads.

Walking made it harder for her thoughts to run rampant. She had to pay attention to where she was stepping. Her world on foot was much narrower than when she was riding. The brush continued to close in around her. Tarbh didn't need a path cleared high enough for someone on horseback, and apparently no rider had been through here for a while. She continued to walk, pushing up overhanging branches so they wouldn't catch on the saddle.

"Look, Rocky." She stopped and rubbed the sorrel's neck. "Open ground." The trail left the bottom and climbed up the left side of the canyon. Lee scrambled up the rock steps, hurrying to stay ahead of the horse. When she reached a little bench of level ground, she checked her cinch and mounted, glad to be able to ride again and more glad to be able to see the surrounding terrain so she could figure out where she was.

She looked back over the thickets she had come through with a nagging feeling she should be seeing something. She got out the map, studied it, and looked around again. She shouldn't be on the left side of the canyon. The draw she wanted to go up was to the right. She had missed it somewhere in the tangle back around a bend or two. She could see no sign of a gap going the direction she wanted to go.

She muttered a few choice words. Lost and on her first day out on her own. She would never live it down. She took a deep breath and then another. Not lost. She was right there. She put her finger on the map. It was her trail that was lost. She could fight her way back through the bottom and hope she spotted the right path. On the other hand, the Ridgeline Trail crossed the heads of most of these canyons. It was going to take some time, but she could keep going up the trail she was on. The map showed it staying up on the hillside where she could see where she was going, crossing to the other side higher up, and tying in, just as she thought it would. It didn't look too much longer than her original route.

"Sorry, Rocky. So much for your easy day." If she was lucky, Seth would be with his colts and not even notice if she was a little late getting back.

Two hours later, she sat on a boulder, head tipped a little to catch as much of the slight breeze as she could. She wiped the sweat from her face and gazed back down the canyon that snaked interminably off to the southwest. Her feet hurt. She'd walked more than ridden. Rocky had proven impressively sure-footed but, on a path that often seemed narrower than he was, Lee found herself scared to be on his back looking down the long, steep, rocky hillside to the slender chartreuse strip of brush in the bottom. She was hot, tired, and sore. Now her decision to go up instead of back seemed doomed. A jumble of boulders too big for her to shift by hand blocked the trail, and she could see no way around.

She rubbed her face, wiping away more sweat or maybe tears of frustration. "Rocky, you need a better partner. It's going to be a long way home." The worst part was she could see the ridge line ahead, not more than half a mile away, and the trail looked easy if she could only get beyond this rock pile. What had she gotten herself into? She was no rider; she had no business wandering around this wilderness alone.

"But I'm not lost," she told herself with a wry laugh. "I know exactly where I am." As if that mattered when someone had to come looking for her.

She stood up and wrapped the reins around the rock she'd been sitting on. "Wait here a minute," she told the horse. She edged around him, grateful for his stocky bulk between her and a long slide to the bottom. Maybe she could find a way to get around the outcrop and its barricade, someplace a rough-walking but agile sorrel horse could get through. There — a trace barely a horse-hoof wide led up. The local wildlife was not stopped by the obstacle. She picked her way through the verdigris rock and pale-yellow brush until she stood on top of the outcrop, looking down on her horse. "You better be good, my friend, or we'll both roll out of here like rocks," she said and made her way down the slope to get him.

Once she got the horse started, he bounded up the slope past her. All she could do was get out of his way and catch up to him when he stopped. She led the horse across the top of the outcrop and turned down, both of them sliding and scattering rocks, coming to a stop on the narrow stability of the trail.

"Rocky, you are great!" She rubbed his face and let her heart settle into a normal rhythm. She'd done it. Clear sailing to the Ridgeline Trail. She reset the saddle and mounted. The horse, unrattled by their scramble, plodded steadily up the narrow track.

She let him stop when they reached the broader trail along the ridgetop and looked back the way she had come. It didn't look bad from that vantage point.

Rocky's head came up, and his ears pricked. Something caught her eye, high on the slope above where the trail was blocked. A horse and rider standing just far enough from the crest not to be skylined. Was Seth checking on her? But the shape was wrong, the rider too bulky, and wouldn't Seth have been on the camp side of the draw?

She swallowed the lump in her throat. Just a passing rider. It didn't mean someone was spying on her. Jerdix was on the run, probably off world, and his crew was scattered. But when Rocky wanted to trot homeward, she made no effort to slow him down.

Long shadows relieved the day's heat as she rode up to the tack shed at Trego and slid slowly to the ground, holding onto the saddle until she was certain her legs would hold her. Her seat bones hurt; the insides of her knees were raw; her shirt was stiff with dried sweat; but she felt good. She talked herself out of the fright when she had seen the strange rider. Now if she just had enough strength to unsaddle Rocky.

She lifted a halter from the wall and slipped it onto him before limping inside to get him a generous serving of grain. She dragged the saddle off his back while he ate, carrying it in and flipping the saddle blanket wet side up over it. Then she went out to brush away the sweat from his coppery hide. That done, she led him to the pasture and turned him loose. He went directly to a sandy spot, dropped down and rolled vigorously, waving feet in the air as he turned clear over a couple of times before he scrambled to his feet and shook off a cloud of dust. Lee slung her saddlebags over her shoulder and headed for the cabin. Someday maybe she'd be able to laugh off the mishaps of her day, someday when she knew what was normal and what was dumb mistake. She'd survived. Anyway, no point in worrying Seth.

Chapter 26

Seth

Routine — that was what Seth wanted. Bring in his colts and Lee's saddle horse; back to the cabin for a light breakfast; go to work while Lee left for the day; take a long break at midday with a good lunch; work with the colts until evening; check over the saddle horses; get back to the cabin in time for dinner; braid horsehair for a while; go to bed and start over in the morning. Safe, predictable.

The two-year-olds were teenagers, not ready for any real work but needing their respect for a human reinforced. They were full of energy and tested boundaries. They made him laugh. On rest days sometimes he sat in the pasture where he could watch them. Which ones were buddies. Who was bossy and who was timid, adventurous, curious, or lazy.

Seth couldn't see the tack shed from the round pen, but he could tell when Lee came back. The horses in the pasture always gave her away. He watched for her, then he got impatient if she was late. Once she was there, he was reluctant to actually see her. He looked forward to evenings when he could sit with his attention on his braiding but know she was nearby, cleaning up the camp or trying to teach the rock rat tricks. She impressed him with the way she slipped so easily into her new job. They rarely spoke unless she had a question about something she'd seen or where she was riding the next day. Evenings were peaceful, with the breeze flowing down the canyon to cool them, and the sunset tinting the blue-green rock with gold.

"I saw the roan today," Lee said as she finished putting the dinner dishes away and began straightening up under the arbor.

"Where?" Seth looked up from his horsehair braiding, his full attention on her for a change.

"High up in Cuneo Creek with two others."

Just the news he'd been waiting for. Cuneo Creek — he tried to picture the drainage. "Where's the map?" he asked. The roan had evaded other riders repeatedly. With just Lee, who had never run horses, how could he trap the colt? He studied the terrain on the map. "Exactly where did you see them?" He pushed the map toward Lee.

"Here," she said, tracing a basin near the head of the creek with her finger. "I came down this way. They watched me for a little while but, when I got close, they circled around behind this little knob."

The horses would go uphill to escape, if given a chance, just as they had when Lee saw them. If they stayed in that little basin and he could get in place without them seeing him, he might have a chance. Lots of 'ifs' but the best plan he had until they actually got on the ground.

"We'll go after them tomorrow, before they move," he said decisively. "Ride the big red gelding. He's your best for this kind of run. I'm going to rope that roan."

"You think you can get that close?" she asked.

"You and Bo are going to run him around that knob right into me."

They left Trego in the dark the next morning. For the first time in days, Seth felt like himself. Focused on the task at hand with no unexpected reactions popping up to unsettle him. He wanted to get there while the horses were grazing before the heat drove them off the hillsides.

It took a couple hours of steady riding to reach the little basin above Cuneo Creek. He stopped in the trees by the creek and dismounted, tying Jester. He led Lee on foot along the edge of the thicker vegetation to a spot where they could look up slope to where she had seen the horses the day before. The knob stood out, a rock outcropping topping a little hill near the upper edge of the basin.

He asked Lee where the horses had been when she'd seen them and what they had done when she'd gotten close, how they'd gone around the hill and vanished. As he studied the ground, he saw movement on the hillside right where he had hoped. The three horses grazed calmly in the morning sun. He pointed to them. It took Lee a minute to find them. If he dropped down Cuneo Creek before climbing over the ridge, he could slip around and come out on the other side of the knob without being seen.

"Stay low down on the slope but in plain sight," he told her, pointing out where he wanted her to be. "Let Bo graze. Get their attention on him."

"Won't they spook?"

"Not if all they see is a strange horse in the distance. Don't move toward them. Let them come to you if they want. Give me time to get in place; make it twenty minutes from when I leave. Then run Bo at them. Push them hard. I want them thinking about being chased. If I'm right, they'll run up the slope and cut around one side or the other of the knob, right into me."

"That's it? Just that simple?"

"If we're lucky."

They hurried back to their horses. Seth checked his cinch and got on. "Wait here a few minutes, then move out onto the slope, slow and easy. Ready?"

Lee nodded. The gold in her eyes sparked, and she looked alive, so alive. He pushed away feelings that threatened, turning his attention to the business at hand. He gave her a thumbs-up and rode off.

He got in position just as he'd hoped, but he couldn't see what was happening. Waiting was the worst part. All he could do was to sit and listen. Sound would tell him which side they were coming from, if they came at all. He got out his rope and checked the coils to be sure it would not tangle. He rubbed Jester's neck and watched his ears. The horse would know before he did. What was taking so long? Where were they?

Jester tensed, his ears flicking, trying to locate a sound. Seth heard it, Lee whooping and yelling, then the thud and rattle of bare hooves in the rocks. Which side of the knob? He wanted the roan; neither of the others mattered. Jester looked to the left, and Seth trusted him. He turned the horse away from the on-coming animals, poised to jump out and go after them as they passed. The pounding of his heart felt good for a change. Ready; set.

The first horse charged into sight and flared away when it saw him. The roan! He put his heels to Jester who leaped forward, almost colliding with the other horse. Seth swung his rope and sailed it out where it settled neatly over the horse's head. Seth jerked the loop snug, but let Jester run with the roan, slowing him gradually. As the rope tightened, the roan slowed too. Seth brought them to a stop. The roan backed away and faced him, head up and tense.

He'd done it. It had worked perfectly. Seth wanted to shout to the heavens. He sat still, letting the adrenaline rush fade. The other two horses, both bays, stopped a little way off, watching uneasily. No sign of Lee — where was she? There — she rode into sight.

"You got him," she said.

"Right and tight," he replied with a laugh. "Question is what to do with him now." The colt had been halter-trained as a baby, so Seth hoped he could lead him. If he left the loop loose though, the colt might slip out of it. Time to see how wild the horse had become.

Seth secured the rope to his saddle and got off, trusting Jester to keep it tight. He untied the halter he had brought and eased his way up the rope toward the colt. The animal pulled back, trapped and defensive. Not a good start. From horseback then.

Seth remounted and began shortening the rope between Jester and the roan. With only a few feet left, he turned Jester, moving him forward past the colt, breaking the stare-down and encouraging the colt to walk along with him. Once in motion, he continued to reel in the colt until he was snubbed up close to Seth's knee. He eased the halter over the colt's neck, caught it around his nose and fastened it. The colt started to back away but gave in to the pull around his neck rather than fighting it. Seth gave him some slack, letting him move away a couple of feet, then switched the tension to the rope tied to the halter. Leaving well enough alone, he left the original rope in place.

"Now we go home," he told Lee. "I'm hoping he'll lead, but follow behind him and let Bo push him if he needs it."

"What about them?" Lee nodded to the other two horses.

"If they follow, great. If not, we'll worry about them later. He's the ringleader."

It was a day for miracles. After a couple of tug-of-wars, the roan settled in behind Jester and trotted along. As they got deeper into the yellow brush along the creek, Seth heard a clatter of hooves behind him. When he looked back, he saw the two bays crowding in behind the roan. Lee dropped back to give them room. Seth chuckled. Perfect.

He slowed to a walk once the colts calmed down. In the narrow confines of Cuneo Creek, he didn't worry about them trying to escape. Once they got to the Mainline Trail, he urged Jester into a trot. The roan sat back against the halter, then jumped forward and trotted with his nose just off of Jester's tail. The two bays stayed with him and Lee brought up the rear, holding in the long-strided red gelding. She'd been right where she needed to be all day.

A quarter mile or so out from Trego, Seth called back to Lee, "Push them. Now we run!" He wanted momentum to carry them on when the colts saw the camp. Lee let the red horse out, driving the loose horses ahead of her. As the colts sped up, Seth kept ahead of them until they were all loping down the trail. He led them past the tack shed and into the open gate of the round pen. "Gate!" he hollered at Lee. She slid to a stop in the opening and jumped down, letting Bo go as she swung the gate closed.

"We did it!" she shouted.

He let the horses circle the pen a couple of times before slowing them down. He brought the roan into the center and snubbed him close to Jester. The colt tried to avoid his hand. Seth patiently rubbed on his neck until he stood still. With a quick move, Seth slipped the loop over the roan's head. Then he released the halter and let it slide off. He held Jester in place until the roan turned away and sought refuge with his buddies. Seth studied the three for a moment, thinking about where to start. By evening he'd have a plan in mind. He walked Jester to the gate. Lee swung it open, just wide enough for him to get through, and closed it behind him.

He took a deep breath and let it out slowly. He felt good; everything was right and tight. He turned Jester back so he could watch the colts settle in. It didn't take them long to begin looking for something to eat. Seth dismounted and loosened the cinch, lifting the back of the saddle for a moment to let the breeze cool Jester's back. Lee stood by the fence, watching the roan. He walked over.

"He is gorgeous," she said without looking away from the horses. "Four years old? He's not going to be easy to train, is he?"

"Once he gets some trust back, he'll be fine." Seth stood next to her and, without thinking, put his arm around her, pulling her against him. Such a good day!

Abruptly he was back in the stall with Jerdix and the rod and his body's overwhelming reactions. He pushed away, stumbled, threw up his arms to protect himself, and backed into something where he cowered, waiting for the next touch.

Far in the distance he heard a startled voice calling his name. "Seth, you're safe. You are safe. It's all right."

The thing he was leaning against shifted. Putting out a hand, he felt sweaty horsehide. Jester, his horse. He was ... he was at Trego Flat. They had just brought in the roan colt.

"Seth." He identified Lee's voice. "Seth, buttonweed. Buttonweed will help." She was right. He fumbled in his shirt pocket for the dried pods.

"Okay," he muttered, to himself as much as her. "I'm okay." He kept his eyes closed. If he saw her, it might all come back again.

"Seth, go unsaddle Jester. I'll stay here. Go now." Her voice again, calm and rational.

He should take care of his horse. He opened his eyes, avoiding looking toward her. He took the reins and led Jester around the corner of rock to the tack shed. He leaned against the horse's shoulder, breathing in the hot, horsey smell and letting the animal re-anchor him. Methodically he unsaddled. He thoroughly brushed the sweaty horse before leading him to the pasture gate. He couldn't go to the cabin, couldn't face Lee. He walked down the stream to the swimming hole, stripped out of his clothes and immersed himself in the cold water.

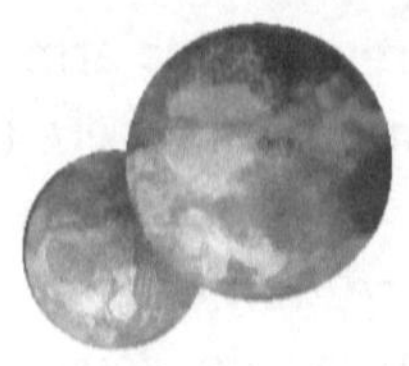

Lee went after Seth, stopping behind the rocks where she could keep him in sight without intruding. He'd been so relaxed and confident. His change, his flashback, shocked her and scared her. She didn't know what he would do next. Torn between worry and guilt at spying on him, she followed him when he didn't go on to the cabin. She stayed long enough to reassure herself that he was just trying to pull himself together. She went back to look after her own horse. All the thrill and euphoria had evaporated. Her spirit wilted. He needed help, and she couldn't give it to him. She cursed Jerdix, wishing he was still on Carico where she could confront him. Unsettled by the strength of her anger, she focused on the motions of unsaddling and grooming her horse.

She made a salad for lunch, left Seth's share in the cooler, and took hers to the shady niche where she had her bed. In the privacy of that retreat she picked at the food, passing tidbits to the rock rat who came out of hiding to join her. He parked his rotund form just out of her reach and extended his agile tail to take what she held out for him. His middle eyes focused on her but the side eyes kept watch, giving him a comical look.

"What am I going to do, Teapot?" she asked the creature. "I can't help him. Maybe I shouldn't even be here."

The little animal whistled and reached out with his tail. She gave him another treat. "I don't know why you like this stuff. You eat mostly insects." He transferred the chopped root from his tail to his nimble paws and nibbled at it. "Silly creature." She couldn't help laughing a little. He was so unconcerned, but she knew he'd be gone in an instant if she tried to pet him.

She thought about calling Dougherty, maybe asking him to send Kiri up on some made-up errand. She wanted someone to talk to, a human person who could carry on a conversation. She should leave, remove whatever trigger she represented, but she couldn't abandon Seth.

Teapot dropped the root and scampered into the rocks. Lee heard the cooler door close. Seth — should she leave him alone or go out? She got to her feet and went back to the cabin.

"We got him," she said, hoping to regain a little of the day's earlier success. "What now?"

Seth avoided looking at her. "I'll go move the two bays to the pasture with the other colts. Stay away from the roan. Nobody but me goes near him for now."

"All right," she said, puzzled.

"I need him to depend on me." He looked up, directly in her eyes. "He needs someone to rely on."

She didn't think he was talking about the horse. "He's all yours. I'll be here if you need any help with anything."

"I know."

Lee went along when he went back to the pens as soon as the evening shadows began to stretch. He saddled Jester and led him into the corral with the three colts. She found a seat on a boulder where she could watch while Seth used his saddle horse to separate the roan from the bays, working them until they stayed on opposite sides of the pen. He opened the gate into the alleyway and let the bays out, cutting off the roan's attempt to follow. He herded the bays out of the alley into the pasture. They went cautiously until they saw the other horses in the field and then galloped off, leaving the roan nickering anxiously.

Seth went back and moved the roan into one of the small pens off the alleyway. He went away to unsaddle Jester and turn him loose, ignoring Lee. He carried hay and a bucket of water to the roan's pen. He put both out for the horse, then leaned against the fence a few feet away and waited while the colt sidled in to eat and drink cautiously.

Lee went back to the cabin. Seth appeared ready to spend the rest of the evening just standing there. What had Dougherty said about the roan? He'd been treated for injuries? Apparently, the treatments were painful, and the horse had gotten to the point that he didn't want to be handled. Then he'd managed to avoid capture for a couple of years. So he had been handled but had lost confidence in people. Seth ought to be able to relate to that.

Chapter 27

Seth

Seth set a plank on the fence rails across one corner of the roan's pen where he could sit while the horse ate. Sometimes, when he knew Lee was gone, he talked to the horse about the things he couldn't tell anyone else. Just sitting, being there without asking anything of the horse, gave him too much time to think. Seth did not want to think; he just wanted to do his job and feel something close to normal. It did not seem to matter to the horse who persisted in keeping his distance day after day. He'd tried everything he knew to reach the animal.

In the round pen, if Seth roped him, the colt stood, tense, twitchy, always ready to step away if he could. A hand on his neck caused him to quiver and swish his tail. Seth backed off, left him loose, and did everything he knew to overcome the horse's resistance. The dark head stayed high, reflecting the animal's tension.

"Come on, horse," Seth said in frustration, after another session. "Just relax." But the horse did not relent.

Seth gave the colt a couple of days off. He added the two bays to the group of two-year-olds he was working with, lavishing them with attention in front of their old partner, leaving him alone. Then he put gentle old Buster in with the roan, hand feeding him while the roan used the old gelding as a shield. He spent every minute he could spare somewhere near the horse, even moving his bedroll to a spot just outside the roan's pen. The roan moved away when he could and stood alert and defensive if he couldn't. Seth persisted, and the colt learned, but Seth knew there would always be a huge hole in his training that threatened wrecks in the future if the horse remained distrustful.

And Seth began to feel like he was being watched. When the roan's attention locked on the ridge above the camp or rowdy fowl flew from the trees with their wild squawks. But he couldn't see anything. Maybe he was as distrustful as the horse.

"What's up?" someone said. Lee started and let down the horse foot she had been studying. She turned to see Kiri standing at the end of the bridge across the creek.

"Problem?" the older woman asked.

"Rocky knocked a chunk out of his hoof," Lee answered. "I didn't hear you get here."

"I brought you some supplies. The skimmer's by the cabin. Want me to look at that foot?"

"Go ahead."

Kiri walked over, ran a hand down the horse's shoulder and picked up the questionable hoof. "Big chunk," she commented. "When did his feet get trimmed last?"

"Too long," Lee said with disgust.

"Where's Seth?"

"Training colts."

Kiri let the horse set the hoof back on the ground. "He'll need a few days off but doesn't look like he did any serious damage. Want to tell me what's going on?"

"How long do you have?"

"Boss told me to see if you needed help with anything before I go back. I thought I'd ride with you tomorrow if I can borrow a horse."

"That would be nice." Lee scratched Rocky's neck thoughtfully. "Come look at something." She led Kiri up to the overlook under the copper trees, gesturing for her to be quiet. Seth, shirtless as usual, was in the round pen with one of the two-year-olds.

"First ride?" Kiri asked in a whisper.

Lee shrugged. She had no idea. They watched quietly for a few minutes before Lee withdrew. Kiri followed.

When they got back to the tack shed, Lee sat down on a rock. "He's doing fine, right? He and the colt and their dance."

Kiri nodded. "I've seen him with lots of colts, just like that. But you don't think so?"

"He never leaves them. If it's not one of the two-year-olds, he's with that roan."

"The one the boss wanted him to catch?"

"Yes, he's obsessed. And the horse is just as determined to be left alone."

"Seth gets that way," Kiri said. "Stubborn, you know."

"Right." Lee's shoulders slumped. "I'll turn Rocky loose, and we can go put the supplies away."

"Whoa," Kiri said. "It's not that I don't believe you. Give me a chance to see for myself."

"If he bothers to come to the cabin later."

Lee let Rocky loose in the pasture. The two women walked to the cabin in silence. Lee wanted to be wrong about Seth. She wanted Kiri to convince her Seth was just focused on a challenge, not withdrawing from everything and everyone, using the horses as his shield. But she knew in her heart that she was right.

"Goodies!" Kiri declared, pulling the top box out of the skimmer. "Cook sent up a big fresh salad for dinner, and this we'll take to the creek with us." She held up a bottle of wine wrapped in a cold pack.

They unloaded and put supplies away. Lee stacked the dirty dishes by the sink. "Left from his lunch," she told Kiri. "He eats at midday if I leave him something to heat. Never washes a dish or the laundry, but I guess I am officially the camp tender." In a rare fit of rebellion, she left the dishes where they sat. "Let's go cool off."

Minutes later, they were shoulder-deep in the swimming hole, shaded by a contorted old vine tree that trailed leaves to make ripples across the surface. Lee lay back, letting the tension out of her shoulders, feeling the contrast of the hot air and cold water. She ducked under and brought just her face to the surface for a moment before sitting up and shaking drops from her hair. Kiri handed her a glass of wine.

"You ought to come down to HQ once in a while. Settlement Day is coming up soon. It'll be a good party."

Lee shook her head, watching drops splatter across the surface of the wine. "He won't come."

"Then come without him. Give yourself a treat."

"I'm fine, Kiri, really. I just get frustrated sometimes."

"Want to talk?"

Lee took a mouthful of the slightly sweet, golden wine and let it slide slowly down her throat. "He thinks he's doing fine, but he's just closed himself away. Maybe I will come down and party. He won't even notice I'm gone."

"He'll notice when dinner's not on the table."

"Maybe." Lee drained her glass and sank back under the water again. Coming up, she poured more wine.

Kiri looked at her intently, like she could see inside, and asked, "How well did you know him before?"

"Well enough." Lee held the wine bottle out to fill Kiri's glass. "Now, tell me about Settlement Day, or your mother's favorite story, barracks myths, stories without morals, at least that apply here and now." Anything except her or Seth or mysterious riders that she hadn't mentioned to anyone.

"Okay," Kiri laughed. "How well do you know Joe Reilly?"

"Joe? Pretty well, I suppose. He's the Marshal for Under Rim; he was my safety contact for the undercover I was on. He's also an old friend of my parents."

"He's worried about both of you. We've been trading blips."

"Oh?" Lee grinned. "You and the Marshal?"

"Me and the Marshal. I'm looking forward to meeting him one of these days."

"I think maybe you should do that." Lee held her breath for a moment. She dreaded opening the subject. "Did he say anything about a man he's looking for?"

"Jerdix?" Kiri asked. "He's the one? He was behind whatever happened?"

Lee nodded.

Kiri looked grim. "He hasn't surfaced. It's driving Joe crazy."

"Does Joe still think he's off world?"

"That's what he says."

"But you don't believe him?"

"Hard to tell from a blip, but he just doesn't sound confident."

Lee stared into the wine glass. "I'm being watched. Followed when I'm riding."

Kiri sat up. "Seth?"

"No. A lone rider in the distance but not him."

"You're sure?"

"I know how Seth sits a horse. I know our horses. It's not him." Lee took a swallow of wine. If Jerdix wasn't gone ... That man stalked through her dreams far too often. She shivered at the thought that he could show up at Trego without warning.

"Seth needs to start riding with you. Isn't he worried?"

"I haven't told him."

"You haven't?"

"He's jumpy enough as it is."

"You be careful," Kiri said.

"I am. I've only seen him a couple of times," Lee said. "I'm probably making too much of a stray rider."

"Maybe." Kiri let it go at that. The conversation trailed off into their days before Carico, Lee with Central Services and Kiri with the Coalition Defense Service. When the shadows got long, they left the water and strolled back to the cabin.

Later, in the half-dark, they sat at the table under the arbor, the last of the wine in their glasses and a depleted bowl of salad in front of them, browsing on the leavings with their fingers. Kiri choked down laughter over some silly incident and gestured into the gloom with her nearly-empty glass.

Lee looked around to see Seth glaring at them. "Fresh salad in the cooler," she told him, still half-giggling. Without a word, he went into the cabin. Kiri shrugged. Lee got up and followed him, her good mood dashed.

"Nice to see you too. You might have at least said 'hi' to Kiri," she said, her voice low and tight with exasperation.

He turned his back to her, pulling off his boots. "You were having a good laugh," he said. "Wouldn't want to break that up."

"I'm not allowed to laugh now?"

He mumbled something indecipherable.

"Scorch it! I am so tired of this. Shut me out if you want, but be civil to Kiri. She's your friend." She took a deep breath and held it for a moment before releasing it. "You need to tear yourself away and work on some horse feet. Rocky took a huge chunk out of his hoof today."

"Tomorrow," he said without looking at her.

"After Kiri and I get back then."

"Back?" he said with surprise.

"She's riding with me."

"To do what?"

"Help me with some things you won't concern yourself with. Oh, and I'm going down for Settlement Day."

"That's not for a while, is it?"

"A couple of weeks."

"But I need you here," he said unexpectedly.

"For what?" She turned her back and walked out before he could respond.

"You two need some time off," Kiri said. She leaned her elbows on the table, fidgeting with her glass.

Lee locked her fingers behind her neck and stretched. "I feel like I'm not even here most of the time."

"Stay down at the Wells for a few days," Kiri suggested.

"I told him I was going down for Settlement Day. He said he needs me here. Don't ask me what for."

"Are you managing all right with the riding?"

"Let's see. I haven't gotten so lost I couldn't find my way back, and neither my horses nor I have gotten crippled, so we must be doing fine." She fiddled with a leaf from the salad, shredding it into tiny pieces. "You saw him with the colt, Kiri. He is so centered and in tune with them. That should give me hope, but it doesn't."

"You may be right," Kiri said. "I don't know what he went through, but it does sound like he's using the horses as crutches. You should tell him about that stranger, make him ride with you."

Lee shook her head. "Not yet. I don't want to scare him. Even though he avoids me, I think I'm his security in a weird sense, like your old service weapon. You have it; you keep it safely put away out of sight; but you'd be nervous without it."

Kiri chuckled. "I'm a year or two beyond that point. I turned it in when I went to work at the Wells. Still, I understand what you're saying.

"Wine's gone," Lee said mournfully. "Want some iced tea?"

"That will have to do."

Over the next couple of weeks, Lee called herself a coward often for not dislodging Seth from his fragile comfort zone or pushing him to face reality. She continued to depart early, get back late, and leave Seth with his horses. When she didn't see any strange riders for several days, she began to relax.

Afternoon heat gave way to frequent thunderstorms. She adjusted her riding to keep off ridge tops as much as possible, and also away from narrow canyons that showed signs of past flash floods, just as Kiri had warned her. Her good sense urged her to return to Trego any day when the storms threatened, but she didn't listen.

Driving a reluctant handful of tarbh that were intent on going back to an area she had already removed them from a few days before, Lee didn't notice the rapidly developing thunderheads until she was well up on a ridge. Before she could find a way down through the jagged rim rocks, the first rumble of thunder crashed around her, followed by drenching rain. Wind whipped the fronds of the palm-pines and drove rain into her face until she could hardly see. She urged Creamy ahead, trying to hurry the animals she was pushing.

One tarbh cow at the back flared her fan at something unseen. When the cow ducked off into a thicket, Creamy ran after her. Lee hung on, laying low on the horse's neck to avoid whipping branches. They caught the cow in a small opening. She turned to face them, flashing her fan like an umbrella in Creamy's face. Just as Lee drove the horse forward with a yell, a burst of rain engulfed them. Thunder cracked with a blinding flash. The horse collided with the tarbh and went down, tumbling Lee across the ground. Hitting the mud in slow motion, all she could think was to hang onto the reins.

A black bulk loomed over her. She curled into a ball, waiting for trampling feet. A flash of lightning showed heavy boots inches from her face. Something shielded her from the rain momentarily and her bridle fell on her face.

She looked up into a face leaning over her. "Go home," a hoarse voice said. "Oasis."

"What?"

"Off Carico. If you know what's good for the Reilly cub."

The face was gone. Where had she seen it before? A knife-wielding drunk in Under Rim. Bull. One of Jerdix's riders. She was dreaming. Had to be. Bad memories coming out of the dark to scare her. To threaten Seth?

She pushed herself up in time to catch sight of Creamy's pale rump heading down slope chased by a rider on a dark horse. She hung the bridle over her shoulder and ran through the mud, trying to keep her horse in sight.

She found Creamy holed up under a vine tree in the bottom of the draw. The steady little gelding let her get the reins around his neck and the bridle on. Good thing it had been Creamy and not Bo. The big sorrel would be halfway home.

She couldn't see any sign of the strange rider. When the storm passed over, she led Creamy into the open. The horse came reluctantly, limping on his off fore. Scorch it. She traded bridle for halter and trudged through the mud. At lame-horse speed it was going to be a late night. And somewhere out there was a rider, a doer of Jerdix's dirty work who ordered her off Carico. If she left, would they really leave Seth alone? She was the one they'd been watching.

Chapter 28

Seth

Seth sat on the board, leaning back into the fence corner. He'd ridden the roan for the first time, forging ahead in spite of the horse's stubborn reserve. Maybe the horse would never fully trust people. At least he behaved politely for the most part. But the ride had been a disaster; well, disappointing. The colt simply refused to move with Seth on his back. He was going to need help with this horse, and he wasn't sure Lee had the skills. So Seth sat in the corner of the corral while the roan picked through the hay and munched contentedly.

Seth woke with a start. Must have dozed off. He hadn't been sleeping well. The roan's nose was inches from his boot, ears pricked with curiosity. The horse delicately took the boot toe in his teeth and tugged. He let Seth's foot drop and lifted his head.

"Are you laughing at me?" Seth asked softly. The horse stretched his head out to snuffle at Seth's legs. Seth extended his hand slowly toward the horse. The roan met it like he would the nose of another horse, neck arched, drawing in Seth's scent before retreating a few inches. Seth kept his hand still. The dark, soft nose came back, and strong lips nibbled at his fingers. Seth withdrew carefully. "Enough of that, colt."

Moving slowly, Seth stood up, keeping his hand extended to the horse. He moved around to the roan's shoulder, reached up and rubbed the horse on the withers and neck. "Oh, you're a fine one," he said soothingly. He stood there, with the dark head under one hand and the relaxed body under the other for a long moment. When he turned away and walked across the corral, the horse followed. He walked circles in both directions, made figure-8s, and the roan horse walked calmly with him. Seth opened the gate and led the way along the alleyway into the pasture with the horse's nose by his hip.

"You go see your friends, and we'll have another little talk tomorrow." Seth stepped away from the horse, breaking the fragile, invisible link between them. The roan walked a few steps, looked back as if to ask if Seth was coming, then galloped away across the field toward the other horses.

Seth stood and watched the roan until he joined the herd with squeals and jostling. The whole herd took off to run a circuit of the pasture. A new horse in the group always stirred things up and made Seth nervous. Horses could get hurt in the process. He waited. The saddle horses settled down first. Roan and the two bays wandered off a little ways away from the other colts. Then horse heads popped up, staring up the ridge with ears at attention. The hair on the back of Seth's neck raised. Something up there sure caught the horses' attention a lot. Slowly they went back to grazing. Probably just swine-deer ... or was it?

Thunder rumbled in the distance. The sun was down. Seth started back to the corrals, eager to tell Lee about the colt's breakthrough, but something bothered him. He looked over the horses again. The cream-colored gelding wasn't there. With a growing sense of urgency, Seth went to the tack shed. Sure enough, Lee's saddle was gone. She hadn't come back yet, and it was almost dark.

He stood by the hitch rail, running through things in his mind. He needed to check and see where she had planned to ride that day. Maybe she was just waiting out a storm. Did he go looking for her with neither moon up for hours and on-going thunderstorms? Did he get on the comm and call the Wells for help? Now, or wait until morning? If she was hurt, he needed to find her.

He paced uncertainly before heading to the cabin. He started putting together a pack of food and first aid supplies, stared at the comm, went out to see if the sky had cleared, paced some more, unable to decide what was best. The old Seth, pre-Jerdix, never had problems acting decisively in a crisis. He hated himself for his dithering.

Taking a deep breath to steady himself, he studied the map. She intended to follow the Mainline out, make a loop up Grassy Canyon, down Stumblerock, and come back the way she'd gone. If he reversed that route, he should find her.

He rolled the pack in a waterproof cover and went back to the tack shed. Grabbing a halter, he ran to the pasture, whistling for Jester. The horse came but slowly, unused to being caught after dark. Impatiently, Seth went out to meet him and rode him in bareback. He fumbled to saddle the gelding, clumsy in his hurry. Finally, he was on his way up the well-traveled trail.

The horse walked surefootedly, unconcerned by the dark. Seth ran things over in his head as he rode. She'd be on the Mainline, making her way home after the storms had let up. Any minute those horse ears he could make out in front of him would prick, and Jester would nicker a greeting ... any minute.

He felt like he'd been riding for hours when he came to a looming rock outcrop that he knew was barely a mile from the cabin. Not being able to see landmarks disoriented him. He thought about Lee, new to the country. She would be completely lost. She should stay wherever she was and wait for daylight. If she did that, he had no hope of finding her. He'd feel a double fool if he got lost searching for her. If he didn't meet her on the main trail before he reached Stumblerock, he'd better camp until he could see. He tried counting his horse's steps to measure time and distance, leaving it to his mount to stay on the trail. The horse dropped his head now and then, like a hound on a scent, and walked steadily on. The smaller moon rose over the hills, peeking between thunderclouds. That would help.

An accusing voice in his head kept distracting him. "Not doing as well as you thought, are you?" it said. "You got her into this, after all. Lots of help you've been, sending her out day after day all alone." And what about that feeling he had of being watched? Was there really someone around? If — when — Lee was back safely, things would be different. Somehow, he'd look after her the way Dougherty expected.

He realized his horse had stopped, standing at a fork in the trail, the mouth of Grassy Canyon. "Right, old man. We go right." He urged the gelding up the main trail, but the horse pulled to the left. Seth rubbed the tense neck. "I know they went that way, but she won't be coming back down Grassy."

He was drowned out by a blaring neigh. A ghost-pale horse came out of the trees to his left. He could vaguely make out a person walking just ahead of the animal.

"Lee?"

"Who else?" she snapped as she came closer. Her horse limped slowly after her. "Good thing you weren't a little faster getting here. You would have missed us."

The real Seth, the old, buried Seth, wanted to leap from his horse and hug her off her feet. He sat where he was. "Are you okay?"

"Creamy's banged up a bit. I don't suppose you brought a camp setup?"

"Just food and first aid."

"That'll have to do. This is as far as I plan to go tonight." She led her lame horse a few steps to a palm-pine and tied him.

Seth dismounted and dug a flashlight out of his pack. He found an old vine tree whose limbs trailed to the ground. Years of leaf-fall padded the relatively dry surface under the branches. He put the pack in its shelter and opened it. "Here. There's hot tea."

Lee crawled in and snatched up the thermos, filled the cup lid and wrapped her hands around it. "If you'd told me this morning how good something hot could be, I would have said you were crazy."

"Nothing like a good storm to cool things off." Seth stayed just outside, reminding himself to breathe. Not enough space.

"I didn't expect you until morning."

"How bad is the horse hurt?" Horses were a safe topic.

She shrugged, shadows from the flashlight creating hard edges on her face. "Not too bad. He's been moving along all right."

Seth couldn't tell shadow from mud or bruising on her face. "What happened?"

"We collided with an uncooperative tarbh," she said. "In a downburst." She seemed about to say more then turned away and applied herself to emptying an emergency hot-pack of soup.

He let it go. "I'll go take care of the horses. Will you be okay without the light?"

"Fine."

He went out to unsaddle the two horses. He couldn't find any obvious injury on her gelding. Muscle strain or bruise he guessed, something he couldn't see easily. He'd take a better look in the morning. He gave both animals a little grain. Steeling himself, he brought the saddles into the shelter of the tree.

She pulled her saddle out of his way, spread her saddle blankets, and pulled an emergency blanket from her pack.

He laid out his own saddle blankets and stretched out as far from her as possible.

"You can turn out the light," she said.

He did, laying the flashlight in the gap between them where she could reach it if she needed it.

"'Night," Lee mumbled. He heard the velvety sounds of her shedding clothing. Then she lay quiet, but it took a while for her breathing to settle into sleep.

Seth's mind refused to still, running through what he could have or should have done differently. He let that frantic static override feelings stirred by her presence that he couldn't deal with. A knot tightened around his heart, a jumble of tangled emotions. He'd had a breakthrough with the roan. He wanted to enjoy that, share it. Instead, he was angry at himself for not looking after Lee, at her for picking that day to need rescue, at the All for the mess his life had become. He crawled out of the shelter, found a boulder near the horses, and sat, listening for far away thunder and watching the little moon zip across between clouds.

Chapter 29

Seth

Under clear morning skies, Seth walked, leading his own gelding. He stopped every few steps to wait. Lee let her limping horse take its time. Last night's slow progress up the canyon in the dark began to feel like a race by comparison. His horse, used to moving out, stomped and pulled impatiently. As soon as Lee caught up to them, he started walking again only to have to pause again in a few yards.

"Stop!" Lee said when he began to move before she had even reached him. When he turned back to her, she laid a restraining hand on her horse's nose. "Either follow Creamy or just go on ahead. I'm tired of chasing after you."

He shook his head. "I'll slow down."

"Get on your horse and go," she said, waving a hand at the trail. "Once you're out of sight, Creamy'll settle down and quit walking on my heels. It's not like I'm going to get lost between here and the cabin."

Seth took her at her word. "Okay. Take your time."

"Go!"

He mounted and pushed his horse into a trot toward home, relieved not to be plodding along on foot and to be away from her grumpiness. The sooner he was out of sight, the sooner her horse would stop worrying about keeping up. It was only about three miles to Trego. She'd be there in a couple hours. And he'd be able to work with the roan before it got too hot.

As he rode, he thought about the last few hours. Dougherty had told him to look out for Lee. She hadn't complained or asked him to go ride with her, so he thought she was doing fine. She'd had one of those wrecks that happened but was okay. She'd get over it. Still, maybe he should start riding with her for a while. That's what he'd do.

Seth brought the colts in from the pasture and then turned Jester out. The colts he was working with now were ready to start riding. Lee would have to help, do some groundwork for him, catching them, brushing them and getting them ready so he could spend his time riding them. Then he'd have time to go out with her.

But first, he wanted to see if the roan's new trust had lasted the night.

When the heat finally sent him to the cabin for a midday break, the clouds were building slowly, unthreatening yet. They might escape another round of thunderstorms. He crossed the log bridge and looked for Lee. He hoped she would have something ready to eat. She should have gotten back a while ago. But she wasn't under the arbor, and the pale horse wasn't in the shaded pen where he expected her to put him. What was taking her so long? He started for the tack shed, muttering about having to ride out and find her again.

"Over here."

He started at the unexpected voice and looked around. Downstream from the bridge, in the shade of a vine tree, Lee sat on a rock with her feet in the creek, holding Creamy's lead rope. The gelding stood knee-deep in the water, casually grazing along the bank. The girl stood up. "I'll put him away."

"Okay," he said, irritated at his relief. He went to the cabin to change into camp clothes. The cave-like stone walls kept the heat at bay, but he preferred the arbor where the shade and a slight breeze tempered the hot, dry air. Insects hummed softly in the leaves overhead, and the chuckling creek ran in the background. Relaxing to the lazy sounds, Seth got out fruit, cheese, biscuits and a cold drink. After lunch, he'd go down to the swimming hole, cool off, and nap in the shade until the sun dropped and the heat eased.

He had almost forgotten he didn't have the camp to himself until Lee trudged in, kicking up dust. She hadn't changed clothes yet. Of course she had seen to her injured horse first thing. She had a scrape on the back of one hand

and remnants of mud on her clothes. She favored her right leg. He hadn't noticed that when he'd left her on the trail to walk her horse home.

"What happened to you?" he asked sharply.

She stopped abruptly and reached out a hand to lean against a post. "I told you I had a wreck." She glared at him. "So, if you don't mind, I'll go wash off the mud. I've had a long morning." She walked past him without another word. What was that all about? But something in the set of her shoulders told him to let her go.

He finished eating and stuck his head in the cabin door to tell her he was going to the creek. She was still in the shower. He could hear the water running. He headed down to the swimming hole, hoping her humor would improve when she got clean and rested.

Late in the afternoon he returned to the arbor with a couple of frog-eels he had caught for dinner. He put them in the cooler and fixed a snack. By now, the corrals would be in the shade, and he could work a couple more colts before dark. He went in to put on riding clothes. A soft catch of breath, almost a snore, warned him that Lee was sleeping in the cool dark of the cabin. He changed quietly and left.

It took a while to get the colts in. All the horses were edgy about something that he couldn't see. If they thought something was there, maybe he wasn't imagining being watched.

A gong sounded in the failing daylight and distracted Seth from the colt he was working with. Lee had dinner ready. He turned the animal loose and shuffled toward the cabin, not at all sure she would be in a better mood. Maybe the change in their schedule that he had in mind would warm that cold shoulder he had gotten earlier.

He needn't have worried about it. Food sat on the table, but she was nowhere to be seen. What had he done to deserve this? Just gone out in the middle of the night to find her and wasted half his morning getting back. Instead of thanks, he got shut out. Was she hurt worse than she showed? She'd say something if she was. Wouldn't she? He ate and dropped the dirty plate on the counter. Fetching his bedroll from the cabin, he headed around the rocks to find a quiet place for the night.

Lee was dressed to ride when Seth got to the cabin in the pre-dawn light. She kept cutting up a melon without looking at him. Her saddlebags lay on a bench, already packed.

"Stay here today," he said. "I'll ride with you tomorrow."

She looked at him, laid down the knife, and straightened. Crossing her arms tightly, she said, "No."

He shook his head in surprise. "What?"

"No, I will not stay here today. No, you will not ride with me tomorrow."

He ran a hand through his hair. "Look, you should take a day off," he said, trying to reason with her.

She uncrossed her arms and picked up her saddlebags. "I am going to the Wells for Settlement Day. I won't be coming back here."

"You ... what's going on? What do you mean, you won't be coming back?" He felt like he'd been punched in the gut. "I know you had a bad day, but that's no reason to quit."

"This isn't working. No point in me hanging around any longer." She shifted her feet, took a couple steps, fumbled with a buckle on the saddlebags.

"What's wrong? I thought things were going fine." His voice rose. Fear made him angry.

"Exactly. You think things are fine." She jabbed her hand at him. "Because you eat and you sleep and you go work your colts every day, you think you're back to normal." Tears came to her eyes, and she folded her arms again. "You didn't notice I was late until dark. Yesterday you left me to walk back with a lame horse and didn't notice I was hurt. You're doing so well on your own that you don't even see me these days, so go ahead and get by on your own. I'm gone." She glared at him for a moment, then turned and stalked away.

"But ... Lee, wait!" He started after her. She didn't look back. "Lee!"

She kept walking, crossing the bridge, throwing the saddlebags onto the white-splashed gelding, catching up the lead of a loaded pack horse, and trotting away, fading into the dawn.

He sat down, focused on breathing, trying to control the panic threatening to overwhelm him. He remembered how relieved he had been when he had found her waiting at Seven Wells. Even when he avoided spending time with her in the weeks since then, he had known he wasn't alone. She was somewhere not too far away. Her presence kept him in touch with here-and-now; she kept him from falling into the void.

"I am okay," he told himself, releasing his grip on the table. "I do not need her. Just keep doing what I've been doing." Just get up in the morning, eat, bring in the morning's group of colts, one step at a time. Hadn't he finally gotten through to the roan without any help from her? It took him a long time to stand up and start to the horse pens, and he skipped the 'eating' step.

Creamy nickered at him when he passed the gelding's corral. When it got too hot to train, he should take the horse to soak its leg in the creek for a while. It was up to him now with no one else to do it.

He rode the roan, taking the colt out into the pasture where he needed all his concentration to steady the animal. He managed to carry that focus over to the next colt and the next. Somehow, he got through the day.

He lay awake late into the night in the quiet of the cabin, trying to get a grip on how Lee could see things so differently than he did. She'd come after him, stayed with him. She wouldn't leave him now. She would spend a couple of days at the Wells, partying with Kiri. Then she would come back, and he would try to ... to do what? Talk to her? Show some interest in what she was doing? Quit acting like he lived by himself? When she came back ...

Midday the next day, the horses in the pasture alerted him to a rider coming up the main trail from Seven Wells. He tied the colt he was working with and headed to the tack shed.

But the rider coming in wasn't Lee. It was a tall old man on a tall brown horse. Ike Allred, oldest of the Seven Wells riders.

"Ike." Seth forced himself forward to take the lead rope of the same pack horse Lee had taken the day before.

"Glad I caught you here," the man said. "Boss sent me up to take the girl's place."

"Oh." She really wasn't coming back. Seth couldn't think of anything to say.

Ike dismounted and tied his saddle horse. "Mind helping an old man with those packs?"

"Oh, sure." Seth led the pack horse to the arbor by the cabin and unloaded the packs while Ike unsaddled his horse. How was he going to manage? How could he be in this space with someone, anyone, other than Lee? No one else understood.

Days passed. Each morning Ike saddled a horse and rode out on another circle, keeping his distance and asking no questions. He did add to the menu, baking bread from his famous yeasty starter. On the fifth day after Lee had left, Dougherty rode in, leading two loaded pack horses, and stopped outside the pen where Seth was getting ready to ride the roan.

"Morning, Boss," Seth said, coming over to the fence, trying to sound unconcerned. "You tending camp now?"

Dougherty sat on his horse, looking down at Seth. "I brought two more horses for Ike. Figured I might as well bring supplies too. I'm short-handed."

"What did Lee tell you?" Seth clutched a fence rail.

"Not a thing I couldn't see by looking at her."

Seth turned his back, seeking support from the roan, who uncooperatively edged away from him. Seth half-turned, kicking the dirt. "She and I can work things out. The work's been getting done."

"She's gone."

"What?"

"I dropped her in Under Rim yesterday. Kiri went with her." Dougherty gathered his reins. "Take these two and get them unloaded. I've got to get back."

Seth tied the colt and left the corral to take the two pack horses. "I'm glad she's gone."

"That so?"

"It's not safe around here. There's been ..." Seth sucked in a breath and braved Dougherty's disbelief. "There's been someone hanging around, off in the distance. I'm afraid it has to do with what happened to us, before."

"Why didn't you say something sooner? That must be what she meant about you being safer if she was gone."

"Lee said that?" Seth wondered what she'd seen that she'd never shared with him.

"Look, you stick close to Ike for a day or two. As soon as I can get another rider up here, I want you at headquarters."

"I ... do I have to?"

"No argument. And keep your eyes open. I want to know about anything unusual. Anything." Dougherty spun his horse and left at a trot.

What had really happened to Lee the night Creamy had gotten hurt? "Sorry, Boss. I'm not coming." But he was talking to himself at that point. Dougherty was gone.

Seth pulled the packs and left them in the arbor. He took the horses to the pasture where he whistled up Jester and Buster. Of course Lee would go back to his father's, the only place she knew on Carico. And Kiri was with her. Kiri would take care of her. With his two personal horses in the corral with the roan, he hurried to the cabin to pack his gear. He hoped Dougherty would forgive him taking the roan.

Chapter 30

Seth

Sixteen hard days later, Seth stopped the roan at the edge of the trees and looked across the meadows at his childhood home, the log house tucked against the trees, the big barn with corrals opening onto pastures, dark and silent now in the middle of the night. He had pushed on into the night, eager for the end of his long ride, but he and the horses were overdue for a good rest. Three times in six months — he didn't want to see the trail between Seven Wells and Under Rim again for a long while.

But now that he could see his destination, he was torn between the need to know Lee was safe and his own rush of anxiety about facing people at all, much less her after the way she had left. Were Lee and Kiri there? In the bunkroom in the barn or in the house? Of course they were. Where else would they be? He turned back into the trees, made camp out of sight of the stead, and hobbled his horses to graze. They were as gaunt and tired as he was.

He woke well before daylight in spite of his late arrival. In the habit of getting up early to travel in the cool morning, he couldn't go back to sleep. He collected a few things from his packs and walked across the meadow to the house. His father would be awake soon enough. And Lee. He told himself he wanted to get cleaned up before he saw her. He didn't want to admit he was terrified that something had happened to her or that she didn't want to see him.

He left his boots on the porch and opened the door carefully. The house was quiet. He'd always loved the way the old place felt when he was alone in its dark, a calm refuge embracing him. He soft-footed his way to the kitchen and turned on one light over the stove, just enough to make some tea. He filled the kettle, put it on the heat, and sat on a stool at the counter facing the room.

Dishes sat on the table, uncleared remnants of a dinner for two, complete with candles burned down to the nub, two unfinished drinks on a table by the couch and a shirt trailing off a chair. Nah, couldn't be. His pa and a woman? He went over and found a rumpled piece of fabric abandoned on the couch, one of Lee's wraps, the black one with red swirling across it that he remembered vividly.

He picked it up in disbelief and staggered back like a fist had caught him just under his ribs. He couldn't breathe. Lee hadn't just come back where she knew someone; she'd run to his father. Why not? Joe had given her the saddle, proof of his feelings for her. They were upstairs now.

The rolling boil of the kettle cut through. He ran to pull it off the heat before it whistled. He tried to imagine them coming down, finding him there. He could go out, saddle up, and be gone before they even knew he had been there. And he would be haunted by the wreckage of any hope he had left. He might as well confront them, see the proof, make himself believe.

A bottle of whiskey sat on the counter. He stared at it; let the thought of the smoky taste roll around on his tongue. He poured a glass, took a generous swallow, sat in the quiet, and watched the first faint gray appear in the morning sky.

Quiet footsteps came down the stairs, and the living room light came on. Joe stood there, wearing only a pair of drawstring pants. "Son!" he said in surprise. "When did you get in? Dougherty said you were headed home. But we didn't expect you this soon."

"Obviously." It took everything Seth had to look him straight in the eye, reminded of what a powerful man his father was physically. Still sitting, elbows on the counter, he held up the black and red fabric and spoke more calmly than he thought possible, "Feels like I'm out of the picture, but I suppose I earned that." He dropped the wrap on the counter and let it slide off the far side onto the floor.

"Wha ..." Joe had the grace to glance back up the stairs. "It's not ..." He seemed to rethink what he was going to say. "I suppose you did," he answered. "She is her own person. If she chooses to come to me, whose fault is that?"

Seth looked down, swirled amber liquid around in his glass. "Mine, I —"

Joe cut him off, crossing toward him with the look Seth always thought of as his professional face. "Enough! You are going to listen to me now, boy! You have abused that girl. You kept her out in some lonely camp away from other people and away from help she needed because you couldn't face what you needed to do. I'm just glad she finally got smart enough to take care of herself."

"What did she tell you?"

"Not a thing, but she came back here. That's all I need to know."

"So you take her to bed? That's how you help her?" Seth slammed his fist on the counter.

"Take it easy, son." Joe eased back, looking concerned. "I'd better clear this —"

Another voice intervened from the top of the stairs, "Hey, Joe, honey, is someone here?"

Joe turned and went to the foot of the stairs, shedding all sign of his marshal's attitude. "Darlin', seems we didn't have the house as much to ourselves as we thought. My son has been making bad assumptions about who I choose to bring to my bed."

The woman came down the stairs, wearing one of Joe's shirts, rubbing at her thick red hair with a towel. Seth stared at Kiri dumbstruck.

She looked at Joe, puzzled, then her eyes found the black and red pool of fabric on the floor. "Lee? By the Elements, Seth, you are a mess if you really thought she was the one up there. And you, Reilly, you thought you would take the chance to make a point?" Kiri said, tucking herself in against Joe and kissing him. "Relax, Seth, Lee went up to Fallen Pine."

Seth pushed the whiskey away, opened his mouth but couldn't think of anything to say. He teetered between shock and relief that he was just a fool. Maybe not Lee but Kiri was almost as bad. She'd been his best friend not so long ago. Seth couldn't believe the way she was looking at his father. She'd only met him a few days ago. Seth groaned and turned away. "Tea?" he asked weakly, starting the heat. He kept his back to the two, struggling to gather some composure. "Moving pretty fast, aren't you?" he muttered.

"I'll have you know I've been very patient," Kiri protested. "I have been blipping with this man for months. I was about to invite him to the Wells to check on you, just so I could meet him face-to-face, when Lee finally came to her senses." She began to clear the dishes from the table, cornering Seth when she brought them to the sink. She stopped abruptly as he withdrew against the wall.

She backed off. "Sorry." She put the dishes on the table, picked up the wrap from the floor, and went to Joe. He ran his fingers along her jawline and took the wrap from her to drape around her shoulders. The two sort of melted together.

Seth gulped, shaken by a weird mix of rod-induced physical reactions and feeling swamped by the new love rapidly filling the room. He'd never seen his father like that before. "I ... I'll just go ..." He headed for the door, snatching up his things. Then something sank in. "Lee's alone at Fallen Pine? She's not safe."

"Easy," Joe said. "We've had no sign of trouble in weeks, no strange riders, no break-ins, none of the trouble we were having before."

"That's right," Kiri said. "And I've been up there with her most of the time. Until ..."

"Until last night," Joe finished. "I wouldn't have let them go up there at all if I was worried about Jerdix or his crew. He's off world as far as we can tell."

"You're sure?"

"I'm sure she's safe at the cabin. Son, the bunkroom is all yours. Get cleaned up and then come back for breakfast," Joe said, his eyes on Kiri.

"Don't wait for me," Seth said and exited as fast as he could. Bringing his horses and gear to the barn weren't enough to settle his turmoil. Twenty minutes under the shower, mostly cold, began to give him some control over his physical reactions but not his thoughts. His brain still couldn't grasp the thought of Kiri and his father. Seeing them act like a couple of teenagers was more than he could handle.

He tried to rationalize it. His father had been alone a long time. Kiri was a veteran with law enforcement experience, so they had something in common. She was getting older too. She had to be in her thirties. Not many women on Carico were still unmarried at her age. With a whole world to occupy and much of a generation gone in the pandemic, having children was important. Women had an unfair advantage, given their role in that activity. They chose their mates, and the men knew it.

Oh, Void! Was he going to end up calling her 'Mom' and be surrounded by little half-brothers and -sisters?

At least it wasn't Lee.

He got out of the shower and dug into his pack for the buttonweed he had picked the day before. He'd been out for weeks. He popped half a dozen pods in his mouth and waited for the calm warmth to spread. He had come here after Lee. She was at Fallen Pine, so he was going there too — that afternoon. He could leave most of his gear here; get there at dusk so she wouldn't send him packing. But first, he was tired. The buttonweed drained all tension out of him. He stretched out on a bunk and fell asleep.

When he woke, muzzy-headed from too much buttonweed on an empty stomach, he dragged himself to the tack room. Midday. He had plenty of time to ride to Fallen Pine. First, he'd missed breakfast, and he wasn't going back to the house. He dug into his pack for the remnants of his food supplies from the trip.

He heard the bunkroom door close and stepped out into the barn aisle. Kiri stood there in her usual riding garb. "I brought you some food," she said tentatively.

"Okay," he replied, not sure how to react to her.

She took a couple steps toward him and stopped when he backed away. "Right, no hugging. Seth, I'm sorry about this morning. We had no idea you were here."

"Quite a surprise," he said, trying to make his body language match the understatement.

She blushed. "For us too, honestly. We didn't know where things were going until I came down yesterday for supplies, and we were alone."

"Don't let me get in the way."

"You know me better than that." She unexpectedly smiled with a devilish look he remembered well. "You just have to learn to live with this, Sonny."

He dredged up something of their past teasing. "Yes, Mom. There, how does that sound?"

"Downright disturbing."

"Ma? Mommy?"

"Can I throw something at you?" she asked, looking around for a likely item.

"Hey, Kir," Joe called, appearing in the doorway of the bunkroom and putting an arm around her. "Hi, son. We're headed over to help Gwyn and Nick lay out their new house site. Did you get the word that they were married? Anyway, come along with us."

"House?" One more new thing — his sister and old friend were getting ready to build a house. "No," Seth said. "I'm going to Fallen Pine."

"I just thought you might want to see them."

"Not today." Later, when he could handle being around people.

"What do you plan to say to Lee?" Joe asked with a rough edge to his voice.

"Whatever comes to mind." Seth tightened up, unwilling to talk about it.

His father let go of Kiri and stepped toward him. "Just tell her you are ready to get some help. That's all any of us wants you to do."

Seth met Joe's stare. "May I borrow a horse? Mine are tired."

Joe held his eye for a moment. "Sure, take Ratchet." He brought Kiri back against him. "Come on, darlin', we'd better get going."

"Wait." Seth surprised himself. "Just, well, don't hang all over each other until you explain things to Gwyn."

"Are we that obvious?" Joe asked, drawing a giggle from Kiri.

"Like a supernova," Seth answered.

"Then she probably figured it out before we did, but I'll try not to shock your sister. You go make peace with Lee. And Ran Cory should be on world in a day or two. She called him before she left the Wells."

Seth nodded, absorbing that information. Weeks alone on the trail brought the realization that he needed help, but actually getting it was something else. He shifted his feet uncomfortably. Facing Lee was the first step. And now he knew what he would do. "Can I borrow the skimmer?"

"To go to Fallen Pine?" Joe asked.

"No. Into town. I need to pick up something for Lee."

"Sure." Joe stepped away from Kiri. "I ... well, anything I can do, you just ask."

"I know." He did but too much was happening too fast. He stepped around them and went into the bunkroom,

shutting the door on all the things he couldn't quite handle.

They took an unusually long time to saddle their horses with lots of laughter, and he didn't want to imagine what else. Only the lingering headache kept him from downing another half dozen buttonweed pods. He settled for one and ate the lunch Kiri had brought. Then he got in the skimmer and headed for Under Rim.

When he got back from town, he found the little brown gelding Ratchet in the pen by the barn, waiting for him. His pa and Kiri must have brought him in when they got their own horses. He wasted no time saddling him. In ten minutes, he was trotting toward Fallen Pine with his surprise for Lee packed securely in his saddlebags.

Three hours later, he rode slowly across the meadow toward the Fallen Pine cabin. He'd expected to see Lee sitting on the porch in the afternoon breeze. Had she seen him coming and gone inside to avoid him? He walked his horse across the meadow where the spring flowers had given way to tall, golden grass that rattled against the horse's legs. Insects hummed in the heat, and honeymoths flitted by. A horse nickered loudly from the pasture behind the cabin. His gelding pricked his ears but didn't answer.

Seth dismounted and tied the horse in front of the cabin. A knot deep in his chest tightened. She'd left him at Trego. Would she refuse to talk to him now? He'd played out variations of their meeting about a million times on the trail from the Wells. Anxiety filled him; his heart thudded raggedly, and it was hard to breathe. He bent over, hands on his knees, and concentrated on breathing in and out. One last deep breath let out slowly, and he straightened, climbed the steps, and knocked at the door.

Chapter 31

Seth

Seth saw Lee peering out the window, mussed like she had been sleeping. She looked away, ran a hand through her hair, and opened the door.

"What are you doing here?" she said.

"Kiri didn't blip you that I was coming?"

"Maybe," she said. "I haven't looked."

He didn't know how he had expected things to go, but this wasn't it. "I'm sorry," he said.

"Not your fault."

"No." He tried again. "I'm sorry for the way I treated you at Trego. Sorry I ignored you. Sorry I didn't help you. I am sorry."

"Oh." She ran her hand through her hair again.

She was wearing typical camp clothes — a light-colored tank top, drawstring pants, bare feet, and she looked incredible. He stepped back. "I just wanted to tell you that."

"You rode all the way from Trego to say you're sorry?"

"And that I missed you. I needed you even when I couldn't admit it to myself. I'm a wreck." There, days' worth of mulling things over while he rode, all boiled down. "And I'll come back once I've gotten the help I need."

"You'll ..." She studied his face. "Come in." She walked into the cabin, leaving the door open wide.

He left his boots on the porch, came in, and shut the door against the summer heat. Afternoon storms rattled in the distance. The cabin was cool.

She went into the kitchen, putting the counter between them. "You should have stayed at Trego," she said. "You were supposed to stay at Trego."

He rolled with that punch. "I guess I didn't get that message."

She gripped the edge of the counter. "He told me to leave Carico if I knew what was good for you. But I only made it this far."

He shook his head. "What are you talking about?"

"The night Creamy got hurt, that you had to come looking for me."

"I remember."

"There was a man, one of Jerdix's riders. When Creamy fell, he was there. He told me to leave Carico."

"You never said anything." That had been the day he'd had a breakthrough with the roan. He'd been eager to tell her about it, but she hadn't come home and he'd finally, unexpectedly, been worried about someone other than himself.

"I don't remember you wanting to talk." She crossed her arms tightly.

"I was angry," he said, "because you scared me so bad. And I couldn't deal with it."

"I'm scared too, now," she said. "Joe's wrong. Jerdix, or at least his people, are still here."

He wanted to go to her and hold her for both their sakes. He couldn't. "Then why are you up here by yourself?"

"I wasn't until Kiri went down for supplies yesterday. She blipped me about not coming back until today, and I said okay."

"You know why she stayed?"

"Yeah. It's about time." Her mouth quirked in a lop-sided grin. She let her arms drop. "There's iced tea. Do you want some?"

"Please."

"They've been dancing around for days, pretending it was nothing. So I came up here. But Kiri wouldn't let me come alone."

"I thought for a minute it was you he was with." Better to tell her before Kiri made some joke about it.

She nearly dropped the pitcher of tea. "Me?"

"Your wrap, the red and black one, was laying on the floor with the remains of dinner for two on the table. Candles, wine, the works."

"But me and your father? Really?"

"He gave you my mother's saddle that he has kept clean and oiled and unused for years." He shrugged. "I told you I'm a wreck. Don't expect me to be clear-headed."

She shook her head. "I suppose him with Kiri is a big enough surprise."

"Like a couple of teenagers, hanging all over each other." He shivered at the thought and tried to stifle his other reactions, the debilitating expectation of pain following pleasure following pain. "I guess that's why they forgot to warn you I was coming."

She set a glass of tea on the counter and backed away, giving him space just like she'd done at Trego. "Does anyone else know you're here?"

"I didn't see anyone but Pa and Kiri. They probably told the rest of the family."

"Good. We'll ... we'll have to leave in the morning. Split up. Disappear until they do catch Jerdix."

"You really are scared."

"Terrified. You didn't know Jerdix like I did. He was set on revenge against Joe and my mother. He hasn't given up on that."

"Yeah, well, I got a pretty good dose of Jerdix." He tried to force away the memories. His hand shook so hard he had to put the glass down.

"Breathe," she said. "Just breathe." She reached a hand out toward him, then withdrew it. "Um, hey. What about the roan? Tell me about the roan."

The roan. His anchor. "He's down at Pa's."

"So you're riding him?"

"Yeah." Firm ground. "He's doing great. The boss will be wanting him back, I guess."

She leaned back against the sink and fiddled with her glass. "I'm the one who should be sorry. If I hadn't made a mess of my assignment, if I'd acted sooner, lots of things wouldn't have happened."

He skirted the panic-laden memories. "I will not run from him now." He picked up his glass, mostly to prove to himself that he could, and took a drink. "Tomorrow we can go down to Pa's and see what we can do to end this."

She extended her glass. "Together?"

He found the will to clink his glass against hers. "Together."

She eased back. "Not much around here to eat. My camp tender went AWOL."

"I've got it covered."

"What did you do?"

"Just wait and find out."

Seth went out and took his horse to the pasture behind the cabin. So Lee had left him at Trego because of a threat, not because she couldn't stand to be around him anymore. That she carried that threat in secret instead of going to Dougherty or his pa with it and tackling it head on was a hint to how damaged she still was. What a pair they were.

He brought his bulging saddlebags back to the house and plunked them down on the table. Lee watched him without a word. Until the first container came out.

"You went to Rajir's!"

"Dinner for two. We did have a date we never got to keep."

"For when you got back from Migration."

"Right. So I asked Tam what you liked. All we have to do is heat it up."

She wasted no time taking charge of that.

So far, their reunion was going well. Somehow that made Seth nervous. He sat at the counter and laid down a handful of buttonweed pods. He'd had one a little while ago when he had picked them. Now just one more. Just to settle the tension thrumming his nerves. "Doc's prescription," he recalled when she looked from him to the pods. She pushed the remaining pods around on the countertop with a finger, then helped herself to one and turned back to the salad she was putting together.

They sat at the counter and ate. He managed to put aside everything else and appreciate the flavors and textures of the familiar dishes, spurred on by her enthusiasm. Finally, he sat back and just watched her breathe in the aromas, savor the flavors, and look forlorn as she cleaned the bottom of each dish.

"I didn't know you liked the cafe food that much," he said.

"Especially Tam's more exotic dishes. Tarbh steak, spinxi eggs, all the usual fare is good, but Tam's curries are superb."

He dared to reach toward her, and she stopped. It took strength he didn't think he had to put his hand over hers, actually touch another human being. She held very still, wide-eyed like a colt unsure what would come next. He touched his finger to the cord around her wrist, squeezed her hand, and held it for a long moment before letting it go.

She wiped her eyes. "Potent spices," she muttered.

"Yeah." He turned his back and wiped his own eyes. He'd held her hand without collapsing in a flashback. One small step. Still a long way to go.

Chapter 32

Lee

Lee lay alone on the couch. They'd slept there, her on the couch, Seth in the big armchair, feet touching. No more. That much was a miracle.

He'd slipped away at first light, thinking she hadn't noticed. She'd let him go. They both had a lot to think about. She got up and stretched, poured a mug of tea from the pot Seth had made, and settled on the kitchen stool. They would go back to Joe's where they would be safe until Jerdix was caught. And then Seth would have to leave to get treatment, but he would come back and they would be together.

The back door creaked open, and she heard boots coming down the hall.

Boots! Seth never ever wore his boots in the house.

She sprinted for the front door. She barely made it around the counter before something stabbed her in the butt. She made three more steps before she lost all control of her muscles and collapsed. Darted like a wayward tarbh. Whatever it was paralyzed just her voluntary movement. She was completely aware. She cursed her complacency.

Someone plucked out the projectile and rolled her over with a booted foot. "Hello, sweet Anni." Jerdix holstered the dart gun and leaned over her. "Nice to see you again." He fastened ties around her wrists and ankles, shook out the light material of an emergency extraction sled and rolled her onto it. Taking hold of the pulls, he dragged her through the house and bounced her down the back steps. She caught a glimpse of Seth lying by the tack shed, apparently victim of the same drug used on her, at least she hoped so. Jerdix continued to tow her down the path to a jumper parked a little way to the west of the cabin. His pull on the front of the sled kept her head off the ground, but the rest of her felt every root and rock she went over.

"There's a nice trail for someone to follow whenever they quit chasing the phantoms I planted Portside." Jerdix took her by her upper arms and lifted her into the passenger seat like she was a small child. The memory of those harsh hands flashed through her mind. He strapped her in, lowering the back of the seat enough that her head didn't flop forward. Running a handheld scanner over her, he located her Ranger-issued ID implant just below her collarbone, jerked her shirt down, and inserted the tip of a knife to pop out the pea-sized device. He pitched it into the forest.

"The trail ends here. Enjoy the ride." He got into the driver's seat and took off, turning toward the rim and climbing above the treetops. Still unable to move, Lee had a fine view of the upper edge of the windshield and the sky. Her heart pounded. Her mind pictured all kinds of scenarios, none of them with a good outcome. If the drug didn't wear off soon, she was worse than dead.

The jumper climbed steeply, and she saw the turquoise rocks of the rim out of her peripheral vision. Why would he go up there?

He chuckled, as if reading her thoughts. "The mistake they have made and will continue to make is looking for me where they expect me to be. What they don't know is that I was born on Carico. Sent away to relatives off world after the pandemic killed my parents, just like your mother was. But I buried that identity so deeply that they'll never find it. So you and I will just make ourselves comfortable in the middle of nowhere until they quit looking. Can you just picture Joe Reilly's face, not to mention your cat of a mother, knowing I have you, and they are helpless to find you? Convenient that I can inflict so much pain on them by doing something I will enjoy so much."

The jumper leveled out and a minute later settled to the ground. Jerdix picked her up and carried her into a small cabin, little more than a shack, put her down on a bunk and left her alone. She heard the jumper hum briefly, like he moved it, maybe out of sight. She could see enough of the room to realize the shabby exterior camouflaged a state-of-the-art prefab building, the kind used as base camps by long-term survey teams. How long had he been here, snug in this hide-out? How had he gotten by everyone looking for him?

She grimly accepted that she was on her own. They might never find this place. He could have taken her anywhere. A jumper left no tracks. Besides no skimmer could maneuver up the cliffs, and jumpers weren't common. How long would it take for them to think of looking up on top?

Blink, blink. She could blink, the first sign of returning control. She savored that little success, although she expected Jerdix had a very good idea of how the drug progressed. Tied as she was, it didn't make much difference. How could she get him to release her? Would he find the 'Anni' persona convincing anymore? Had he ever? Or would he just drug her again? Be submissive, frightened — that part was easy enough — and wait for an opening. Survive and escape. The drug kept her from controlling her heart rate and breathing, and both gave away her terror. She'd just have to use that. If she could keep her head, she'd find a way out of this eventually.

The door opened, letting in early morning heat. She could see thunderheads already building. Jerdix came to stand over her, grinning with satisfaction. "Welcome home, sweet Anni. We'll have some fun later, when you are more, uh, responsive." He reached over to scratch off the scab where he had cut out her implant and smeared the rising blood across her chest. He ran his big hand up to her throat where her pulse pounded and laughed, then turned his back and crossed the room.

The aroma of food came to her, causing her stomach to growl. He sat at the table and ate, making a show of his enjoyment. With him watching, she refrained from testing her returning muscle control. The longer he thought she was under the drug, the better.

Done with his breakfast, he came back to where she lay. Her eyes widened, and she tensed when he pulled out the rod from a holster on his belt. Casually he held it toward her bare foot. She jerked away. He laughed.

"See, you can move on your own, although you'll need a bit longer to regain fine motor control. No point trying to speak yet." He ran the rod up the sole of her foot. She waited, holding her breath, but he didn't activate it. He smirked. "Are you Anni? I did kind of like her, but things will be more interesting if you have a little more fight in you than she did."

Lee tried to pull away, to curl into a ball. He took hold of the tie around her ankles and jerked her straight. She might be regaining control, but she had no strength.

"First lesson," he said coolly. "Do as you are told, and you will be rewarded."

She could guess the other half. It took everything she had to nod when she wanted to plant her feet in his grinning face. She had to mislead him into underestimating her. This time, though, she had no intention of letting him have everything his way.

"You will lay still. Do not move."

She nodded. He slid her pant leg up and stroked her leg, holding the rod under his own jawline and activating it. The hand on her leg tightened sharply as he reacted to the quick pulse of the pleasure setting. On himself? She cringed in horror.

He loosened his grip and smoothed her pant leg down. "Very good. You obeyed." He released the ankle bindings and let them fall to the floor. "That's your reward. Oh, don't try to walk yet. You'd just fall on your face. And know that the door is locked. No point in trying to run barefoot anyway." He holstered the rod.

Suddenly he dropped his controlled front, grabbed her throat violently, and lifted her up. "Lesson two, same as the first. Do as you are told." He flung her down and left her lying there, gasping. He paced the length of the room with hurried steps. Gradually, Lee saw his shoulders drop. He stretched his neck, shook off the tension, and stopped.

Lee held very still, wishing herself invisible. Just then a voice boomed clear and strong. A comm, she could see a comm unit out of the corner of her eye. She recognized Seth. He was alive. Jerdix grabbed the headset and silenced the speaker so she couldn't hear.

"There's the crippled cub, begging for help, right on schedule." He rubbed his hands together in anticipation. "And the intrepid Marshal will come to the rescue. Now all we need is your dear mother. Where is your mother?" He spun and stared at her. "You will answer now."

She knew that no answer she could give would satisfy him. She stalled, moved her lips and tongue, and stammered, "I don't know."

"Where is she?" He came two steps closer, looming over her. She brought her arms up defensively. "Speak!" he ordered.

"On assignment," she croaked with uncooperative muscles. "Two-year survey sweep."

"You lie," he said softly. "Speak."

"You aren't her current assignment." Lee huddled back, waiting for him to strike, telling herself to show no fight, not yet.

She stared at his hands as he clenched and unclenched his fists. She let him see her fear. He backed away, regaining his control. "I believe you. She should have been here, but this may be even better. She'll suffer that much longer knowing what's happening to you." He paced across the room and back. "Your mother and Joseph Reilly ruined my life," he said vehemently. "They killed my wife and my elder brother; they deprived my family of my leadership. They locked me away and did everything in their power to dismantle what I had built. They deserve whatever pain I can inflict upon them."

He loomed over her. She huddled down. He reached out. She held her breath. He took hold of the tie around her wrists and clipped it to a snap on the end of the bed. She let herself breathe.

"Be good and lay still. I have things to do." He went into another room, closing the door behind him. She could hear his voice but not make out the words. He must have taken the headset with him. She'd known he must have contacts providing him with information. What arrangements was he making now?

While he was out of sight, she worked first at improving control of her arms and legs and then trying to decipher how to free her hands. Both the tie and the snap were high tech gadgets that needed something she didn't have, probably his thumbprint, before they would release. Finding no way out short of chewing off her own hand, she tried to wait calmly, saving her energy. That may have been the hardest thing she'd ever done when her mind screamed at her to do something.

She couldn't hear his voice anymore. Water was running. Was he taking a shower? She was baffled. She tried her bindings again with no more success than before. Cautiously she sat up and tucked her feet under. The room was warm, but she was chilled. She still wore the camp clothes she had on the night before. Why hadn't she put on some socks when she got up?

The door clicked, and she huddled back against the wall. Jerdix came into the room in one of the business suits he had always worn to the office, perfectly tailored, expensive material, and totally out of place. Instead of shoes appropriate to the costume, he had on the heavy boots he'd worn earlier.

He came over. "Stretch out," he said. When she hesitated, he grabbed her ankles and put the binders back on. Yanking her feet down, he hooked the ankle bindings to the foot of the bunk. "Sorry, sweets, but I need to go out for a bit." He ran his hand up her leg again, activated the rod against himself, and stood enraptured for a breath, clasping her thigh hard enough to leave marks. Then he straightened her pant leg and stepped away. "I'll be back," he said, "and you'll be fully functional by that time." He turned off the comm and left.

With him gone, she relaxed a little. She tested the ties unsuccessfully. The bunk was attached to the wall. No chance of breaking it apart enough to get loose.

She studied the room. He'd been there a while, a long while, and was a poor housekeeper. The open cabinet was full of supplies, so someone was helping him. He couldn't just walk into the store in Under Rim. Well, maybe in West End, the next district over on the edge of settled territory. He did have the jumper. He could even be going into Portside. And where had he gone now, all dressed up?

The longer he was gone, the more she began to fear he had just left her there. But he had other plans for her. He'd made that clear. Had he gone after Seth? Is that what he was doing?

She struggled with her bonds, succeeding only in cutting into her wrists. From vengeful he'd progressed to what? Could he be ... was he addicted to the rod and its pleasure? It was possible. Had she caused that, when she left the rod lying next to him in his barn?

The day dragged on. By late morning, thunderheads filled the limited view from the windows. Early start. What would a thunderstorm be like high up here on the rim? They could be wild enough down in Under Rim.

Jerdix didn't come back. Seth would have help by now. She'd heard him on the comm. He would be safe. And they would be looking for her. They would.

Thunder rumbled nearer and nearer until it crashed around the hut. She heard the crack of a nearby lightning strike. Plenty of tall palm-pines up here, natural lightning rods. The downpour hammered the roof and pelted the windows. Even a jumper would be grounded by this. Then in moments it was gone, and sun blasted between the clouds. Lee hoped it was steam, not smoke, she could see rising into the sky.

She was thirsty, hungry; she ached; she listened for the returning jumper, half-terrified of what would happen then; half-terrified it would never come and she'd die there slowly from dehydration.

Another storm cell moved over, the thunder and rain hammering her nerves. The door burst open. Rain blew in followed by Jerdix. "Think you can keep me down, do you?" he yelled out into the storm. He slammed the door behind him, laughing. "Miss me, sweets?"

Rain turned to hail, drowning out any answer she might make. Lee buried her face against the bunk, afraid the roof would cave in, not wanting to see when Jerdix came for her.

And he did, without waiting for the deafening storm to ease up. He forced her over so she could see him, freed her feet, attached a lead to her wrists, and released the snap that held her to the bed.

"Stand up," he shouted over the hail. She complied, finding she was about as steady on her feet as a drunk. No chance of taking him down and running for it, not this time.

"It's almost time. We'll have front row seats for the show." In a ludicrous gesture, he ushered her toward the front door with a sweep of his arm.

She looked at the door rattling in the wind. He laughed. "Go. Walk ahead of me outside and straight forward."

"Out in that?" she dared to question.

"Forgive me," he said with a half-bow. "Your wrap, my sweet." He flung a blanket over her and settled it into place around her shoulders.

Barefoot and stiff from being bound, she didn't trust herself. For now, she meekly did as he instructed. She thanked the Elements when the hail let up just as they went out into it. The rain continued but not as hard. An inch of hail carpeted the opening in front of the cabin. Under the trees, branches and rocks scattered on the ground. She stumbled along. Whenever she began to steady, Jerdix gave a sharp tug on the leash, twisting her half around. She fell several times to his great amusement.

They didn't go far before the trees opened up, and they came out onto a rocky point. The storm cell sailed off to the east, revealing a vast expanse all the way from the rim down to the lower desert miles away. The gritty surface of the blue-tinged rock was easier on her feet than the forest floor but was slick with hail. Wind whipped against her. She shivered uncontrollably, one more thing preventing her from fighting her way out.

"Right out to the edge," Jerdix told her. "Look carefully. Your haven at Fallen Pine is right there. Out there's the ridge west of the Reilly stead and their long barn roof. And that tiny, inconspicuous cluster is Under Rim. Too bad it's not clearer, but this will do."

She couldn't make out most of what he pointed to. The sun peeked between the storm cells, teasing with its momentary warmth. Mist hung around the rim and drifted across the vista, rising in smoke-like plumes from the canyons below. She shifted, putting one foot on top of the other. They burned with the cold. It was summer; it wasn't supposed to be cold.

He stripped the blanket off her, wrapped one arm around her, and pulled her back against him. She almost welcomed the warmth. Then she saw the rod in his hand.

"Not long now," he said eagerly. "Joe Reilly has smeared my family for the last time. Once he is reduced to the nothing that he really is, I will be free to show the people of this backward rock all the opportunities they are overlooking. Carico will be an economic power. And I'll keep you at my side, hostage to the good behavior of your interfering friends. You ... all of them ... will thank me in the end. You'll see what it looks like to properly exploit potential." He stroked her jawline with the tip of the rod, stopping with it just under her chin. She lifted her head up and back to avoid it. He had her arms pinned with his iron-hard forearm just under her rib cage so tight she could hardly breathe. The only weapons in her arsenal that she might apply were her feet, bare feet against booted shins and insteps. All she could do was to wait for an opening.

Clouds moved in around them, concealing the world below. "No!" he protested, tightening his grip until she gasped. "No! We have to see!" He stepped closer to the edge, lifting her feet off the ground momentarily. She squirmed, trying to loosen his grip. He shoved the rod against her throat and thumbed the control, sending a jolt of agony streaking along her nerves clear to her toes.

"Behave," he said. She held still, straining her head away from the rod tip, terrified of touching it again.

He paced along the cliff edge, dragging her with him, cursing at the obscuring clouds. His anticipation became fury. He seemed indifferent to her, like she was just a load to carry, but he didn't loosen his hold.

The brink of the rim was a step away, a harsh freedom for her, if she could over-balance him. She pushed that thought away. She would find a chance. He couldn't keep her helpless forever. She shivered; her feet were numb; she sagged until her chin touched the rod. She jerked away from it even though it did nothing, the memory of the pain fresh in her mind. He brought it up against her. She held her breath, waiting.

Chapter 33

Seth

The little brown horse clambered up the last rocky steps and halted on top of the Rim. Seth looked around. Which way now? If he guessed right, Jerdix would be out on the overlook. He dismounted and rubbed Ratchet's neck. The animal was breathing hard. Seth hoped he hadn't pushed too hard to get here. He dropped the reins over a branch and left the animal in the shelter of the trees.

A few steps into the woods, Seth found fresh scuff marks in the litter and a clear boot print in a bare spot. Quickly, as quietly as he could, he followed the signs toward the rim. Mist thickened and drifted eerily through the forest. He heard Jerdix shouting. From the concealment of the trees, Seth looked out to see the man standing at the far edge of the rocky opening facing out toward the edge. Lee, where was Lee? Jerdix shifted a little. He was holding her in front of him.

The fog broke into tatters, and Jerdix eagerly said, "Come on, come on. Almost time. We'll be able to see. We have to be able to see."

Seth stepped into the open, maybe ten paces from him. "You won't miss anything," he said loudly. "Nothing's going to happen."

Jerdix spun, pointing the rod like a gun. "You!" Jerdix howled. "What are you doing here?"

Seth's eyes locked on the rod. He struggled to refocus on the man's face, not to look at that rod. "They found the weak link in your organization," he said. "He spilled your plan. Nothing's going to blow up today."

Jerdix looked toward Fallen Pine. "No, that can't be."

Lee struggled, twisting against the arm that threatened to crush her. Jerdix stepped back to get his balance.

"It's over." Seth managed to speak boldly, but his eyes kept going back to the rod. It threatened to paralyze him.

"You forget my nice little rag doll." Jerdix lifted Lee's feet off the ground. "I still have her." He started to bring the rod back toward her.

Lee moved then, smashing her head back into Jerdix's face. She twisted and went limp, slipping out of his hold, stripping her shirt half over her head, and landing sprawled on the rock. Jerdix reached toward her with the rod.

Seth fought to pull his eyes from that torturous little device. *Get away, Lee.* She tried. She rolled. She got her feet tangled with Jerdix. The rod came closer. She kicked herself away, still on the ground. Jerdix grabbed her ankle. Jabbed her foot with the rod. She rolled in agony-ecstasy.

Seth couldn't force himself forward, couldn't risk the rod. Unable to watch, he looked away, saw a broken branch on the ground near his feet. He snatched it up, stumbled forward. Swung it.

It struck Jerdix's elbow. The rod flew, hit the wet rock, skittered toward the edge. Jerdix scrambled after it, reaching, reaching. The rod sailed into space. Jerdix dove after it and vanished over the edge.

Seth stared, half expecting Jerdix to reappear over the brink. He heard a meaty thunk on the rocks below. "He's gone."

"Gone?" Lee lay at the edge, digging in heels and elbows to keep from sliding on the slick rock.

"Down there. Elements! Hold still." Seth grabbed the tether attached to her wrists and pulled her back from the edge, going down on his knees. She was soaked, barefoot. She trembled uncontrollably.

Lee took a deep breath. "Gone. Along with the key to these." She held up her bound hands. Suddenly she was laughing hysterically.

"Easy, easy." Seth saw the blanket and passed it to her. He couldn't make himself get close enough to wrap it around her.

"Summer on the rim and I'm freezing." She choked back more laughter.

He reached into the pocket of his raincoat and pulled out a pair of thick socks. "I saw these on my way out the door and grabbed them for some reason." He tossed them to her.

"Socks." She caught them, pulled them on. "My hero!" Her trembling subsided a little.

"Can you walk?" he asked.

"Give me a minute."

"Haven't got minutes." He wanted to pull her to him and kiss her. He managed to take her hand and squeeze it. "Ratchet's hot from the ride and shouldn't be left standing in this breeze. I'll get him, and we'll go find that key."

She shuddered. "What happened? I didn't see what happened."

"I hit him with a stick."

"Where it hurt the most, I hope." She giggled, then took a deep breath to keep from losing control again.

"He dropped the rod. It slid off the cliff. He dove after it, right over the edge."

"He was addicted. He was going to ..." She choked back whatever she started to say and eyed the turquoise rock disappearing into space a few feet from her.

"Did he hurt you?"

She shook her head. "No damage, just hypothermia and hung over from the drug he used. But I need to see that he's really dead."

He let it go at that for the moment. Time later for the full story. "Then let's get out of here."

Seth ran to where he had left Ratchet and brought the horse back. In the few moments he was gone, the mist parted. Lee sat in the sun, holding the blanket open to let in the warmth. The vista before them was painted gold and silver as the mist fled. Suddenly it was a beautiful afternoon with a promise of rebuilding heat. A light breeze smelled of damp earth and freshness. He wanted to make love to her right there in the sun and the clean air. The thought threatened to overwhelm him with anxiety.

"Come on," he said. He shortened the stirrups and led the horse to a log. She hobbled to it, struggled up, and slid her leg over the saddle, leaving her feet hanging.

"Hold still," he said. It took all the control he had to pull off one of the socks and inspect her icy foot. The sole was scraped and scratched. He pulled a big splinter out of the heel. Putting the sock back on, he went around the horse and repeated the inspection on her other foot, finding an inch-long slash on the tender arch. The visible wounds — he wondered what invisible damage Jerdix had inflicted.

"Let's go," Lee urged. "I want to get these binders off."

"Right." He took the reins and led the tired horse to the head of the steep trail. "Hey, where's Jerdix's jumper?"

"A cabin just back into the trees a little ways." She pointed.

"Do you want to go there? You could take the jumper."

"No!" she answered. "Anyway, it probably needs his thumbprint just like I think these binders do." She lifted her hands.

"Would have been nice if he'd unlocked those before he jumped off the cliff." Seth dared to lay his hand on her leg. "Hang on. This first bit's rough. Are you ready?"

"Give me the reins. Easier to let him pick his own pace." She rubbed the horse's neck.

Seth did as she suggested and followed the horse down. He hated to ask the tired animal to pack a rider, but Ratchet had no trouble negotiating the rocks and mud of the steep downgrade. The horse picked his way cautiously, never tripping, showing Seth that he was in good shape.

When they reached the bottom of the upper cliff, Seth led the way off the trail, working through the boulders and trees to reach the place where Jerdix had fallen. Under the crag, Seth found the body twisted and broken on a pile of rocks. The rod lay a few feet away, unscathed by the fall. The horse snorted and refused to come near the smell of blood and death. Lee rode him far enough away that he settled down.

Seth helped her off. She reached down and stripped off the socks before picking her way over to the body. Her ability to think about things like keeping socks dry amazed Seth.

Jerdix lay face down with his head turned too far around. Lee reached out and touched one of the blank eyes, getting no reflex blink. "Dead. Now, get these off me." She held out her bound hands.

Gingerly, Seth took hold of the flaccid right hand and pressed the thumb to the release. The bindings dropped off, and Seth let the hand fall. He felt unclean from the brief contact.

"What about that?" Lee pointed to the rod. He saw the shudder that ran through her.

He took her hand. "Go keep the horse company. I'll stack rocks over it to keep it safe until someone comes for it." He didn't care if something disturbed the body but doubted anything would find that carcass appetizing.

It took him more than one false start to get close enough to cover the rod with rocks. The sight of it turned him to mush. But he did it. With a sigh of relief, he went back to Lee and the horse and led the way down the next steep stretch to a semi-flat opening big enough for a skimmer.

"We can wait here. Pa should be along in a while."

Lee slid to the ground and found a place to sit. Seth unsaddled the horse and laid out the saddle pad against a boulder in the sun. Once Lee was settled there, Seth gathered the driest wood he could find to build a fire. As he did, he watched her. What had Jerdix done to her? Used the rod on her? Raped her again? But she seemed unconcerned about being touched or about the sticks he moved close to her.

"No," she said finally.

"What?" He quickly looked down at the fire he was coaxing to life.

"I am not suffering from post-rod trauma. That is what you're worrying about, isn't it?"

He blew gently on the fire and fiddled until it was burning well before answering, "Yes."

"I do have a whole new appreciation for that device, but he only used it once, no, twice, on the pain setting."

She took a deep breath. "I'd almost forgotten how bad that could be."

He chewed on the inside of his lip, letting the memory slide past him. "Yeah, well ..." He fed a little more wood to the fire.

"You said something to him about nothing blowing up. What did you mean?"

Seth refocused. "Jerdix. He planned to blow up Fallen Pine, and I don't know what else. He was waiting up there where he could watch."

"What happened? What stopped it?" she asked.

"I don't know for sure. When the drug wore off enough for me to move, I tried to call Pa on the comm. Then I saw a blip from him that Jerdix was monitoring audio, to get away from the cabin, and to wait for ordinance disposal. I took that to mean explosives. I stuck a note on the porch post and headed this way."

"How did you know where to look for me?"

"I listened when the jumper took off. Once I had an idea what he had planned, I just hoped he was coming to the overlook. You said he had a cabin?"

"State-of-the-art base camp prefab disguised as a shack."

"When did he set that up?"

She shrugged. "Could even have been when he first came to Under Rim."

Seth shook his head. "I sure would like to hear the whole story."

She shifted restlessly. "We don't have to stay here because of me."

"Someone will be looking for us any time now. This is the nearest place to Jerdix that they can land a skimmer."

"So we wait?" She leaned back against the rock.

"We wait." He put a couple larger sticks on the fire and gathered some green branches.

"Smoke signals?" she asked when he laid a bough over the flames.

"Got a better idea?"

She laughed, a strong, good-humored laugh that relieved his concern about her more than anything she could say.

Once the fire was going well, Seth went to the horse and rubbed off the drying sweat, scratching the itchy spots and checking him over. Seth had worried about how hard he had ridden to reach the rim, but the animal seemed to be fine.

Lee sat back against the boulder, soaking up the sun with her eyes half-closed. She was safe now; they were safe. He went back to sit near her, not quite close enough to touch. Suddenly he couldn't wait to get through treatment, to be able to actually put his arms around her.

"Warm enough?" he asked.

"Getting there," she answered.

"I love you, you know."

"I'm glad you remember. You forgot for a while."

"I did."

"But you're still wearing the cord." She held out her hand for him to take. He could do that much.

"Almost worn out," he noted.

"In some cultures, a cord like that is a promise. Couples have the life of the cord to decide whether to stay together."

"So we take things one cord at a time?"

She laughed. "One cord at a time."

"Then let's make the next one out of permasilk."

"I'm glad we have that settled."

They sat there, dozing in the afternoon sun that drove the storm's cold away, hands touching, until the Marshal's skimmer appeared and settled to the ground.

"Ready?" Seth asked. Reprieve over. Now came the explanations.

She nodded. "It's going to be a long day."

By dinnertime, hours of shuttling around from one place to another and answering questions left Seth completely exhausted. The Marshal had immediately turned the investigation into Jerdix's death over to more impartial eyes but that hadn't kept him from wanting to hear all the details. One good thing for Seth — everyone was too interested in Jerdix to pay too much attention to his homecoming. And Lee ran interference, making sure he had space. Too many people; too much activity. He balanced on the edge of panic half the time.

Late in the afternoon, the ordinance disposal team from Portside released the Reilly stead as safe and clear of explosives. The team packed up their gear and assorted evidence, had a quiet word with the Marshal, and left. Fallen Pine and the hut on the Rim were still under the control of investigators, following up on the removal of explosive devices and evidence of the kidnapping.

The whole family gathered for dinner — Seth and Lee, Joe and Kiri, Nick and Gwyn, and Teri and Lije. Thankfully, the thunderstorms blew themselves out, and the evening was suited to grilling outside so Seth didn't feel trapped.

"It was really one of Jerdix's riders that gave away the whole plan?" Kiri asked.

Joe nodded. "One Willem Willemsen, better known as Whip."

"Whip?" Seth remembered the cocky rider from Tobin Canyon. One of the two who had delivered him to Jerdix.

"Yeah," Joe said. "He apparently helped deliver a cargo load to Jerdix up at that hut and began to have second thoughts about some of the equipment. He showed up at Marshal's Office HQ in Portside with the story."

"Barely in time," Kiri said. "I was glad to see the ordinance disposal team show up. Never was my specialty."

Joe grinned and put his arm around her. "I hear you had things under control at the house when they got here."

"Not much to control."

Joe kissed her. "You can look after the place for me anytime you want."

She melted against him. "So, what now?" she asked.

"Jerdix is gone," Joe said, "but Emerging Territories Business Consortium has taken over his property. He's been connected to them for years."

"That was one of the things I was looking at back when ..." Lee let the rest go unsaid.

Joe nodded. "I'm afraid we're going to be busy for a while."

"Well, I don't want to think about that tonight," Lee said. "I just want a bunk and about ten hours undisturbed."

"I set the bunkroom up for you," Kiri said. "Both of you."

"Oh good," Lee said with a grin. "The house feels kind of crowded."

"Yes, it is," Joe said, kissing Kiri.

Seth shook his head and stood up. "Just keep the party down so we can sleep."

"Ran Cory will be here in the morning," Joe said.

"Okay." Seth skirted the gathering of his family, still clutching Lee's hand. Today he'd made progress. He had been able to physically deliver a critical blow to Jerdix, and he could hold Lee's hand. Tomorrow he would follow through with his promise to get the help he needed. That wasn't as frightening as it had been a day ago.

Chapter 34

Seth

Less than a day later he stood by Ran Cory's surf-or, a pack at his feet and Lee by his side.

"Sorry to rush Seth off." Cory rubbed Lee's shoulder gently. "But we have a narrow navigation window to get him on board the CSHS Pierce. We couldn't get him into better hands if we had the choice of every hospital ship out there."

"Better do it then," Seth said. His family stood on the porch of the house. He'd already said goodbye to them. He and Lee had said their goodbyes privately. Not the way he would have liked. Touching hands was about the most contact he could tolerate. But that left a welcome-home to look forward to.

Lee squeezed Seth's hand. "Love you. Now go away."

Cory kissed her cheek and entered the little craft.

"Only a blip away," Seth whispered and blew her a kiss.

She smiled. "Miss you."

He nodded, unable to answer, and followed Cory.

Carico hung above him, filling most of the ship's view screen, blue, turquoise, and bronze. Seth reached out toward the white clouds that obscured the sparsely settled patch of mountains and deserts where he had grown up, the home he was leaving. He felt exiled, temporary though it would be. He hated leaving Lee to face the aftermath of Jerdix's death, but she was hardly alone. He felt lost without her. He didn't even have the roan horse to lean on.

The surf-or rolled slightly and settled into its cradle to become the control cabin of the clumsy-looking interstellar survey boat. He felt the connections click into place. The smell and feel of the ship's air changed. Carico slid out of the viewscreen to be replaced by an incredible array of stars. Gripped by a weird sensation of falling into infinity, panic rose in him.

"Close your eyes," he heard Cory's calm voice. "Use the med pump."

As instructed, he found the patch on his wrist and tapped it to send a dose of drugs into his system. He hunched in his seat, shivering until the calming haze spread through his mind.

"Good," Cory said quietly. "I turned the screen off."

Seth opened his eyes a crack and was relieved to see a blank wall where the abyss of stars had been. The tiny cabin began to close in on him.

"We have a few minutes before we exit orbit. Settle into your quarters. Sleep a while. And don't try to tough it out. Use the drugs. I promise you'll be ready to experience the trip on your way home. Now, let's just get you there."

They spent a week en route, and Seth rarely left his berth. He could watch the star field on a tiny screen over his bunk where it looked more like a picture than like the universe swallowing him. At first, he tried to get by without drugs but, in this alien place, he couldn't get grounded. When claustrophobia threatened to engulf him, he finally chose the mental fog. He couldn't focus enough to make sense of his surroundings when Cory led him from the survey ship onto the massive hospital ship through indistinguishable beige corridors.

"Trust them," Cory repeated as they walked. "You'll be isolated in a sensory-deficit environment at first while they evaluate you and plan your treatment. Give yourself as much patience as you would a mistreated colt, and you'll get through this."

"Normal?" Seth managed to ask.

"Not the same but able to live your life normally, yes."

"Tell Lee ... just ... well, she was there for me, you know."

"Tell her yourself. You'll be able to send her blips. Here we are." Cory led him into an empty, featureless room. "You won't see anyone at all for a little while, but you are only as alone as you want to be. Someone will always be available by comm. You can adjust the lights and temperature. One of my old friends will be working with you. He'll talk to you in a few minutes."

"Like a bug in a jar," Seth muttered.

"More like a horse in a stall. Think of this as a haven where you are protected from all those stimuli that threaten you. You are one tough young man. This will be easy compared to what you've been through already. So, ready to do this?"

"I guess so." Even through the drugs, Seth felt like he was taking the first steps onto a slippery slope.

"I'll leave you here then." The door swished closed with a thump, and Seth was alone.

Bare walls, disembodied voices, interactions by way of a screen. He couldn't tell how long he had been there when they let him have the first blip from Lee.

Seth, Doc's got me in a post-trauma counseling program. Lots of quiet time. Patience. Lee

Seth, 2 weeks since you left. Progress on finding underlings. Whip gave up names. Lee

Seth, Nick & Gwyn's baby's due at New Years. Hope you blip soon. Worried. Lee

Finally, they let him reply. The exchanges were his only contact with home.

Lee. Isolation; Slow increase in sensory input; meds make it hard to focus. Stay safe. Seth

Seth, Gwyn back to school next week. Nick moping. Joe+Kiri=LOVE. Lee

Seth, Rider reported at Trego begging for work. 'Bull' Bellinger, Whip's partner. In custody. Lee

Lee, Brain scan normal. Out of isolation. Fewer meds. Mind-body training. Hate it here. Seth

Seth. Whip negotiated 3+ years restitution service. Rest of organization fled Carico. Relieved. Lee

Lee, In barracks now. No panic. Mind clear. Walls driving me crazy. Seth

Seth, Staying at Fallen Pine now. First signs of autumn. Miss you. Lee

Lee, SPARRING in martial arts practice. Take hits; no sweat. Seth

Seth. Impressed; other contact good too? Want you here. Lee

Lee, Feel real again. Big test soon, then home I hope. Need horses. Need you. Seth.

Forty-six days after the door had closed behind him, committing him to treatment, Seth balanced firmly on his feet in the middle of the training mat, waiting for his instructor to initiate an attack. The man facing him gestured him to wait and acknowledged someone entering the room. The newcomer stepped into place opposite Seth. "May I?" Ran Cory asked.

Seth grinned and settled into position. Relax; let the tension go; watch with a soft focus; let his core be strong. Assess. Cory was older, smaller but wiry and no doubt fast. Seth was a novice and knew it, but maybe he could get in one or two touches. "Light contact?" he asked.

"Light contact," Cory confirmed and took his stance.

"Begin," the instructor said.

Seth held his own for the first couple of exchanges. Cory tested him, keeping it more of a training bout than a competition. Seth let go of caution and moved surely, with confidence.

Cory passed near the instructor who handed him something. Seth's world narrowed to the black object in Cory's hand. All his terrors right in front of him. A solid kick to his ribs followed by a tap to his head brought him out of it. He blocked the next kick, struggling to regain his composure. Cory held the rod like a knife, came at him, and hooked his foot while driving him back. Seth went down on his back, kept moving, and rolled to his feet.

Cory stood at ease. "Catch," he said, throwing the rod. Seth somehow overcame his revulsion and snatched it from the air. Looking at it, he saw a plain black baton the length of his hand with no controls.

"Just a kubotan," Cory told him. "But you didn't know that. Well done. You just passed your final exam."

Seth clutched the baton. He'd almost lost himself again. But he hadn't. Loosening his grip, he tossed the little self-defense stick back to Cory. He couldn't think of anything to say.

Cory caught it and passed it on to the instructor. "Are you ready to go home?"

"If they'll let me go. Are you my ride?"

"I am. Get your things together. We have a marginal window. It'll take a bit longer than the trip here, but I thought you'd prefer that to waiting for a quick trip."

"Just get me home." Seth acknowledged the instructor before leading Cory into the hallway. He spent two hours jumping through hoops and untangling red tape. He stopped long enough to send a last blip to Lee that read simply, "On my way." He whistled softly as he strode onto Cory's ship, not cured — there was no cure — but with the tools he needed to have the life he wanted.

Chapter 35

Seth

Cory had them cleared for takeoff by the time Seth got aboard. He wasted no time getting underway. "Better get settled in your berth and have something to eat before the first transfer."

"Sir ..." Seth began hesitantly.

"Yes?"

"I've been wanting to ask some questions for a while."

Cory settled back. "Then let's clear things up now."

Uncomfortably aware that this was Lee's father, Seth plunged in. "I understand now what happened, that the repeated use when I never knew what to expect made the rod so bad for me. But he used it on Lee too." He waited to be sure this wasn't a surprise before going ahead. "Is she okay?"

"Why wasn't she as traumatized as you? Because it wasn't used on her often enough and in close repetition. It's the repetition and the expectation."

"She never talked to me about it," Seth admitted. "But if the pleasure setting is used consistently when someone expects it?"

"Addiction. Like Jerdix at the end. In one way it's like adrenaline. You go into a situation that makes you nervous and that you know will be exciting, like getting on a colt for the first ride. Whatever that animal does gives you a rush, and you expect it. You enjoy it. But if you are riding quietly along with no reason to expect excitement and your horse loses its footing or spooks, you get a rush but probably don't enjoy it nearly as much. It's out of synch with your expectations of a relaxed ride."

"So when Lee got the pleasure stimulus?"

"It just made the trauma of the situation worse and left no desire to repeat it."

"And she's really okay?"

"She's doing well," Cory said.

Seth accepted that until he could see for himself. He stared at the blank view screen that had threatened to engulf him on the earlier trip and dared to turn it on. The star field appeared but no panic set in, no feeling of falling, no pounding heart. He could enjoy the enormity.

They spent ten days getting to Carico. Seth spent a lot of the time in the tiny gym, going through the *batayr* martial arts forms he'd learned to practice mental and physical control. Cory joined him sometimes. Twice Seth's age, smaller and lighter, he regularly reinforced the value of experience and speed when they sparred. Seth soaked up the training, watching his opponent the way he watched a colt, reading hints and improving his reactions. He enjoyed the activity more than he ever had on the Pierce when his whole focus had been recovery.

At last, they came out of the final transition, and Carico appeared in the view screen. A few more hours and he'd be home. Seth closed his eyes and tried to remember the smell of the desert after a rain or of the forest around Under Rim on a spring day, open skies, breezes, dirt and dust and animals.

"I miss it too, sometimes." Cory sat in the control chair, watching him with a grin.

"You lost your family in the pandemic?"

"No, I'm not originally from Carico. Different world, different disaster. Cris wanted to come back here at one point, and we stayed for a while. But she couldn't settle down, and now, well, I know what I do is important, so I don't regret past choices."

"Exactly what do you do?" Seth let his curiosity surface.

Cory laughed. "I don't know how to explain that very well. Dig into secrets; sometimes help people like you; generally try to make life less risky. I'm addicted to information and try to get it into the hands of those who can make use of it to keep people like Jerdix from spreading too much pain."

"Sounds ..." Seth searched for a word.

"It's challenging. Always something new." Cory shrugged. "What about you? What do you plan to do now?"

Keys to recovery — goals, plans, direction to his life. Seth had spent a lot of time thinking about his future. "Go back to Seven Wells," he said confidently. "Stay there at least two years, maybe even five, learning to run the horse side of the business until I can qualify for import-export permits and a breeding permit. Study the markets. Get set to go into business for myself."

"Those permits are hard to come by."

"I had thought I might take over Pa's, but now he may want to keep his. I'm just guessing, but he might retire from law enforcement to raise kids."

"You could partner with him."

"I have another partner in mind." Seth looked down at his hands, at the worn cord he still wore around his wrist. He was intensely aware that this was Lee's father as well as someone he respected. Deep down, he feared a discouraging response.

Cory didn't answer, and Seth looked up. "Son," the older man said. "That is between the two of you, but I don't think she plans to leave Carico anytime soon."

"A lot's happened. I hope we can get past that, but we'll have to see."

"Do you need her to make your plan work?"

Seth considered his response, wanting it to carry the weight it deserved. "No, I don't. She'll be a big help, but we ..." How to say this to her father? "Before this started, we seemed truly good together. And that spark still seemed to be there when I left. But I won't hold her if she doesn't want to stay."

Cory studied him silently long enough to make Seth shift uncomfortably, then nodded, apparently satisfied with something he saw. "I'll drop you at Fallen Pine then. You two can reacquaint yourselves before you face the whole family."

"I'll get my things together." Seth stood and slid between the seats. "How will I ever repay you for all your help?"

"Just make good use of what you've been given." Cory smiled. "It's autumn at Fallen Pine, and it looks like there's a storm over the rim. I thought you'd need appropriate clothing. You'll find a pack in the storage lockers."

"What time will we get there?"

"It'll be late afternoon, local."

"Good." Seth collected the pack from the locker and hurried to his berth. He changed into warm, durable clothing, thankful for Cory's thoughtfulness. He stuffed his light-weight shipboard clothing into his bag. He gathered the bag and the jacket Cory had provided and took a last look around, saying goodbye to ship walls and confinement. Then he returned to the control cabin.

As Cory separated the surf-or from the main ship, Seth watched the view of Carico passing beneath them, blue and verdigris and yellow under bright white clouds in swirls and banners. The settlements occupied such a tiny piece of one massive continent. He'd never given that much thought. It felt like a huge area when he was horseback or even in a skimmer.

As they lost altitude, he closed his eyes and ran through mental exercises, seeking the delicate balance he had learned. So much rested on the next few hours. He had to read Lee correctly. She'd seemed sure before he left. But had they both changed too much?

"Almost there." Cory's voice cut into his concentration. "Looks like rain. The ride down could be a little bumpy." They dropped through the clouds, coming out not far above the treetops. Seth was glad the Rim, the overlook where Jerdix had died, was hidden. Cory landed the craft in front of the Fallen Pine cabin. The autumn meadow was drab brown. Smoke curled from the chimney.

Seth saw Lee come out onto the porch, pulling on boots and coat. His heart pounded. Cory squeezed Seth's shoulder and advised, "Breathe," as he went to open the hatch. "I'll be at Joe's for a few days."

Just plain, ordinary fear, that's all it was. Not debilitating panic, just fear. Seth got up, put on his jacket, and slung his bag over his shoulder. Sucking in one last deep breath, he stepped out into the light rain.

Lee saw him, tensed, flashed a smile followed by a frown as she started toward him, arms open to hug him before she stopped a couple steps away, uncertain. Of course she couldn't know how he would react to her touch.

"Hi," he said. "You look good." He held out his hand, palm up, inviting her. She came closer, shoulders tight and high, and slowly reached out to rest her hand on his. He closed his fingers firmly around hers. He couldn't read the eyes that studied him.

She blinked, looked down, and nodded. "You look good too. Come in out of the rain." But she slid her hand away when she turned. Seth's heart sank. He followed her to the cabin.

She waved at her father, standing in the door of the surf-or. "Is he coming in?" she asked.

He shook his head. "He'll be down at Pa's."

"Okay." She stopped on the steps with her body language carefully controlled and watched the craft lift away and vanish into the low clouds.

Seth set down his bag. "Thank you for the blips," he said. "I looked forward to them."

"You're welcome." She paused. "How are you?"

A question he knew he'd be asked repeatedly. "Functional," he answered. "Pretty good most of the time. And you?"

"Good. Well, good enough that Vinz convinced Doc to let me out of regular counseling."

"Are you sure that was a good idea?" Seth asked. He had come to believe in the value of professional help.

"Vinz thinks so."

They stood in uncomfortable silence for a moment. Seth opened his arms. "I would like a hug if you can manage one." Slowly she came to him, buried her face in his chest and wrapped her arms around him. He held her close. The contact warmed some spot deep inside him.

He let her ease away when she wanted. "Welcome back," she whispered with her face down so he couldn't see it.

"Lee, if you aren't all right with my being here, please, tell me. I'll do whatever you want."

"What I want?" She studied him for a moment, then raised her wrist to show the worn cord tied there. "I want the same thing I wanted when I tied these cords on — I want us, together. You just took me by surprise. I was planning to have something special set up to welcome you home."

"Just being here is special enough." He took her hand and kissed her palm lightly. "Right now, I want to take a walk. I've been inside walls forever. Come with me?"

"I think I'll take the chance to shovel out my clutter. Go see your roan horse. He's such an imp without you to keep him in line."

Seth hugged her quickly and jumped off the porch to stride around the cabin toward the horse pasture. The cold touch of the rain felt strange after weeks on a ship. The world smelled wet and old. The woods were still, empty of the summer insect life. The air felt clean and rich.

He found three horses watching hopefully for treats, his roan, Clown, and Ratchet. Jester and Buster must be in the lower pasture or at his father's stead. He got some grain from the shed and spent a few minutes surrounded by the smell and touch of horses. He had missed that almost as much as he'd missed Lee.

Rain fell harder, and the wind picked up. He gave the animals a last scratch and walked back to the house. He'd looked forward to this day for so long. She said she wanted to be together. Nervous anticipation replaced his earlier fear. He brought his things from the porch and dropped his bag at the foot of the loft steps. The scatter of unwashed dishes and clothing reminded him of her apartment in Under Rim when she'd been 'Anni'. Lee had been neater at Trego. More controlled maybe.

Lee came from the hallway. "No one warned me I had company coming this soon."

"So I see." He opened his bag and lifted out a small, neatly wrapped package. "I brought you something." He held it out to her. "Please, open it."

She took it, tested its weight and laid it on the table. She unwrapped it, careful not to tear the heavy, dark-red paper. She touched the enclosed fabric lightly with a fingertip before picking it up and shaking it out. A cascade of whisper-light silk tumbled free, a wrap in a rich bronze color shot through with gold.

"It made me think of your eyes," he said.

"Oh, Seth, it's exquisite." She ran it through her hands, then wrapped it around her shoulders and rubbed her cheek against it. "So beautiful."

"Will you put it on?"

"Yes, of course. Oh, wait!" She dashed out of the room and came back with the red shirt he had left at the stead in the spring when he'd gone to Seven Wells. She handed it to him. "Do you know, I carried that with me all summer?"

"You did what?"

"Waiting for the right time to give it back to you."

He took it. "Looks like I get to dress for dinner too."

"Yes, dinner. Good thing Kiri brought supplies yesterday."

"Go change. I'll see what I can put together."

He took his time getting started. Once he had ball tubers roasting and steaks ready to grill, he built up the fire in the fireplace, wanting its soul-warming comfort. He hauled his gear upstairs and put on the red shirt. It didn't fit as well as it had. He'd lost weight. But he was strong. And hungry.

He went down and knocked on the shower room door. "Should I put the steaks on the grill?"

"Go ahead," she answered. "I'll be out in a minute."

He took the steaks to the fireplace and swung the grill into place. With the meat sizzling over coals, he checked the ball tubers. He wanted everything to be perfect. Then she came into the room.

"Elements and All!" he whispered. "You look fantastic." She'd done something different with the wrap, draping it over her left shoulder and leaving her left leg bare almost to the hip. The soft fabric clung and moved with her.

"You were right. It really brings out my eyes, don't you think?"

He forced himself to look up. "Sure does," he stumbled. "I didn't realize how it would look. You are so beautiful."

"Thank you." She cautiously put her arms around his neck. "Are kisses tolerable now?"

"We'll have to try it and see," he said weakly, dazed by her reaction. "Not something I practiced back on the Pierce."

"A little one then." And she did kiss him quickly on the lips. "You know, I think Kiri knew you were coming. Look what she brought with the rest of the supplies."

She opened a cupboard and produced a bottle of celebration-quality tempranillo wine.

"Let's go sit on the couch," he said. "We can try some of that wine while the steaks finish."

They ate good, Carico-grown food; they drank wine. He let Lee talk about life around Under Rim. Gwyn and Nick's house was half-finished. Gwyn was Portside for school, and Nick was helping his mom put the gardens to bed for the winter. Kiri was running the Reilly stead, and the Marshal stayed close to home except to chase down loose ends of Jerdix's business.

Lee lay back against Seth, swirled the deep ruby wine. He held her a little closer, enjoying the sleek feel of the fabric over her skin. "Should we let them know we'll be down in the morning?" he asked.

"Da will tell them."

He kissed her neck under her ear. "More wine?"

"I don't think so. I'd like to keep my head."

"This has been the best." Seth set both their glasses aside. "I've been starved, and this is a feast."

"The food?"

"Touch," he replied.

She twisted around so she could look at him. "I couldn't help. I wanted to."

He wiped a tear from her cheek. "But you did help. You were there even when I didn't admit that I needed you to be." He kissed her deeply, relishing how good it felt. "I will never forget the way you look in that dress."

"I do love it. And I love that you thought to get it for me."

"I know I'll have bad days, but this is not one." He held her, drinking in the feel of her warmth against him, intoxicated with knowing he felt no anxiety. "This is where I am supposed to bare my soul and tell you how the last few months made me feel, at least that's what they told me to do back in my rehab sessions."

She laid a hand on his face. "One of these days soon, we'll go up on the Rim, and you can shout it to the wind."

"I'm beginning to hope we can salvage something out of this mess."

"Pretty good treasure in salvage sometimes."

He couldn't resist taking her hand and kissing her palm. He breathed deeply and let it out slowly. "I'm going to need to take this slow."

"Me too," she said.

"Okay." Of course. He wasn't the only one with baggage.

They sat facing each other on the couch. He took her feet in his lap and massaged them gently as they talked. The contact soothed his ragged nerves. At some point warmth and wine and contentment kicked in, and they both dropped off to sleep.

Sometime later he woke up and slipped away. Outside the night was quiet. The clear sky arched over him, speckled with stars. Lander, the larger moon, rose full and orange on the horizon with the smaller Damele speeding past it. A chill breeze caressed him.

Lee came out and stood next to him. "You okay?" she asked.

"Yes. How about you?"

"I am. It's good to have you back."

He took her face in his hands and ran his thumb along her cheek bone. "What now?"

She looked up at him. "How soon can we get out of here?" she asked.

"Where to? Down to Pa's?"

"There first, I suppose, but I was thinking about the long term. Were you planning to stay here for a while?"

"No, not for long. How does Seven Wells sound?" He put his hands on her shoulders and waited for her response.

She relaxed and put her arms around his neck. "Sounds right and tight. When can we leave?"

Winter was coming. It would be warm down on the desert. "Tomorrow?" he suggested.

"How about next week?" she answered more practically.

He drew her in against him, cherishing the feel of her after the long drought. They would work things out. "Okay, next week," he agreed.

Stepping back, he brought out two slender circles of braided horsehair from his pocket. "There," he said. "Knots for us to hang onto."

She held her hand out so he could slip one around her wrist. She took the other, and her brown-gold eyes flashed as she put it on him. "Yes, useful things, knots."
He pulled her close and held on tight.

END

About the Author

Nan C. Ballard's *Under Carico's Moons* series of science fiction cowboy stories reflects her love of places where vehicles yield to cows, towns are hours apart, and hills climb clear to the sky. She's written and edited environmental assessment reports, written an arts column for a small town paper, and collaborated on adaptations of plays for community theater. Her poetry has been published in the online *Willawaw Journal* and the anthology *Mount Shasta Reflections.* She supports her fellow writers as a chapter co-chair and online Coffee co-host for Willamette Writers. She does quick pen-and-colored-pencil doodles to practice mindfulness. Her current just-for-fun project with her husband is to visit interesting places in every county in Oregon.

You can find her at nancballardwriter.blogspot.com or @NanCBallard on Twitter and Instagram.

www.ingramcontent.com/pod-product-compliance
Lightning Source LLC
Chambersburg PA
CBHW030704190726
48286CB00001B/161